MY BROTHER'S DOMINATRIX

B.B. LAMETT

Broodleroo

First published by Broodleroo 2024
Copyright © 2024

All rights reserved. No part of this book may be reproduced in any form or by any electronic or mechanical means, including information storage and retrieval systems, without written permission from the author, except for the use of brief quotations in a book review. It is illegal to copy this book, post it to a website, or distribute it by any other means without permission.
This is a work of fiction. The names, characters and incidents portrayed in it are the work of the author's imagination. Any resemblance to actual persons, living or dead, events or localities is entirely coincidental.
B.B. Lamett (a.k.a. Suzi Bamblett) asserts the moral right to be identified as the author of this work.

First edition
Paperback ISBN: 978-1-8382550-4-6

For P.A.B.

GLOSSARY OF TERMS

BDSM – bondage, dominance, submission and masochism *(catchall for anything kinky)*
Breath control play – restriction of oxygen heightening sexual arousal and orgasm. Methods include strangulation, suffocation *(gas masks)*
Dildo – non-vibrating phallic-shaped toy designed for penetration. Made of silicone, rubber or glass *(come in wide variety of skin tones and sizes…)*
Dominatrix – takes the sadistic role in sadomasochistic sexual activities *(sole beneficiary of brother's estate)*
Dungeon – room or area with BDSM equipment *(brother's play space)*
Hypertensive heart disease – high blood pressure *(reason for armband found in wardrobe?)*
Intermeddling – interference in something that is not one's concern *(too late, too late…)*
Nitrous oxide (a.k.a. noz or laughing gas) – colourless gas sold in pressurised metal canisters *(explains balloons and cream maker)*

Poppers (a.k.a. amyl nitrite) – liquid drug giving instant high *(relaxes anal muscles)*

Pulmonary thromboembolism – heart attack *(killed my brother)*

Safe word – codeword used to decrease intensity of BDSM *(alternatively say STOP)*

Submissive – compliant, yielding, spineless *(lying, deceitful brother)*

Vanilla – Someone not into BDSM *(me?)*

PROLOGUE

Simon's smile taunts me from the framed photograph on top of his coffin. It was my sister Wendy who suggested we lay a rose beside it. I wish I'd argued more. A small spray of flowers would be more appropriate. The symbolism of a single rose conveys the wrong emotion.

The congregation titter at something the celebrant says. Are they even referred to as 'congregation' at a humanist funeral? Si once joked he wanted 'Highway to Hell' as his coffin was carried in but Wendy vetoed that. She's Christian; she's allowed one veto.

I must stay focused.

'When Simon was seven…' The celebrant recounts a prepared anecdote. When she gets to the part about Wendy and I dressing him up in a tutu, they laugh. I want to howl. Perhaps it was our fault?

I find myself counting heads. There must be eighty or more. An eclectic mix of family and work colleagues and, lurking at the back, people I can't identify.

'Simon was well regarded at work,' she continues. His

colleagues nod encouragingly, one lady dabbing her eyes with a tissue. 'Kind, patient, always at the end of a phone…'

I'll invite them to stay on afterwards for a cuppa and a chat. They'll queue to speak to me, gushing with earnest condolences. Clasping my hand and telling me how wonderful my twin brother was.

If they only knew…

I could tell them the truth. I could share all Simon's sordid little secrets. I could reveal that my brother was, in fact, a great big liar.

CHAPTER ONE

Making a peephole in the fogged-up window, I stare out at driving rain and try not to cry. 'I really wanted to do The Three Peaks.'

Tom settles Brodie, our springer spaniel, under the table. 'I doubt we'd even see Batty Moss viaduct in this.'

A rosy cheeked waitress emerges from behind the counter. 'Shall I bring you a nice pot of tea while you decide?'

I paste on a smile. 'Yes please.'

My husband raises an eyebrow. 'Since when do we drink tea?'

'What do you expect in a Yorkshire village? Costa Coffee?'

The waitress returns with an enormous brown teapot. 'I'll bring you some hot water. Tea's proper Yorkshire. Might be a bit much for you Southerners. You decided?'

Quickly I scan the menu. 'Cheese toasties?'

As she bustles away to prepare our food, Tom retrieves an abandoned newspaper from the next table. 'Why do we have to have such a packed itinerary anyway?'

'Because it's a walking break.'

'You and your bloody hiking. We don't have to climb every hill.'

I reach across the table and take his hand. 'We're here now. Can't we make the best of it?'

My mobile rings and I scrabble to retrieve it from my rucksack. 'Wendy. Good timing. We've just stopped for lunch.'

'Tom with you?' asks my sister.

'Yes, but it's pissing down with rain and…' A sound down the line. 'Wendy?' I sit up straight. Is she crying. 'What's the matter?'

Detecting my tone, Tom lowers his paper.

'It's Simon. Oh dear, there's no easy way to say this… Simon's dead.'

My mind won't process the words.

'Did you hear me, Sarah?' she repeats. 'The police scared Bob half to death… he thought it was one of the kids…' Her voice fades as my phone drops to the table.

Tom reaches across to pick it up. 'Wendy? This is Tom. What's happened?'

The bell over the tearoom door chimes as an elderly couple step inside and stare about, trying to decide where to sit. Under the table, Brodie whimpers.

I watch as Tom traces fingertips across the tablecloth. 'Give me the number.' He looks at me mouthing, 'Pen?'

I should be doing something, but I can't move.

Tom locates a stub of a pencil in one of the rucksack pockets and scribbles a number down on the newspaper. 'Okay, we'll keep trying this end. Yes, we'll call you back.' Ending the call, he sets the phone carefully on the table.

'Si's dead?' I don't recognise the voice as my own.

Tom reaches for my hand. 'I'm so sorry.'

'Told you I had a feeling something wasn't right.'

He rubs his fingers across my knuckles. 'You did. It's the twin thing. You always pick up when something's wrong.'

'What happened?'

'Sounds like he had a heart attack.'

'When did it happen? Where?'

'I don't know.'

The waitress interrupts us, setting two cheese toasties on the table. 'Here you go.'

'Thanks,' says Tom.

The sweet smell of Wensleydale assails my nostrils and I crinkle my nose. 'I feel sick.'

Tom pours tea and pushes a cup towards me. 'Here. Have a sip. Wendy says the police gave her a number for the coroner, but it keeps ringing out. I said we'd try.'

'Why did the police contact Wendy?'

'I guess because we weren't home.'

I sip the tea and wince. 'It's too strong. Let's try the number.'

'In a minute.' He adds sugar. 'Try now.'

The waitress looks across questioningly. 'Everything all right?'

'Sorry,' says Tom. 'We've received bad news and have to go.' He pulls a twenty-pound note from his wallet and slips it under the sugar bowl. 'Ready?' He gets up, tucking the newspaper under his arm. 'Let's go outside and see if we can get a better signal.'

'Mind how you go, my lovelies,' calls the waitress.

As we step outside, sun breaks through a cloud.

'It's stopped raining,' I say.

'Yes.' Tom guides me to a wooden bench overlooking a small village green. We sit down and he pulls me into a hug.

'I don't believe any of this,' I say. 'Si wasn't even ill.'

'Let's see what we can find out.' Unfolding the newspaper, he taps the number into his phone.

I scroll through my contacts until I find Si's number. I press call and it goes straight to voice mail. *'Hey Si. It's me,'* I say, after the beep. *'Look, can you call me? It's urgent. Love you bro.'* I hang up. 'He'll ring back in a minute,' I tell Tom. 'God, how he'll laugh about all this.'

Tom has given up on the call and is now Googling.

'What are you doing?' I ask.

'Trying a different tack. Looking up numbers for hospitals and mortuaries.'

As he makes more calls, Brodie creeps out from under the bench and I gaze into his soulful eyes.

Tom waves a hand to get my attention and I lean in, my ear close to the mobile.

'Yes, I can confirm we have Mr Simon Foster,' says a woman's voice.

My legs begin to shake.

Tom squeezes my knee before speaking into the phone. 'Sorry, who am I speaking to?'

'Paula Clark, Mortuary Manager for Brighton General Hospital.'

'When did he arrive?'

'This morning.'

'Si's dead.' I'm about to throw up. 'Oh God. Si's dead.'

CHAPTER TWO

It takes an hour to hike back to Chapel-le-Dale. As we step inside the cottage, Tom wraps his arms around me. 'You're shivering. Must be the shock.' He kneels in front of the wood burner to build a fire.

I put my phone on charge before sinking down on the chintzy sofa with Tom's mobile. Repeatedly I try the coroner's number, but it rings out. 'Still no reply. Oh God' – my hand flies to my mouth – 'we need to let Jamie know.'

'I'll do that. Why don't you take a bath?' says Tom. 'It might warm you up.'

Hauling myself up, I walk slowly through to the bathroom. I place the plug in the bath, turn on the taps and while it's filling, stare at myself in the mirror. Who am I? Am I even a twin if there's only one of us? When the bath's full, I peel off my clothes and step into the warm water. Lying back, I close my eyes. I can't believe Si's dead. He'd seemed fine last time I saw him. On good form…

. . .

I'd taken the glass, eyeing the bright pink concoction with suspicion. 'What the hell is it?'

'Porn Star Martini.' Si winked. 'Nothing without the secret ingredient.' Clumsily he sloshed vodka into my glass. 'Try it.'

Cautiously I sipped before wincing. 'It's very sweet.'

Si grabbed the glass and took a slurp. 'Strewth! A work in progress, I fear. Perhaps I'll make another jug of Margarita.' He yanked a bag of ice from the freezer and, as he ripped it open, ice cubes spewed across the kitchen floor. 'Oops.'

I smile at the memory. Si was ever the clown. But he wasn't always okay. Since his marriage break up three years before, I'd made the effort to phone or text him regularly, meeting for a Thai meal or a cocktail night every couple of months. Should I have done more?

Climbing out of the tub, I dry myself and pull on a white terry bathrobe. Sliding my feet into slippers, I pad into the sitting room.

'Feeling better?' asks Tom.

'Not really. Did you manage to speak to Jamie?'

'Yes. He sends his love. I told him we'd call again in the morning.'

'Thanks.' I wrap my arms around myself. This is one of those moments when I really need a hug from my boy. Although I really should stop thinking of him as a kid. Nineteen now and heading back to uni in September... I check my phone. The battery's up to twenty per cent. 'I'd better call Tina.' Si's ex-wife's number goes to answerphone, so I leave a message asking her to call me back.

'Bob rang,' says Tom.

'Oh hell.' I flop down on the sofa, rubbing my brow.

'He's spoken to the police and the coroner.'

This is so typical of my brother-in-law. When Dad had to be moved into a care home, it was Bob who dealt with everything. I shouldn't complain. I was working full time and would have struggled to make the arrangements, but it still pissed me off.

Tom opens the wood burner and prods the logs. 'He told them he'll be point of contact.'

'But I'm Si's next of kin.'

'It's only temporary. Just until we get home.'

I sigh. 'I hope he won't go charging over to Si's.'

'Would that be such a bad thing?'

I scowl. 'You know it would.'

Tom heads out to the tiny kitchen and I hear him bustling around. He returns with a tray and sets it on the table. 'Here you go.' He passes me a coffee. 'I was thinking… If the paramedics had to break in, I wonder if the property's secure?'

'How can we find out?'

'I'll call Michael.' He takes his phone into the kitchen to make the call.

Cradling the mug in my hands, I stare into space. It's not the first time we've had to call the downstairs neighbour. There've been times when I've needed to check up on Si. I sip my drink, feeling so helpless. Wendy was first to receive the news and now Bob's dealing with the police and coroner.

Tom returns with a plate of toast. 'The paramedics didn't break in. Michael had a spare key. We'll pick it up when we go over there.' He offers me the plate. 'Try and eat something.'

'I still can't believe it.' I pick up half a slice of buttered toast and take a bite, but it tastes like cardboard. 'We need to go home.'

While Tom pops next door to explain everything to our

holiday cottage host, I close my eyes, listening to logs crackle and hiss in the wood burner. Si's my twin. I'd sensed something was wrong. Why didn't I call him?

Tom comes back, stamping his feet on the doormat. 'Mrs Morgan's making us sandwiches for the journey.'

'I suppose we'd better pack then.' I blow my nose. 'Part of me doesn't want to go home. It will make it real.'

'We could pack everything up and head off first thing?'

I force a smile. 'Sure.'

I can't sleep, so wrap myself in a blanket and wander around the garden. As I gaze up at stars in a dark, unpolluted sky, I reflect how much Si would love this. An avid stargazer, he had a proper telescope. Now it's him who feels a million miles away.

Si was a staunch atheist, just like his favourite author Terry Pratchett. Needing connection, I pull out my phone and Google to find a quote. *'No-one is finally dead until the ripples they cause in the world die away.'*

CHAPTER THREE

After stopping off at home to unload our cases, we head over to Lewes.

'I'm so sorry about young Simon,' says Michael, handing Tom the spare key.

Tom pats his shoulder. 'We're just grateful you were here to let them in.'

'It was like a scene from *Casualty*.' Michael pulls a handkerchief from his pocket and dabs his eyes. 'They had one of those defibrillator things. His face was that grey' – he shakes his head – 'I scarcely recognised him.' He blows his nose. 'After they'd gone, I popped back up. Carpet's a bit of a mess where they trolleyed him out.'

Tom, with the foresight to bring boxes and rubbish sacks, carries them up to Si's flat. When I dawdle behind, he glances back at me. 'You going to handle what we might find?'

Am I? When my brother and his wife split up, Tina met me for a drink. "I want you to understand," she said, "he left me no choice. His behaviour was intolerable. You do know he was gambling?"

I shook my head.

"Addicted to it. And that's not all. He watched dodgy stuff online. Disgusting. No one could be expected to put up with that."

'Did you hear what I said?' asks Tom.

'Most men watch a bit of porn.'

Tom grins.

'Single men,' I continue. 'Don't think you've got *carte blanche*.'

He unlocks the door and I stare at the tell-tale black marks where the paramedics manoeuvred Si through the narrow doorway. Trying not to think about it, I step over them.

Tom's pragmatic. 'I hope you're not intent on clearing the whole flat today.'

'No, I just want a quick look around.' I gaze about Si's sitting room. A typical bachelor pad – leather sofa, TV, music system, games console. The windows are fitted with efficient blinds and prints of abstract art adorn the walls. Si moved in about eighteen months ago. "Downsizing," he'd said. "Now I'm single again, I don't need such a big place."

'Where do you want to start?' asks Tom.

'In here, I suppose. We need to find any paperwork I may need and remove anything that might distress Wendy and Bob if they show up. I'll start on the cupboards.' Kneeling down, I swing open the doors. The first cupboard is packed with stationery – paper, pens, stapler. The shelf above contains photo albums. I slide one out and open it. It's brimming with family snaps. 'Oh look, these were taken on holiday in Eastbourne when we were kids.'

Mum leaning against a breakwater wearing a floppy hat; Wendy squinting with sun in her eyes; me and Si filling buckets with pebbles, building sandcastles, paddling in the sea…

'Let's not get into those now,' says Tom.

I close the album and stow it in a box to take home. Turning my attention to the second cupboard, I haul out a home office file. 'Hopefully something useful in here.' Flipping the catch, I pull out a bundle of documents – bank statements and utilities bills. 'These are all years old,' I say, checking a few dates. 'I suppose his bills are online now.'

Tom, going through paperwork on the sideboard, pulls out something.

'What's that?' I ask.

'Porn,' says Tom.

'Good job we came, then.' As I set the file aside to take home, my phone rings.

'Hello? Mrs Edwards? This is the Coroner's Office.'

'Oh, yes. Thank you for calling back.'

'You wanted some details about the circumstances of your brother's death.'

I sink down on Si's sofa. 'Yes, please.'

'I can tell you what I know. Mr Foster called the emergency services at 01:05. He was unresponsive when they arrived, and they failed to resuscitate. His body was moved to the mortuary at Brighton General Hospital.'

It's like listening to an afternoon drama on the radio. None of this seems real.

'Are you aware of any circumstances that might have led to your brother's death?' she continues.

'No. Simon was forty-six and healthy.'

'No previous illnesses or underlying health problems?'

'Not that I know of.'

'Well, as this was an unexpected and unexplained death, it's likely there will need to be a post-mortem.'

Silent Witness pops into my mind. I imagine the pathologist up to her elbows in Si's body cavities. I swallow. 'Do I need to identify his body?'

'No. The police were able to ascertain your brother's identity at the scene. I believe his neighbour, Michael Johnson, confirmed he lived alone.'

'Okay.' I let out a slow breath. 'So, what happens now?'

'I'll be in touch. When the post-mortem's been completed, a death certificate will be issued. If your brother's death goes to an inquest, you'll be issued with a temporary death certificate. You'll be able to use this to sort out the funeral arrangements.'

'Right. Thank you.'

'If anything else should occur to you, or you have further questions, please don't hesitate to call me back.'

As I end the call, I see Tom rolling up electrical cables. 'Assume we're taking the laptop?' he says.

'Yes.'

I'm lightheaded as we move into the kitchen. Si's mobile and Filofax are on the worktop, and Tom adds them to the box.

I fill a glass with water and take a sip, noticing for the first time a bedside cabinet inexplicably standing in the middle of the kitchen. 'Why's that in here?'

'Perhaps they moved it to make more room?'

Trying to rid myself of the image of Si being wheeled out on a gurney, I head through to the bedroom, coming to an abrupt halt when I spot blood on the quilt cover and bottom sheet.

Tom offers me a pair of rubber gloves. 'Probably where the paramedics removed a cannula.'

Si's blood. I shiver at the thought. Declining gloves, I strip the cover from the quilt, roll it up with the bottom sheet and pillowcases and stuff the lot into a black sack.

Mirror wardrobes take up one entire wall and Tom slides open the right-hand door to reveal a rail packed with hangers. Something long and black catches my eye and I lift it out – a priest's cassock, complete with white dog collar.

'What the hell is that?' asks Tom.

I read the label. '*Rocky Horror.* Si always did love an excuse to dress up.' As I'm returning the garment to the rail, my fingers brush against leather and I extract something else.

'Oh, hello,' says Tom. 'What's that?'

I hold up a black, leather one-piece.

'If it was white, it might have belonged to Elvis,' he says.

'Wet suit?' I suggest.

'That's no wet suit.' Tom reaches into the wardrobe and takes out another outfit in black PVC. This one has a dog collar neckline and shorts rather than long trousers. 'Kinky.'

I tear another black sack from the roll. 'I think we'll get rid of these.' We bundle the costumes into rubbish bags. 'Let's go through the drawers,' I say.

There are two sets inside the wardrobe. The first packed with T-shirts, pants and socks, while the top drawer of the second set contains a tin box filled with miscellaneous jewellery. Buried beneath are two credit cards. 'I'll need to cancel these.' I set the cards aside and yank open the lower drawer. 'Oh, no.'

'Well, well.' Tom slides the drawer from its runners and empties the contents onto the bed.

'Eww.' I stare at an assortment of dildos – flesh coloured to neon pink, average size to hung like a horse. Each one fixed to a variety of straps ranging from jock to G-string.

Some phalli are smooth, some knobbly. One's twisted like a giant corkscrew. 'What the fuck?'

Tom snorts with laughter. 'Something else we didn't know about young Simon.'

'But why would he have these?' I shudder, unable to imagine Si engaging in such weird sexual practices.

Tom shakes another black sack open. 'Better bag 'em up.'

'I need the Marigolds this time.' As I drop the dildos into the bag, I examine them – some squidgy, others firm and erect. One has a cable attached and I dangle it like a dead rat. 'What on earth is this?'

'I guess you plug it in and inflate the…'

'Oh my God! I don't want to know. Thank goodness we emptied this before Wendy and Bob arrived.'

'She'd have had a bit of a shock.' Tom ties up the bag while I move around to the far side of the king-size bed.

I hardly dare open the bedside drawers. When I do, I sigh with relief. 'It's all right – tissues, cold remedy pills and several pairs of glasses.' There are deep drawers in the divan base and I tug one open. 'It's okay. Just blankets and bedding.' I pull open the drawer alongside. 'Oh wait, no it isn't.'

I stare down at bondage equipment – gas masks and gimp masks, some studded, others buckled; leather straps complicated as horse bridles; coloured rope in a variety of diameters; two latex leotards.

Tom peers over my shoulder. 'Enough to stock the shelves of a Brighton sex shop.' As he opens another bag, I lift items out one-by-one, holding them at arm's length.

'We'd better double bag this lot,' he says, checking the weight.

After we've emptied the drawer, we pull the bed from the

wall. Thankfully the drawers on the inaccessible side are empty.

I head for the bathroom to wash my hands. 'You know what?' My voice cracks as I attempt a joke. 'We've found everything except handcuffs.'

'Let's have a coffee,' calls Tom.

'After finding that stuff, I don't really fancy having one here. Why don't we stop for a drink on the way home?'

'Just the kitchen left, then,' says Tom.

Wandering back, I find him clearing pens and odd bits of post from the worktop. 'Don't make it too tidy or they'll know we've been here.' Remembering the misplaced bedside cabinet, I open the top drawer, barely batting an eye at a large packet of condoms, along with three packs of party balloons in yellow, purple and pink. 'Weird place to keep balloons.'

Tom's already preparing another bag.

The lower drawer is full of tiny bottles no bigger than nail polish. 'Some sort of massage oil?' I pull the Marigolds back on and drop the bottles into a bag. At the back of the drawer, I find two pairs of pink, fluffy handcuffs. 'There you go.' My tone is almost triumphant.

The bottom drawer contains two boxes of nitrous sulphate, the capsules used in soda syphons. I lift out a silver cannister with a nozzle on top. 'What's this?'

'No idea,' says Tom.

Rummaging around at the back of the drawer, I locate an empty box and pull it out to study the label. 'It's a cream maker.'

Tom frowns. 'Odd.'

'*For piping cream,*' I read. 'Perhaps Si had his own private foam parties.'

'I wouldn't know.' Tom bags everything up.

'Wait. I'm not sure we can bin those capsules. Aren't they full of gas? They might explode.'

Tom peers into the bag with distaste. 'Well, I'm not picking them back out.'

'Fine, I'll do it,' I grumble, retrieving the capsules and, for good measure, the tiny bottles of liquid. 'It might be flammable. Let's put everything combustible in a cardboard box.'

'Right, do you want to do anything else today?' asks Tom.

'I think we've done enough.' I survey our bounty – two cardboard boxes, a laptop, a home file plus half a dozen bulging bin bags and a pair of size ten high heels from the top shelf of the wardrobe. 'Will we fit this lot in the car?'

'I think so, but better pray Michael doesn't offer to help.' Moving as quietly as possible, we lug everything downstairs and load it into the boot.

'We're definitely stopping at a pub on the way home,' says Tom. 'We deserve it.'

CHAPTER FOUR

Once home, Tom carries the boxes through to the dining room while I plug Si's laptop into the wall socket and clear everything off the dining room table.

'Come on, boy.' After letting Brodie out in the garden, Tom closes the doors and moves towards the sideboard. 'Gin and tonic, I think.' He mixes our drinks before retrieving something from one of the boxes and easing himself down on the sofa. 'Ahh.'

'A little light reading?'

He holds up the magazine to show me the cover – a well-endowed woman in an uplift bra with pouting blood-red plumped-up lips. 'Thought I'd make the most of it before you chuck it out.'

I throw him a withering glare before opening the home file and taking out the paperwork. 'Enjoy your porn.'

'It's not porn, it's fetish.'

'What's the difference?'

'Well, fetish is more kinky…'

'Actually, don't tell me.' My mobile rings. Tina's number. 'Hi, Tina?'

'She doesn't want to talk to him.'

'What? No I… Look, who is this?'

'It's Jill, Tina's sister. We met at their wedding.'

'Oh yes, right. Is Tina there?'

'What do you want?'

'Look, I'm sorry but you leave me no option. I have sad news. It's Simon. He's dead.'

I hear whispered voices, then Jill comes back on the line. 'This for real?'

'I wouldn't joke about something like this.'

More scuffling then finally Tina's voice. 'Sarah?'

'Yes. I'm sorry, Tina. It's true. Si's dead.'

I hear her sharp intake of breath. 'What happened?'

'He had a heart attack.'

'Was he ill?'

'Nothing to predict it as far as I know.'

'I don't think…' Her voice catches. 'Sorry Sarah. I can't do this right now.'

'That's okay. I'll give you a call in a couple of days.'

An hour later, the table's covered. Documents from when Si bought the flat and, more worryingly, a loan agreement. Did Si take out a loan to consolidate debt? How did he get in so deep? Why didn't I know how bad things had become? I should have kept a closer eye, done something to address his gambling problems. I sigh. 'Most of this stuff is years out of date.'

'I'm not surprised.' Tom sets the porn mag aside and picks up the TV remote.

Searching through Si's Filofax, I find more debit and credit cards. 'That's four cards… how am I going to do this without statements?'

Tom glances up from football highlights. 'I guess he stored everything electronically.'

I open Si's laptop and switch it on. Password secured. I try our birthday, Mum's maiden name and birthday. Nothing works. 'I don't think I'm going to get access.'

'I could ask Steve in IT?'

'Would he be allowed to do that?'

'Don't know. I can ask. Can't you contact the banks and get them to send you statements?'

'Yes, but that takes time. I need to know what I'm dealing with. I don't even know if Si's solvent.'

Tom comes over and rubs my shoulders. 'Why don't you leave it for tonight.' He points at a fat, brown envelope on the table. 'What's that?'

'Divorce papers. I haven't plucked up courage to look.'

He lifts my empty glass. 'Want a top-up?'

While he mixes more drinks, I examine Si's mobile. I can't open it without a passcode, but I know the last message is from me.

Turning attention to the home file, I'm halfway through the dividers when I come across an A4 envelope. 'Found his will,' I say, triumphantly.

'That's good.' Tom sits down, scrolling TV channels.

'Oh no!'

'What?'

'Another will.'

Tom gets up. 'Two copies?'

'No, two wills.'

Tom takes the second envelope from my hand. 'What date's the first one?'

I pull three sheets of paper from the envelope. '2012.'

'I win,' says Tom. '16th November 2018.'

I scan through the will in my hands. 'This one leaves

everything to Tina. I suppose it's inevitable he'd want to change that after the divorce. What's yours say?'

'Who's Angela Bentley-Bell?' asks Tom.

'Never heard of her. Why?'

'Si's left everything to her.'

I snatch the paperwork from his hand.

I bequeath all my personal possessions and assets to Miss Angela Bentley-Bell, Flat 3, 67 Forsdyke Road, Brighton.

Simon and Tina didn't have kids. I could believe he'd be bloody minded enough to leave his money to an animal charity or scientific research rather than let Tina get her hands on anything. But this? 'Who the hell is Angela Bentley-Bell?'

'He must have had a secret girlfriend,' says Tom.

'But why wouldn't he tell me?'

'Perhaps they hadn't been together long, and he didn't want to risk her being vetted by his two bossy sisters.'

I thump Tom on the arm. 'If they weren't together long, then why leave everything to her?'

Tom pulls up a chair as I set the two wills side by side. They both look legit, with solicitor's stamps on the last page. The sole beneficiary on the first is Tina and on the second is Angela. 'Poor Tina,' I say. Then, noticing another difference, I gasp. 'Damn it!'

'What?' says Tom.

'On the first, I'm sole executor. On the second, Si's named both Wendy and me.'

'That's okay. You could do with the help.'

'But it means I'll have to tell her something.'

Tom frowns. 'Doesn't that rather defeat the point of rushing over there?'

'I won't mention all the stuff we found. Where are we going to put it, anyway?'

'Dump it.'

'I'm not sure we can. Angela might know it was there.' I tap my chin thoughtfully. 'Do you think Wendy knows who this Angela is?'

'I doubt it.'

'It's odd we've never heard of her.' Why didn't Si tell me about his girlfriend? Was he embarrassed by us? I open my own laptop and Google "Angela Bentley-Bell" and "Brighton". A link pops up for an online legal advice service. I scroll through the advisors' names and get a hit.

Tom reads over my shoulder. 'She's a lawyer?'

'Looks like it. Or she was. The company's gone into liquidation.' I click "Images" and I'm taken to a photo of an attractive red-haired woman. The image is blurry, but she's posing in a yellow, one-piece swimming costume on a pebbly beach that could be Brighton. 'Can this be her?'

Tom whistles. 'Beauty and brains.'

'Hey!' I elbow him. 'That's chauvinistic.'

'Ow.' He rubs his ribs. "Why don't we see if Jamie can find out more?'

'That's not a bad idea.' I grab my mobile and call our son. 'Hi Jamie. We went to Uncle Simon's today and found out he's left everything to someone we've never heard of.'

'Seriously?'

I gulp back a sob. It hurts that Si didn't share his news with me. 'I know how good you are with computers,' I say. 'Her name's Angela Bentley-Bell and she lives in Brighton. I wonder if you could take a look? All I'm getting on Google is that she used to work for an online law firm, but the company seems to have been dissolved.'

'Okay, leave it with me,' says Jamie.

. . .

He messages back within the hour.

> I've found an Instagram account. You'll have to set up your own account to view the whole thing but I'm attaching a link to a photo.

I open the link on my phone. It's a better shot of Angela on the same beach, pouting as all youngsters do in their selfies. 'Wow,' I say. 'She's gorgeous.'

Tom leans over my shoulder. 'Simon was punching.'

I enlarge the image. 'She's young. Twenties, do you think?'

He reaches for the porn magazine again.

'Tom, for heaven's sake. You'll go blind.'

'Hang on. I want to check something.' He thumbs through. 'There, look.'

I stare at the photo in the magazine. It's staged, of course – a girl staring directly into the camera lens, wearing a red basque and suspenders. 'Okay, I know you have a penchant for fishnet stockings, but what exactly am I supposed to be looking at?'

'Look closer.'

'So, she's got a whip.' I push the magazine away. 'Some sort of sadomasochist stuff. I don't see why…'

'Look at her face.'

Reluctantly, I take the magazine back and study the girl more closely. I pick up my mobile phone, allowing my gaze to travel from the girl on the beach to the girl in the magazine and back again. 'It can't be… is it the same person?'

'I think it is,' says Tom.

I flick back to the first page of the article. '*Angelica Belle in her Dungeon from Hell.* Who the devil is she?'

'There's a six-page spread,' says Tom.

I scan through the first paragraph: *Princess Angelica… fetish and sexual… sadistic dominatrix…* 'Oh my God. Si's left everything to a sex worker.'

CHAPTER FIVE

'Are you awake?'

I lift my head from the pillow and squint up at my husband. 'Yeah.'

'I'm away in a minute, but there's something I need to show you.'

I throw off the quilt, pull on my dressing gown and follow Tom down to the kitchen. 'What's so important?' I switch on the kettle, stifling a yawn. I didn't get to sleep until the early hours, turning everything over in my mind.

'I was looking through that fetish magazine again over my porridge.'

'For God's sake, Tom. I'm not sure it's appropriate, given her connection to Si.'

'I noticed something about the photoshoot.'

'What?'

'Simon's in the photos.'

'What?'

'Look.' Tom opens the magazine to the six-page spread. Behind the woman, a man, face blurred and wearing a black latex leotard, is shackled by hands and feet to a bench.

I rub my eyes. 'That could be literally anybody.'

'Turn the page.'

I turn over and gasp. The image in the next two shots is much clearer. On the right-hand page the man is lifting his head. Si's features and wavy hair are clearly visible in the mirror wall. 'Fuck.'

'Fuck indeed,' says Tom.

'I looked at this yesterday and didn't even register anyone tied to the bench.'

'Same,' he says. 'My eyes were on the lovely lady in the basque.'

I slump down heavily on a kitchen stool while Tom makes me a coffee.

'What does this mean?' I ask. 'Could she have been blackmailing him? Is that why he's left everything to her?'

'I don't know, but I thought you'd want to know.' Tom checks the time on the kitchen clock and picks up his car keys. 'I'm sorry, I've got to go.' He pecks my cheek. 'I've put those boxes up in the loft for now.'

After he's gone, I carry my mug through to the dining room. I can't believe it. Why would Si have got involved with that woman? Picking up his leather Filofax, I work methodically through the sections. I don't know what I'm looking for – a blackmail note, perhaps? What I find is a couple of Polaroids, similar to the shots in the magazine. In one, Si's nuzzling up to the dominatrix. In another, his head is between her thighs. He doesn't appear to be protesting. Far from it. Could he really have cared for her?

My coffee's gone cold. I wander back to the kitchen, open the cupboard and stare at cereal boxes. I've no appetite and my head's throbbing. Perhaps it was the gin last night. I perch at the breakfast bar and ring Nicki.

'Sarah?' She sounds surprised. 'You're not home already?'

'We had to cut the holiday short. It's Si. He's dead.'

She gasps. 'Oh Sarah. I'm so sorry. What happened?'

'He had a heart attack.'

'What? But he was so young.'

'Yes.'

'Oh, my goodness. What can I do to help?'

'Nothing, really. I just needed to hear a friendly voice.'

'I'm always here for you.' I can tell she's holding back tears. 'Oh God, what a shock.'

'It happened Sunday night,' I continue. 'He dialled 999, but was gone when the paramedics arrived.'

'Oh my. Well, at least it was quick. He won't have known much about it.'

'I can't bear to think of him being on his own. He'd have been so frightened.'

'Oh, Sarah. I don't know what to say.'

'I know.'

'Have you got to identify him?'

'No, the coroner said the police already did that.'

'And is Tom being supportive? I know things haven't been great between you two lately…'

'To be fair, he's been bloody brilliant.'

As I hang up, Brodie sighs mournfully. 'All right, boy. Once I'm dressed, I'll take you out.' I rummage around in the kitchen drawer for paracetamol and swallow two tablets with a glass of water.

The walk revives us both. On our return, I fill Brodie's water bowl and make myself coffee and toast. After I've eaten, I call my sister. 'Hi Wendy.'

'Hey, how are you doing?'

'Okay. We went to Si's yesterday.'

'Oh dear. That must have been an ordeal.'

'Yeah, a bit.' She has no idea. 'We collected the spare key and I picked up some paperwork.'

'Well, don't you go doing all the sorting yourself. I'll speak to Bob and find out when we can come over. It's Mary, of course. I'm not sure who'll look after her.'

Typical. Since her mother-in-law moved into their annex, my sister has the perfect excuse not to venture west of Robertsbridge. 'Wendy, we found two wills.'

'Two?'

'Yes. In the first he left everything to Tina…'

'Well, I can't say I'm surprised he made a new will. I don't think Simon even spoke to Tina after the divorce. We have a photo of him and Tina at Millie's baptism in one of those multiple framed collages. When Simon last visited, he asked if I wouldn't mind removing it. The cheek. After all, Tina is still Millie's auntie…'

'Wendy,' I interrupt. 'In the second will, Si's left everything to someone called Angela Bentley-Bell. Have you heard of her?'

'Angela Bentley-Bell? Sounds posh. Perhaps his girlfriend? You know, he was texting someone last time he was here. Bob did wonder if…'

I interject again. 'So, you've never heard of her?'

'No, but I'm pleased he had someone special. I hated to think of him all alone.'

'Did you know he'd named both you and me as executors?'

'What? Oh, I'm not sure I want the responsibility. Especially if the beneficiary is someone we don't know.'

'But you just said you were pleased for him?'

'Well, I am, but I'll need to talk this over with Bob.'

Of course she does. Her husband has dominion over all aspects of her life. At eighteen she cast aside her plans for university when she left home to get married. With her support, Bob, a Bible-bashing brother of a strict religious sect, rose quickly through the ranks to elder. Every decision in their lives is governed by adherence to holy scripture and the restrictive rulebook of the patriarchal congregation.

'What shall we do about Dad?' I ask.

'What do you mean?'

'We should tell him, don't you think?'

'Oh, I'm not sure that's a good idea. He wouldn't understand.'

'But it feels wrong. Him not knowing, I mean.'

'You know how he is, Sarah. He's completely withdrawn from this world.'

'He still has better days.'

She sighs. 'It's his birthday next week.'

'I know. Are you going to see him?'

'I might try and call over next weekend if Bob can stay with Mary.'

Don't put yourself out, I think. I'd been leading up to telling her about the sex stuff. She's joint executor and she should know. But I can't seem to raise the matter over the phone. 'Okay. I'll go through Si's paperwork and see what I can figure out.'

'All right, but don't take on too much too soon.'

I return to the dining room table and stare at the papers.

At the sound of a key in the lock, Brodie barks excitedly. Seconds later, my son pokes his head around the door. 'Hi Mum.'

'Jamie!'

He steps into the room. 'Thought you might need a hug.'

'I do.' I stand up and wrap my arms around him.

He leans back studying my face. 'You doing okay?'

'Sort of. Coffee?'

'Sure.' He follows me into the kitchen and sits at the breakfast bar.

I flick the switch on the kettle and spoon coffee into mugs. 'Thanks for the link you sent.'

'Hope it was helpful.'

Once I've made our drinks, I sit beside him.

Jamie helps himself to sugar. 'This Angela. She was Uncle Simon's girlfriend?'

I sip my drink. 'Not exactly.'

He laughs. 'I thought she was a bit…'

'Yes.' I purse my lips. I can't ask my son to do this, can I? It's not appropriate. I take a deep breath. 'Jamie, could you do another search for me? Anything on social media in the name of Angelica Belle.'

'Similar name. Is it the same person?'

'She might be.' I hesitate a moment. 'I think she's something in the sex industry.'

'Porn star?'

'Well, she's in a fetish magazine. Your dad says it's not the same as porn.'

'Okaaay.'

My cheeks flush with heat. I've said too much.

Jamie checks the time. 'My shift at Sainsbury's doesn't start until two. Can I use your laptop?'

'It's on the dining room table. Shall I make you a sandwich?'

'Need you ask?' Jamie winks as he heads into the dining room.

I toast cheese sandwiches and carry them through on a tray. Jamie's engrossed, so I sit opposite, writing 'to do' lists in my notebook. We eat lunch in companionable silence.

After he's finished eating, Jamie pushes back his chair. 'Right, how much do you want to know?'

'Everything.'

'I've found Instagram and Twitter accounts for Angelica Belle. You can't access much unless you request to follow, but you're right. I'm pretty sure from the profile pics it's the same girl.'

'I shouldn't be asking you to do this.'

'It's okay, Mum.'

'I don't suppose there's a contact number or email?'

'No, it's a secured account. The other thing is... I found an Instagram account for Uncle Simon. It's not in his name, so I don't think he wanted it found. There's some dodgy stuff... perhaps it's not such a good idea you read it?'

I feel sick. 'Jamie, I'm so sorry.'

'It's okay.' He checks his mobile. 'Look, I need to go.'

'Do you need a lift?'

'No, I'm good.'

'Jamie?'

He pauses on the threshold.

'We found things at Uncle Simon's. Sex toys and stuff. Your dad's put the boxes up in the loft. I didn't want you to stumble across them and think...'

He grins. 'What? That my parents are a pair of right old pervs?'

CHAPTER SIX

'I'm home.' Tom comes through to the kitchen.

'You're late.'

'Sorry.' He takes a bottle of wine from the fridge and pours two glasses. 'It's been manic today. The Art Deco furniture arrived from Garrick House and Yvette's been rushed off her feet.'

'Poor Yvette.' I try to keep sarcasm from my voice. It seems to me she has both Tom and his business partner Graham, wrapped around her little finger.

'Don't start.' Tom passes me my wine.

Biting my tongue, I drain water from the pasta and dish it into bowls. 'All right to eat out here? The table's still covered.'

'Sure.' Tom perches on a kitchen stool.

'Jamie popped in lunchtime,' I say, changing the subject.

'I wondered if he would.' Tom makes a start on his food. 'Any more info on Angelica Belle?'

'He found a few social media accounts.' I play with my pasta. 'I can't stop thinking about her. If Si's left her everything, she must have meant a lot to him. What if she doesn't know? What if she's going about her day not knowing that Si's dead?'

'It's not your problem.'

'It is if I'm to be executor. I need to get hold of her.'

'Can't you write?'

'That will take time. I think it's important she knows.'

After Tom's finished eating, he heads into the sitting room and slumps in front of the TV. I clear things away and message Jamie.

> Is there a way I can get in touch with Angelica other than by writing?

> Only by setting yourself up with an Instagram account and following her, he replies. Or I suppose I could follow her…

> Don't you dare!

I pour myself another glass of wine and wander through to the dining table. An hour later, Jamie messages back.

> Okay, I have a phone number for Angelica.

> Brilliant. How did you do it?

> Reverse search. Best you don't know.

I have Angela Bentley-Bell's number. Well, I have Angelica Belle's number, and everything points to them being the same person. If Si had feelings for her, he'd want her to know what's happened.

I pick up the phone, but don't feel brave enough to ring. What would I say? Instead, I send a message.

> Hello. Is this the number for Angela? This is
> Sarah Edwards. I have sad news about my
> brother, Simon Foster.

Tom turns off the TV and heads out to the kitchen. Moments later, he sticks his head around the dining room door. 'You've cleared up. I was going to do that.'

Course you were… 'S'okay.' I stare at my phone, willing Angelica to reply.

'I'll take Simon's laptop into work tomorrow. Steve will need possible passwords. Write down anything you can think of – birthdays, pets' names, your mum and dad's birthdays, special places…' He emits an exaggerated yawn. 'I think I'll go up. You coming?'

'Not yet. Got a bit more to do.'

'Night night, then.'

As he heads upstairs, my phone beeps with a text.

> Hi Sarah. Yes, this is Angela. Has something
> happened?

I'm sorry to have to tell you that Simon died suddenly two days ago. He had a heart attack. It's been a terrible shock.

> Oh no, I'm so sorry. Simon and I were good
> friends, but I hadn't seen him in a while.
> How are you coping?

Hadn't seen him in a while? Why the hell has he left everything to her, then? She doesn't even sound surprised. Suspicion flits into my mind. Did she already know?

I don't think it's really sunk in.

> No, of course. Sarah, I'm intrigued to know
> how you got my number.

I'm not ready to tell her she's Si's beneficiary. I'll have to make something up. I reflect for a moment before texting:

> Simon had your name written on a pad. My son helped me track you down from your Instagram account.

> Oh yes. Simon always said he'd leave my details, so you'd be able to contact me if anything happened to him.

If anything happened? That's an odd thing to say. There's a pause before she responds again.

> It must have come as a bit of a surprise, me and Simon.

That's an understatement. But I'm not giving her the satisfaction.

> I guess so, but each to his own.

> I'd like to talk to you sometime. There are things I think Simon would want you to know.

> Okay. I'm busy right now sorting out his stuff. I'll message again when I've more time.

I stay up until the early hours going through Si's paperwork. When I do eventually creep up to bed, I can't sleep. The mortgage application was for two hundred thousand so there should be collateral left in the flat. But what if Si increased it? And there's that loan agreement for twenty-four grand. Just how much more did he borrow? I toss and turn. Without bank statements, how do I know if Si was even solvent? Who the hell is Angela Bentley-Bell? And what would Si want me to know?

CHAPTER SEVEN

It's an hour's drive to Wendy's, but we need to speak face to face. As joint executor, she has a right to know what's going on.

As I pull onto the gravelled drive, she steps out of the front door of their mock Tudor house frowning. 'No Tom?'

'He had to go to work, but I need to talk to you about something.'

'You'd best come in.' Linking arms, she leads me into the beamed hallway and waits while I take off my shoes. Opening a hidden cupboard under the stairs, she hands me a pair of towelling visitor mules. I slip them on and follow her into the new kitchen extension. It always surprises me that accumulated wealth seems to be condoned under the brethren's rulebook.

Today the bifolds are fully open. 'Wow.' I say. 'Those doors really do bring the outside in.'

'They do, don't they?' Wendy pads across the hardwood floor to her top-of-the-range coffee maker. 'Latte or cappuccino?'

'Cappuccino please.' I perch on one of the designer stools

while she presses buttons and the machine obliges with comforting gurgles and hisses. No wonder my sister doesn't like leaving home.

She carries two cups to the kitchen island and lifts the domed lid from a glass cake stand. 'Carrot cake? It's vegan.'

'Please,' I say.

She cuts us both a generous slice and pushes a plate towards me.

I fork cake into my mouth. 'This is lovely.'

She beams.

I put my fork down. 'Wendy, there's something I should have told you a long time ago.'

She perches on the stool beside me, waiting expectantly.

'When Si and Tina split up, Tina and I met for a drink. She told me things about Si. Things I didn't know.' A tear trickles down my cheek and I wipe it away with my hand.

'Oh, bless you.' She offers me a linen napkin.

'Thanks. I feel bad I never told you, but it felt wrong even me knowing. I didn't want what she told me to damage your relationship with Si.'

'Did Simon know you knew?'

'No, of course not.'

'Well, maybe you don't need to tell me then.'

'I do, because it has implications for what we have to do for him.' I take a sip of coffee, wishing that Wendy had something stronger. 'Tina told me Si was gambling. He was also watching some dodgy stuff online.'

She gasps. 'Porn?'

'I don't know the details. Chat lines maybe?'

'That's even worse.'

'Tina wanted me to know so I'd understand why she left him. She wanted me to tell you too, but I couldn't.'

'It's okay.'

'It's not okay.' I hesitate for a moment. 'Me and Tom found stuff. Sex stuff in Si's flat. That's why I wanted to get over there before you and Bob showed up. Tina told me there were things she couldn't tolerate. I thought we might find adult magazines, perhaps a bit of porn on his computer but, the thing is…'

'Go on.'

'Angela Bentley-Bell. We've found out she's also known as Angelica Belle. She's a sex worker.'

Wendy's cheeks pale.

'Angela Bentley-Bell is a dominatrix,' I say. 'Do you know what that is?'

'Of course I do,' she splutters. 'I may not have read *50 Shades,* but I'm not totally naive.'

'Okay, sorry.'

She drums manicured fingernails on the worktop. 'Do you think we should contest the will?'

'I don't know. If it's what Si wanted…'

'Perhaps this Angelica woman coerced him?'

'She says she and Si were friends.'

Wendy's voice raises an octave. 'You've spoken to her?'

'No, I texted. I was worried she might not know Si had died.'

'And did she?'

'I'm not sure. I wasn't convinced she was surprised, but it's hard to tell from text messages.'

My sister pushes her cup away. 'I'll have to speak to Bob about this.'

'Sorry if I've shocked you.' I slide off my stool and pick up my handbag. 'Let me know what Bob says.'

'It's not you, Sarah, but it goes to show that you never really know people.' She sighs. 'Look, I'll talk to Bob, but I'm pretty sure I won't be acting as executor.'

I drag myself out of bed and stumble downstairs in my dressing gown. Tom left early and Brodie, excited to see me, wags his tail. 'Sorry boy. I need coffee first.'

My mobile rings. 'I'm renouncing executorship,' says Wendy, 'and I suggest you do the same.'

This is Bob-speak. He never did approve of Simon's life choices and was constantly inferring he had a drink problem. I can imagine how it went. *"Your brother's a sinner and will not enter the Kingdom of God. Set yourself apart from all things immoral..."* He's such a pious prick! As I flick on the kettle, I try a different tack. 'What about Si's personal stuff?'

Wendy scoffs. 'I'm not bothered about that.'

I spoon instant coffee into a mug. 'We don't want Angelica getting access to family stuff. If she gets his laptop, goodness knows what's on there.'

'I told you, I don't care.'

'What about your kids? If she's a sex worker, who knows what sort of people she mixes with? She might sell our details on to paedophiles. Millie and Rosie could be groomed.'

'Now you're being ridiculous.'

'I'm not being ridiculous,' I snap, irritated my sister doesn't seem more concerned about the risk to her teenage daughters. 'If we renounce executorship, we give up control.'

'Bob's rung Citizens Advice and got me an appointment for tomorrow morning. Why don't you do the same?'

'I'm not sure…'

'Sarah, you don't need to be involved. Bob's furious that Simon has dragged us into his sordid little world. Promise me you won't contact that woman again?'

'I need to think about it.'

. . .

After hanging up, I head into the dining room, fire up my laptop and Google "Renounce executorship". *If an executor intends to renounce, they must do so before any intermeddling.*

The article goes on to define intermeddling as, "Performing some or all of the duties that a personal representative would be obliged to perform if they were administering the estate." Oops. I may have already intermeddled.

Brodie whimpers.

'All right, boy.' I quickly shower and dress.

As I walk Brodie through the park, I call Nicki. 'Fancy meeting for coffee?'

I'm sitting outside Organic Deli nursing a cold latte when she arrives carrying a bunch of roses. She hugs me before stooping to pet Brodie under the table. 'Hello boy. Hope you're looking after your mistress.'

I take the bouquet and set it down on a spare chair. 'You didn't have to, but thanks.'

'There's this, too.' She hands me a card.

I tear open the envelope and silently read the Henry Scott-Holland poem, *Death is nothing at all.* Inside, Nicki has written, "*With love and thoughts from the Humanities Faculty*".

'That's very sweet,' I say.

'I emailed the heads of department. I hope that was all right. How are the arrangements going?'

'Everything's up in the air. They won't release Si's body until they've carried out a post-mortem.'

'Well, they have to check these things out.'

'I know.'

Nicki picks up the menu. 'Have you decided?'

'I'm not hungry.'

'You must eat. Why don't we share a hummus and vegetable panini?' She goes to place our order at the counter, calling back over her shoulder. 'Do you want another drink?'

I glance at the cold froth in my mug. 'Just tap water please.'

Nicki returns to the table. 'I hope your sister's helping?'

'It's not easy with her commitments, the mother-in-law…'

'But she'll come to the funeral? I'm sure she'll support you on the day. Look, I know I wasn't close to Simon, but would you like me there?'

'I'd love it. You're such a good friend.'

A waitress delivers our drinks. 'The panini won't be long,' she says.

'Thanks.' Nicki stirs sweetener into her latte. 'You've let HR know?'

I sip my water. 'Not yet, but I will.'

She stares at me. 'Simon was your brother, Sarah. You're entitled to time off.'

I shake my head. 'It won't be necessary. I'm hoping to arrange the funeral before the end of the school holidays.'

'Well, you're not to worry about coming in for Results Day. I can brief the other heads of department re the results analysis.'

'No, I'll be there.'

'God, talk about soldiering on.'

Tears prick behind my eyes.

Nicki touches my hand. 'Sorry, I didn't mean to upset you. It's just… you don't have to do everything yourself.'

The waitress arrives with a panini and an extra plate.

'Thanks.' Nicki slides one half of the panini onto the spare plate and pushes it towards me. 'Eat,' she commands.

I pick up a slice of red pepper. 'I can't open Si's laptop to access his bank accounts.'

'I suppose that's a common problem nowadays.'

'Not helpful when you're executor.'

'Can't you contact the banks yourself?' She bites into the panini.

'Probably.' I place the pepper back on my plate. 'I've got something else to tell you.'

She raises an eyebrow.

'Si left everything to a woman we've never heard of.'

Nicki splutters and chokes.

'You all right?'

'Went the wrong way,' she croaks.

I pass her my water.

'Ta.' Setting the glass down, she brushes breadcrumbs from her top. 'Simon was a dark horse.'

'That's not the worst of it.' I lean forward to whisper. 'She was his dominatrix.'

Nicki's eyes bulge before she bursts out laughing. I find myself joining in and it's a relief.

'Sorry' – she holds her belly – 'but you couldn't make this stuff up.' She dabs her eyes with a paper napkin. 'Is my mascara smudged?'

'No, you're fine.'

'And you had no idea? What am I saying, of course you didn't. You'd have told your bestie.' She places a hand lightly on my arm. 'So, have you been in touch with her yet?'

'We've exchanged a few texts.'

'But you are going to meet her?'

'I'm not sure. I suppose I might.'

She grins. 'Can I come?'

CHAPTER EIGHT

'Take a seat,' says a young girl in Santander's Haywards Heath branch office.

Perching on a red leather sofa, I check through my file – bank cards, copy of the will plus my own ID.

A young man approaches, hand extended. 'Mrs Edwards? Please, come this way.'

Although it's my local branch, I've never been upstairs. I follow him into a tiny interview room and take the chair opposite the desk.

'Firstly' – he adjusts his tie – 'may I say how sorry I am for your loss.'

'Thank you,' I say.

'Would you like a drink?'

'I'd like a G&T, but I doubt that's an option.'

He smiles politely. 'I understand you've been unable to access your brother's accounts online?'

'Yes. Everything's triple locked. When we try to change the password, it insists on verifying by sending a code to Simon's phone.'

'And you can't access that either.'

'No. I tried the Apple Genius team, but they can't access the phone without a passcode.'

He turns to a computer screen. 'Did you bring ID?'

I hand over my driving licence and a statement from the water board. 'To be honest, I had a job finding a hard copy of my own utility bills. I suppose it's a sign of the times.'

He nods. 'Your brother had three accounts with us – a current account and two savings accounts.'

'And what about a credit card?'

'He didn't have a credit card with us.'

'Well, that's something I suppose. What about payments to other credit cards? He had cards with Barclaycard and MBNA.' I tap my fingernails on the desk as he checks the screen. 'Wouldn't it be easier if you printed me a copy of whatever it is you're looking at?'

'You'd like to request hard copies?' he asks.

'Of course. As I've already explained, I have no access to my brother's bank statements.'

'I'll put in a request to head office. Will the last six months be sufficient?'

'You can't print them now?'

'I'm afraid that's not Santander's policy, but I can check for the payments you've asked about. Ah yes, Barclaycard. A payment went out on the fifteenth of July for five hundred pounds.'

Shit. If Simon was paying Barclaycard £500 a month, what the hell did he owe?

The young man smiles courteously. 'Were you looking for funeral expenses to be released?'

'That would be helpful.'

'It's Santander's policy to release funds to cover funeral expenses' – he pauses – 'where such funds exist.'

There's a sinking feeling in my belly. 'Are you saying there are insufficient funds?'

'Let me print the balances.' The printer to the side of his desk whirs and chugs while we sit in uncomfortable silence. It's obviously too vulgar to discuss actual figures. He passes me two slips of paper. 'These are the balances for your brother's savings accounts.'

I read £00.00 on the first slip and £00.14 on the second.

He hands me another sheet of paper. 'And this is the statement for his current account.'

I scan to the bottom of the page. '£26.87. That's it?'

He nods.

'So, you won't be releasing funds for his funeral?'

'I can release the funds in your brother's account to you today,' he says, 'if you give me your bank account details.'

'I bank here.' I tap the desk. 'Sorry, are you saying this is all that's in my brother's account? Twenty-six pounds?'

'And eighty-seven pence,' he says. 'Plus fourteen pence credit in the saver account.'

I call Wendy. 'There's nothing in his bank accounts.'

'She's cleared him out,' she says. 'Angela Bell, more like Dark Angel from Hell.'

Despite the situation, I chuckle. 'That's pretty good.'

'This is Satan at work, Sarah,' she continues. 'You need to renounce.'

'Renounce what? My sins? Jesus, Wendy, you sound like a bloody priest. This is not some sort of exorcism.'

'Please don't blaspheme.'

I exhale. 'Sorry.'

'I'm sorry too. I'm just worried, Sarah. You don't understand how the devil works. You're most at risk when you're vulnerable.'

'I'm not vulnerable, and anyway, it's too late now. I've been to the bank, so I've intermeddled. You can't renounce executorship once you've intermeddled.'

It's a moment before she speaks. 'Bob and I were thinking. If you insist on going down the executor route, why not hand it over to a solicitor? You don't have to sort everything yourself.'

'But I do. I can't bear the idea of some house clearance company dumping everything into a skip.' I stop short of telling her what's really on my mind. That perhaps there's something in Si's flat I'm meant to find – a clue, a message from beyond the grave, something to help me make sense of all this. 'Anyway,' I continue, 'if the estate's insolvent there won't be money to pay a solicitor.'

She lowers her voice. 'I'm not sure I can help much. Bob's livid about the whole thing. I might be able to put a little aside…'

'Forget it,' I say. 'If it comes to that, I'll sort it out and claim it back off the estate.'

'But suppose there's nothing in his estate?'

'Then I don't know.' I sigh. 'Anyway, we need to make arrangements for Si's funeral.'

'Yes, of course. Perhaps you could claim something towards that? There must be a government fund or some such thing.'

'We're not giving our brother a pauper's funeral,' I snap. I take a deep breath. 'Are you coming to the funeral directors with me?'

'I don't think I can. Mary's not been well and…'

'Right. Well, have a think if there's anything particular you'd like.'

'I'm sure I'll be happy with whatever you decide.'

'What about dates? Do some days work better for you?'

'You'll have to see what they've got. Don't wait on us.'

'But you are coming?'

Her hesitation says it all. 'I'll try, but it does depend on getting someone to sit with Mary.'

After hanging up, I check the time. Tom won't be home for at least an hour. I suppose there's no harm in trying a solicitor. As I Google local firms, I wonder how much to tell them. Oh, damn it. They may as well know the whole story.

'So, your brother has left everything to a sex worker?' says the first guy. 'Well, if the will is legitimate, there's not much you can do about it.'

'I'm not disputing the will. I just want to know what happens to his digital assets.'

'I've never been asked that before,' he says. 'I'll have to take advice.'

How can the issue of digital assets not have been raised before? Everyone keeps everything online nowadays.

'How do I gain access if I have no passwords?' I ask the next.

'You can't,' she replies. 'It's illegal. But if you retain executorship, you have the right to have any computers cleared down.'

'But I need access to his accounts to determine whether my brother is solvent.'

'I'm sorry, we wouldn't take on an insolvency case,' she says.

The third company is more helpful. 'Well,' she says. 'In twenty-three years, I've only come across this sort of thing once before. You're right, you do need to establish whether the estate is solvent.'

'But asking banks for details of his accounts is intermeddling and I read online that if I want to renounce executorship, I can't intermeddle in the deceased estate.'

'That's true.'

'Would you take the case if I paid myself?'

'Yes, but perhaps do a little more digging. Do you have the original will?'

'No, just a copy.'

'See if the solicitor who drew up the will made any notes.'

'We'll have to eat out here again.' I gesture to place mats on the breakfast bar. 'The dining room table's still covered in paperwork.'

'That's okay.' Tom washes his hands. 'Is Jamie back tonight?'

'No, he and Dan have plans. He's coming home Sunday.' I dish up lasagne. 'It's only a *Cook* one from the freezer, I'm afraid.'

'That's fine.' Tom takes a bottle of wine from the fridge and pours us both a glass before sliding onto a kitchen stool. 'How did you get on today?'

I spoon salad onto plates. 'I've made loads of calls. Still information gathering.' I rest my chin on my hand. 'Sometimes I wish we'd never brought that bloody stuff home with us.'

'You're not suggesting we take it back?'

'No.' I pick up a fork. 'It's too late now.'

He tries the lasagne. 'This is good.'

'Did Steve have any joy with Si's laptop?'

Tom shakes his head. 'Not yet.'

I put down my fork. 'If Angela inherits his personal effects, she'll get that, too. How do we know what's on there? Suppose she sells our personal details?'

'You worry too much,' says Tom.

I resume eating, but my mind's in a whirl and I can't stop talking. 'Suppose when we do get into the laptop, I find Si's in debt? Suppose he's insolvent?'

Tom tops up my glass. 'Then I guess there won't be anything for Angela to inherit.'

'But what about me and Wendy? Are we liable for his debts?'

'I wouldn't think so.'

I push back my chair. 'I need to check.' Leaving Tom loading the dishwasher, I head into the dining room and start up my laptop. The Co-op web page *What to do when someone dies,* is reassuring. It sounds as if my sister and I would not be responsible for Si's debts. However, it states in bold lettering: ***We do not handle insolvency cases.***

I look up as Tom brings the coffee through. 'I don't think I'm up to this.'

'Then quit. Your sister has.' He moves the paperwork aside, places the cups on the table and sits beside me. 'Tell me the pros and cons.'

'Well, if I stay as executor, I might be able to influence what Angela gets. Also, I can ensure his debts get paid. But it's a ton of work with no gain.'

Tom sips his drink. 'And what if you bailed? What are you afraid of? Letting Simon down?'

Letting him down… I'm transported back to the 1980s, when Si and I were fourteen. A new girl started at our school and my form tutor, who viewed me as responsible, asked me to look after her. Bianca had moved down from London when her family did a council house swap. With her pink hair, biker jacket and lace skirt, she looked like Cyndi Lauper. We began to hang out and my kudos shot up instantly. Sadly, my streetwise friend was not a good influence. Well-versed in shoplifting, she soon had me pilfering lipsticks and nail polish from Boots and stashing her haul of cigarettes and weed.

When Dad found the contraband in my bedroom, he went ballistic.

'It's not mine,' I said.

'It's under your bed,' yelled Dad, his face puce with rage.

'It's mine,' said Si. 'I hid it there so you wouldn't find it.'

Years later, I asked Si why he covered for me.

'I was always in trouble – drinking, smoking, stealing. One more black mark didn't matter, but you?' He shrugged. 'You were Dad's little golden girl. I didn't want to shatter his illusion.'

'Sarah? I said, what if you bailed?'

I open my mouth but there's a lump in my throat and I can't speak.

'I think you have your answer,' says Tom.

CHAPTER NINE

I order peppermint tea and sit facing the window. Veez, the veggie café on the edge of The Lanes, was my suggestion. I've been here before on shopping trips to Brighton with Nicki. Should I have worn a red carnation? I'm early but want to see Angela arrive.

Eleven o'clock comes and goes. By quarter past, I've decided she's not going to show. The café's heaving with brunch customers. If she doesn't arrive soon, I'll have to order something else. I'm about to go up to the counter when a head-turning woman steps through the door in a purple faux fur coat with a *Louis Vuitton* handbag tucked under her arm.

'Angela?' I say.

She smiles, her lips plump, her make-up flawless. 'Call me Angel.' The drawl in her voice throws me. I hadn't expected the accent. 'I'll get myself a tea.'

I observe her waiting in line. Glossy red hair worthy of a *L'Oréal* ad; black ski slacks disappearing into understated but expensive leather high-heeled boots. She's not just attractive, she's beautiful. Like she stepped off a catwalk. I listen as she places her order, precise in the way Americans often are.

'I'll take an Earl Grey tea please. China cup, no milk, lemon on the side.'

The guy behind the counter smiles. ''Drinking in? Take a seat and I'll bring it over.' He didn't offer me table service.

Returning to the table, she unbuttons her coat but doesn't take it off, as if reserving the option of flight. She smells divine – jasmine and vanilla. Is it *Yves Saint Laurent*? If we were on a blind date, I'd be the disappointing one. No wonder Si was enamoured. As Tom said, he was clearly punching. Or would have been if he hadn't been paying for it, I remind myself.

'How are you?' she says.

Her tone is condescending and I bristle. 'I'm doing okay.'

'I'm glad you suggested meeting. So much better than texting.'

The serving guy brings her tea.

'Thank you.' She turns to me. 'You having another?'

'No, I'm okay for the minute.'

'This feels so strange.' She smiles. 'It's like I know you. Simon talked about you all the time. You and Wendy.'

'He did?' I hadn't expected that.

'Yes. He told me all about coming to you for Christmas last year. He also sent me a lovely photo of him and Wendy when he visited her in Robertsbridge.'

Christ's sake. She knows so much more about us than we know about her. 'How long had you known Simon?' I ask.

'Three years, off and on. We were very close last year. Texting on a daily basis.'

Three years? Was he texting her when he stayed at mine? Were they laughing at my conventional little family? I feel a sudden surge of anger. 'When did you last see him?'

'A few months ago.' She wrinkles her nose and I notice a

smattering of freckles under her make-up. 'I must admit we'd had a bit of a falling out.'

'What about?'

'Simon was seeing someone, and I didn't think she was a good influence.'

Was she jealous? Is that how this works? One dominatrix poaches clients from another?

'I knew her,' Angel continues, 'and guessed she'd get him back on drugs.'

'Drugs?'

'Nothing illegal. Mostly nitrous and ket.'

'Fuck.'

'Please understand, when Simon was with me, I'd virtually weaned him off. Apart from poppers, he was clean.'

Supercilious bitch. Does she expect gratitude? I have no idea of the world she's describing. I don't know this other Simon.

'I was training him,' she goes on. 'Helping him to sort out his life.'

He wouldn't have needed to sort out his life if you weren't in it, you cow, I think. But I smile and nod.

She sips tea. 'He wasn't in a good place financially. I expect you knew that.'

'I know he'd built up a few gambling debts.'

'Did Tina tell you that?' Her smile is patronising. 'It was his cover story. Most of the money went on chat lines and webcam. I was helping him get his life straight. I've got his household accounts. You'll be needing those. I could email them across.'

She's got his household accounts? Jeez. 'Thanks. I haven't been able to access much. Everything's online.'

'Yes. I did have his passwords, but he probably changed them. I'll send you what I've got.'

Did she have total control of his life? 'So, this other woman?' I prompt.

'Lady Layla,' she says. 'Yes, we know each other.'

'And she was a bad influence?'

'Layla's into ket. She also does breath training.'

I nod as if I understand what she's talking about. I'll have to Google it when I get home.

'What really annoyed me, though,' Angel continues, 'was when she posted a video of her and Simon out on a shopping spree. He was really splashing the cash and I knew he couldn't afford it.'

'Did you speak to him about it?'

'We exchanged a few angry texts, but I'm afraid he was pretty much out of control by then.'

'With drugs, you mean?'

'And spending beyond his means.'

Despite best intentions, tears trickle down my cheeks.

'I've upset you,' she says.

'No, it's okay.'

'It feels wrong.' She shakes her head. 'Telling you all this. Like I'm going behind his back. But he said he'd leave you a note explaining all about me.'

I squirm. 'Not exactly.'

She raises an eyebrow. 'He didn't leave a note?'

'Just the will.' I take a deep breath. 'Did you know that you're sole beneficiary?'

There's no change in her expression. 'He did say he was going to do that. He told me I saved his life.'

We leave the café, hugging awkwardly before going our separate ways. I head towards the promenade. I need to think.

Saved his life? She's got to be kidding. It was her who

destroyed it. How do I know she wasn't the one to get him onto drugs? She knows so much about us. God, Si. What were you thinking?

I'm even more worried now about what's on the laptop. Has Angel got access to his online stuff? Will she sell our details to dodgy people? I don't trust her, and yet I must portray the illusion of friendship. She's my only connection to a side of my brother I know nothing about. She was sorting his life out? That was my job. Why didn't Si ask me for help?

My phone buzzes with a text from Nicki.

> How did it go?

Okay I suppose. She was nice enough.

> Pretty, I bet.

Beautiful. And much younger than Si.

> OMG. Was it awkward?

I survived. She seems to know everything about Si, and all about me and Wendy.

> Perhaps they talked while they were doing it? [smiley face emoji]

I walk as far as the i360, sea air blowing the cobwebs away. On the way back, I call Wendy to fill her in on my meeting with Angel.

'You're getting too involved, Sarah. Walk away.'

Like you, I think. Perhaps it would make Wendy feel better if I did. 'I can't.'

At home, I head straight for my laptop to check out what Angel told me. Using the link Jamie gave me to Si's Instagram, I scroll down, quickly spotting a post I recognise. *Shopping in London – perhaps I'll visit the Queen, or at least a Lady?* I remember commenting I hoped he'd have a lovely day. Now the double entendre is obvious. Was he playing with me? Laughing as he posted messages with hidden meaning? That must have been the day he 'splashed the cash'. Were he and Layla just shopping, or did they have a sex session booked?

Si's entries are more frequent in June, which fits with what Angel said about him being out of control. Further down, I find a link to a video of Lady Layla. Skinny little thing, early twenties, perched on the bonnet of a tatty old car and flashing her suspenders at whoever's filming. The camera pans around and I see the photographer's not Simon, thank God.

What Angel told me about drugs plays on my mind. I'm Googling nitrous when my mobile rings. 'Why don't I bring home a takeaway?' says Tom. 'Save you cooking.'

Jamie's out, so we eat in the kitchen again. Tom drinks Cobra but opens a bottle of wine for me. This is becoming a habit.

'So,' he says. 'What's she like?'

I help myself to vegetable biriyani. 'American, slim – petite actually, and every bit as attractive as in the photos.' I fill him in on our conversation – the sex sites, Lady Layla, drugs.

'So, the capsules were nitrous?' he says.

'Uh huh.' After the Google research, I'm an expert. 'It's to make you high and involves the use of balloons and a cream maker.'

'Not foam parties, then.'

'And those little bottles we found in the bedside cabinet? Poppers, not massage oil. Dilute your blood vessels and cause... oh, it doesn't matter.' I'm not going into how they help your anus relax. 'Even opening a bottle runs the risk of inhaling. What will we do with them?'

'Pour them down the drain, I suppose.'

'No, there's a story online about someone disposing of the liquid down the sink and causing an explosion.'

'Perhaps we should drop them off at the police station? Are they legal?'

'I think so, but I don't really know. I almost wish they were illegal, then the police might access Si's phone and I might find out how much he was spending on them.'

'We could try a chemical waste disposal.'

I top up my glass and wander through to the dining room. Opening my laptop again, I Google "Chemical waste disposal near Haywards Heath" and find a number of drop-off sites.

While I'm searching, Tom fetches the box from the garage. He packs the tiny bottles in an old biscuit tin, masking it up with tape like it's some sort of nuclear waste. 'Perhaps I'm being a trifle overcautious,' he says, 'but what do I know?'

The ket is more difficult. From the internet search, it sounds as if it's administered in tablet form. 'We'll have to go through Si's medicine cupboard,' I say.

Tom scoffs. 'I doubt the bottles are labelled as ketamine.'

Next, I research the effects of long-term use of these drugs. 'He covered his tracks so well, I have no idea how long he'd been using. Angel seemed to think Layla got him on to them, but how can we be sure?'

'He may have been on them for years,' says Tom.

'Do you think they caused the heart attack?'

'I don't know.'

'The coroner mentioned that if the post-mortem threw up anything dodgy, there might be an inquest.' I get up and begin to pace. 'Suppose I'm put on the stand? Suppose they say, "Mrs Edwards, were you aware your brother took drugs for pleasure?" What do I say? I can't lie.'

'Sarah, you're worrying about something that might not even happen.'

'Perhaps I should tell the coroner?'

'Do you really want to raise drugs as an issue?'

CHAPTER TEN

Next morning, I call the Coroner's Office. 'Has the post-mortem on my brother been carried out?'

'Not yet. We hope to have it done by the end of the week. There's a bit of a backlog.'

'You asked me to come back to you if anything occurred of relevance to my brother's death?'

'Yes?'

'This is difficult, but it's come to my notice, from conversations with a friend, that Simon may have taken recreational drugs. Nitrous, poppers, perhaps some ketamine…'

'My dear, in my job, I've heard it all. Nothing you've told me comes as a great shock, but thank you for letting me know. I will ensure the doctor who performs the post-mortem is aware. Meanwhile, if anything else should come to your notice, please call.'

I text Angel as Tom and I drive to Si's flat.

> Did you manage to find Simon's accounts and passwords?

> I'm still sorting through everything. I'll send you something as soon as I can.

'She's cleaning things up,' says Tom. 'Making sure she's not incriminated in anything.'

He's probably right. I'm not going to argue after he's taken the day off to come with me.

'So, what are we looking for?' asks Tom, parking behind Simon's Corsa.

'The coroner told me what I need to register the death and Google supplied a list of what the bank needs.' I consult my notepad. 'Passport, driving licence, birth certificate and marriage certificate. I've already got the divorce papers.'

'And none of those things were in that home file?'

'Nope.'

We head up the stairs to Si's flat. The place already feels abandoned and unloved. Tom stands, hands on hips, in the middle of the sitting room. 'Okay, where do we start?'

'Could you empty the contents of the medicine cupboard? We don't know what he has in there. I don't think we should leave anything lying around.'

'On it.' Tom goes through to the bathroom while I check the drawers under the TV. I find various instruction manuals for household appliances, but nothing on my list.

'I've flushed everything, but I didn't see anything illegal,' calls Tom.

'Okay,' I reply. 'How about you check that tin box in the bedroom next? The one in the drawer where we found the credit cards.'

'Good call.'

I move across to the bookcase and start with the lower

shelves. Among the larger books, I locate a couple of A4 folders – one full of walking routes, while the other contains a wad of handwritten notes. 'Looks as if Si was teaching himself Spanish,' I mutter.

'I've found a few things,' calls Tom.

I go through to the bedroom where Si's birth and marriage certificates are laid out on the bed. 'That's good,' I say.

'There's also this.' Tom holds up a gold charm bracelet.

'That was Mum's. Angel's not getting that. Mum would turn in her grave.'

'A ring, too.' Tom opens a small box containing a blue solitaire ring. 'Would it be Tina's?'

'I don't know.'

'Let's take it. If Miss Bentley-Bell asks after it, we'll say we took it home for safe keeping. What else are we missing?'

'Passport and driving licence. I'm surprised they weren't in his Filofax.'

We return to the sitting room.

'What about where you found those photo albums?' asks Tom.

I open the small cupboard near the window. The bottom shelf is crammed full of loose photos spilling out of shoe boxes. I haul the whole lot onto the floor. 'I need to go through these. Some are old family photos.'

Tom loads them into a Sainsbury's Bag for Life. Under the boxes, I find another A4 folder and flick through – plastic wallets with vehicle documents and insurance policies. No passport or driving licence.

'I've just had a thought,' says Tom. 'Perhaps he kept his driving licence in the glove box of his car?'

'Yes, that's possible.' I check my list. 'Well, apart from the passport, that's it.'

'Where would he keep that?'

'I don't know. One of the bags in the wardrobe?'

We go through all the holdalls, emptying every side pocket. We even check the bedside cabinets again, but it's nowhere to be found.

'I wonder if the police took it?' says Tom. 'They must have had something to tell them who he was, and doesn't it say next-of-kin at the back? We were wondering how they found Wendy's address. Perhaps that's the answer?'

When we get home, Tom calls the police while I make coffee.

'Any luck?' I ask as he hangs up.

He shakes his head. 'All they have are his keys. We can pick them up from the station.'

I push down the plunger on the cafetière. 'They're not urgent now we've got the spare set from Michael.'

'What about the morgue?'

'They didn't mention any personal stuff.'

After we've finished coffee, I ring Tina. 'How are you doing?'

'I'm okay.' She exhales. 'It was a shock, you know?'

'I know. Look, do you feel up to talking today?'

'Yes, sure.'

'You know that stuff you told me about when you and Simon split up?'

She swallows. 'I needed you to understand that I had no choice.'

'I know, and I get it. You said Si was gambling?'

'Yes, online gambling. He took out credit cards in my name and wanted to increase our mortgage to cover his debts.'

'I'm so sorry. I had no idea.'

'It's not your fault. He hid it well.'

'Tina, you mentioned other online stuff.'

'Yes.' Her voice catches. 'Chat lines. I couldn't bear it.'

'Was there anything else?'

'I dread to think. Why?'

'It's just… oh, Tina. He left his money to someone the family doesn't know.'

'A sex worker?'

'God, you nailed it!'

'Nothing would surprise me.'

'I'm sorry.'

'For what? Me not getting any money? To be honest, I don't think I'd accept it even if he *had* left me anything.' She blows her nose. 'Is there anything else you want me to do?'

'I don't know.' I sigh. 'I'm wading through his Facebook friends at the moment, but it's hard to know who's who.'

'I'm happy for you to run names by me. I could sort them into friends and colleagues, etcetera.'

'Thanks Tina. You're a star. Will you come to the funeral?'

'I don't think so. I'll think about it, but my instinct is to say no. I drew a line under things three years ago. I don't want to open old wounds.'

'That's okay. I understand.'

Her voice cracks. 'I don't think you do.' She's quiet for a moment. 'Just because we split up, it doesn't mean I stopped loving him.'

CHAPTER ELEVEN

It's six a.m. I have time before Tom wakes. Leaving him in bed, I creep downstairs and open my laptop. In Si's Twitter feed I find videos – Lady Layla extolling the virtues of breath play; a guy wearing a gas mask. How can he breathe? Christ, is that Simon? What the hell is he doing? Inhaling stale smoke? That won't have done his lungs any good.

In another shared post, Lady Layla mentions her birthday. *Thank you to my wonderful sub for the champagne and cake.*

Si made her a cake? I didn't know he could bake, but there she is, flashing a cake in a Tupperware container I remember loaning him, and bragging about the fact it's gluten free. He went to a lot of trouble.

I scroll down. Oh God, my brother dressed in the kinky black number with dog collar and shorts. He's on his knees rubbing oil over Layla's hips and bum. I play the audio.

'My darling sub, Spiro, treated me to this lovely little latex number.'

Spiro?

Layla pats his head affectionately. *'Are you enjoying yourself, Spiro?'*

'Yes, Goddess.' I recognise Si's soft voice. His jaw is clenched as he concentrates on his task. He doesn't seem the least bit embarrassed. I watch the video twice, transfixed. Did he enjoy living a double life? No one knowing who he really was? Keeping secrets from us? From me?

Upstairs, I hear Tom's alarm and pause, listening for the sound of his feet heading for the ensuite. Moments later comes a familiar whirring as the shower's turned on. I haven't got much longer. Opening my emails, I find a new one from Angel. *Here's what I've found. I must have deleted the rest.*

She's attached a letter sent to her by Si. *I'm enclosing my monthly household expenditure as discussed.*

Jeez, did Angel edit this? It reads like he's speaking to an accountant, not someone he's paying for sex.

As well as regular payments for mortgage, council tax, electricity, water, car expenses etc, Si estimates spending £500 a month on web sex and an additional fixed fee of £800 per month for his domme. That's as much as many fathers pay in child maintenance. How did he fund his secret lifestyle?

Not much luck on passwords, Angel's email continues. *He probably changed them after we fell out. They don't seem to work anymore.*

Conniving bitch. She's being selective, giving me only half the information which she knows is of no use. She's determined to hold onto power. How do I know she hasn't doctored this? How do I know Si even sent it?

It's over thirty years since we lost Mum to stage four breast cancer. Now, as I perch on the edge of the two-seater couch at Tranquillity Funeral Home, memories come flooding back.

'Are we waiting for anyone else?' asks the funeral director.

'No, it's just me.' I reach for a tissue from a box strategically placed on the coffee table. I shouldn't be doing this alone, but Tom's gone to an auction and Wendy has a coffee morning at the Church that she simply couldn't get out of.

'I'm not sure how far we can get,' I continue. 'I haven't got the death certificate yet.'

The funeral director tilts her head in a well-practised show of sympathy. 'We can sort out everything apart from the date. Then, when the release comes through from the coroner, we'll collect your brother, bring him here and keep him until the service.'

'Simon didn't want a service as such. He was a devout atheist.'

'That's fine. We have celebrants who will conduct a humanist ceremony. Now, from what you're saying, I assume it's to be a cremation?'

Lifting a folder from the shelf, she takes me through coffin and lining choices. It's like choosing a new couch.

'Good,' she says. 'I've noted all that down. Now, could you bring something in for your brother to wear?'

'What, a suit or something?'

'Whatever you think appropriate.'

I leave equipped with a list of local venues, leaflets on celebrants specialising in humanist funerals and a business card for ordering the flowers.

Once home, I go through Si's Facebook friends to see how many I know. None have names or profiles suggesting they're in the sex game. Si obviously kept the different elements of his life in separate compartments.

I compose a post for his Facebook page, telling his friends I have sad news and inviting them to private message me. It feels wrong to blurt out he's dead, but they'll probably work it out from my post.

Next, I ring Tina with Si's address book to hand, plus a list cobbled together from his Facebook friends. In minutes, she's sorted them into categories – work colleagues, mutual friends, plus a list of unknowns.

'I can let our mutual friends know if you like,' she offers. 'I'm still in touch with most of them.'

'That would be a great help, thanks. Tom and I found some stuff at his flat,' I say. 'Stuff that backs up what you told me. I'm sorry. I never realised how bad it must have been.'

'Have you seen his social media sites?'

'His Facebook page, yes. And Jamie found an Instagram site I didn't know about.'

'Simon had two Instagram sites and a Twitter account. Some of the comments on Twitter are interesting, if you get my drift.'

I don't tell her I've been looking at them.

'I keep reminding myself of the man I married. Good, kind, generous Simon.' She sighs. 'That's how I'd like to remember him and that's how you should try to remember him too. Do you have to be involved? Sorting out his estate, I mean?'

'He made me executor. Well, me and Wendy, but she's renouncing the role.'

'You're a good person, Sarah.'

I snort. 'I don't know about that, but I feel obligated to

sort out his crap. He was my twin, after all. Have you decided if you'll come to the funeral?'

'Yes. Jill's bringing me. We'll come to the service, but won't stop on afterwards. I hope you understand?'

'Of course. Look, I'm sorting out the eulogy. The service will be non-religious. Is it okay if I mention your marriage and trips abroad? Only good stuff.'

'Yes, and please mention Jill's kids, Sophie and Hannah. They thought the world of their Uncle Simon. It's such a shame. In many ways he'd have made a great dad.'

'We found something else at Si's flat – a ring, white gold with a blue sapphire. Would that be yours?'

'Yes. We bought it in a lovely little shop in Battle. Simon had it resized. A commitment ring, for all the good it did.'

'Do you want it?'

'I'd love to have it. Thanks.'

'Is there anything else you'd like? I've spoken to Angel and she's happy for the family to keep anything of sentimental value.'

She scoffs. 'I doubt she wants his old tosh.'

After our call, I settle down with my laptop again. In his secret Twitter account, Si's retweeted posts from a number of dominatrix – what's the plural? Dominatrices? Dommes? I soon spot one from Angelica Belle. *Thank you to my humble sub for fixing my laptop. He also brought me flowers and my favourite perfume.*

She's accompanied the words with an image – a bottle of Black Opium. This was retweeted by Si, I remind myself. No one forced him to share this. He was a good-looking man, but he'd have been lucky to get a girlfriend as gorgeous as Angel. He seems proud of their association. Did he view it as real?

Later posts fail to mention Angel. Is this when she fell from grace? Was this Si's pattern? Strike up a relationship, if that's what it was, become totally besotted, then, months later, move on to someone younger? An uncomfortable thought pops into my head. Suppose there's an even more recent will?

I return to Si's Facebook account and notice a new post from someone called Daniel saying how much Simon will be missed. Immediately, I ping him a private message.

> Hi Daniel. I saw you'd posted something on Simon's page. Would you like me to send you the funeral details when it's sorted?

He messages straight back.

> Hi Sarah. I'm so sorry to hear about Simon. Truth be told, I'm gutted. He was my best mate and meant the world to me. We shared everything and I'm really going to miss him. Here's my number if you want to talk.

I check the time. Tom won't be back for another hour. Entering the number into my mobile, I press call. 'Hi, Daniel? This is Sarah.'

'Sarah. God, I was so sorry to hear about Simon. How're you holding up?'

'I'm okay.'

'I can't believe it. We were supposed to meet up last weekend, then I heard from someone he worked with that he was dead. It's mad. I can't get my head around it.'

'You were good mates then?'

'The best. Simon knew all my secrets and I knew his.'

How much does he know about Si's secret life? 'This is

difficult…' My voice is hesitant. 'I've found out quite a lot about Simon that I didn't know.'

'You've been reading his blog then?'

'His blog?'

'Yeah. Simon wrote about the trials of life, his depression, that sort of thing.'

'I knew he suffered with depression, but didn't know he kept a blog.'

'Yeah, you should defo read it. Heart-breaking stuff, but good. I'll send you the link.'

'Thanks.' I pause. 'Actually, it wasn't Si's depression I was talking about.'

Silence.

'Daniel?'

'Yeah, I'm still here.' He exhales loudly. 'This isn't the sort of thing we can talk about over the phone. They were his secrets, you know? I'm not sure I'm ready to share, especially with his sister.'

'That's okay. I wouldn't want you to share anything you weren't happy about. But if you do feel up to talking, I'd really appreciate it.'

'Yeah, I'll have to think about that, Sarah. It's a tough ask.'

Simon's blog is entitled RAMBLINGS of a DEPRESSIVE VOLCANOLOGIST and consists of a dozen or more posts spread out over the last eighteen months. Many share his love of volcanos, while others describe what it's like living with depression.

. . .

We're all on a journey and mine isn't so different from the next person.

Did you know approximately one in four people in the UK experience mental health problems each year?

I'm one of those people. Like many, I deal with depressive thoughts on a daily basis and, as part of my recovery, I'm going to document them. They're not earth shattering, I'm not looking for sympathy or compassion, and they probably won't change your life, but...

Incidentally, although these are ramblings of my mind, I also find walking helps. During good times, I'll share some of my favourite walking rambles.

Let the journey begin...

CHAPTER TWELVE

Next morning the coroner calls. 'The post-mortem on your brother has taken place and I can confirm his death was caused by pulmonary thromboembolism, with a secondary cause of hypertension.'

'What does that mean?'

'A heart attack, my dear. Although your brother's blood pressure was high, which might have contributed.'

'Would Simon have known about his blood pressure?'

'Not necessarily. Some call it the silent killer. Anyway, I'm pleased to say there's no need for an inquest. I've released the paperwork, so you can go and collect his death certificate and get on with the funeral arrangements.'

My relief is palpable. 'Thank you.'

'You can request a more detailed report if you wish.'

'What does that entail?'

'I send you the full report by email when it's complete, although I'm afraid it might seem gobbledygook.'

After lunch, I head over to Green Valley Care Home, where I deposit a shop bought cake with reception before signing the Visitors' Book and making my way into the lounge. Half a dozen armchairs have been arranged in a semi-circle around the TV and a couple of residents are calling out answers to *The Chase* while the remainder slouch in various stages of oblivion. Dad is in the conservatory, his wheelchair thoughtfully positioned to face the garden. I squat down and give him a peck on the cheek. 'Hello, Dad. It's Sarah.'

Nothing.

I shift, placing myself directly in his field of vision. 'Dad?'

No hint of recognition. I'd hoped today might be better.

One of the care workers – Cinta, I think she's called – lurks in the doorway, smiling benevolently. 'Your sister is coming?'

I shake my head. 'She's hoping to come at the weekend.'

'Okay. You want cake now?' Her tone is hushed, as if afraid of spoiling the surprise.

Yes,' I say, 'why not?' I perch on an adjacent chair and pat Dad's arm. 'How are you today? I brought you some of those fruit jellies you like. I'll give them to Cinta and she can put them in your room.'

Fruit jellies used to be Dad's favourite. Maybe one of the care workers will cut a jelly in half and pop it into his mouth and, once the sugar's gone, the sweet will work its way to the corner where it will stay until someone removes it with a tissue.

Cinta's back, processing in with the Waitrose cake, now festooned with an odd assortment of candles. Two of her colleagues bring up the rear, singing in broken English, 'Happy Birthday to you…'

As she lowers the cake ceremonially onto a side table,

Dad's eyes flit side to side like a frightened animal. I take his liver-spotted hands in mine. 'It's your birthday, Dad. Many happy returns.'

Bleary grey eyes fill with tears and his chin wobbles.

'It's okay, Dad.'

His forehead, brown as old leather, furrows with confusion.

The little gaggle of care staff hover anxiously. 'It your birthday, Mr Foster,' says Cinta. 'We all gonna have nice cake for your tea.'

'Why don't I blow the candles out for you?' I crouch and blow with an exaggerated puff. 'Let's make a wish.' I gesture to Cinta, who whisks the cake away to be cut up and shared with residents and staff.

'Dad?' He's already retreated within, tapping his fingers to some unheard tune. I stare at spidery thread veins on his ruddy cheeks, watery yellow rimmed eyes, eyebrows the colour of steel wool. Are you still in there? Seventy-nine. It's no age really. A wave of anger overwhelms me as I think of all the fit and healthy octogenarians still living life to the full. It's so unfair.

Tenderly, I stroke his calloused hands. 'Tom and Jamie send their love. Jamie's back at uni in September. It's his second year. He might stay on after he's finished his degree. Get a flat up there…'

This is pointless. He doesn't know who I am. He doesn't even know what day it is.

'It's nice outside,' I say. 'Cool for August, but pleasant enough. Shall I read to you?'

I pull a copy of *Moonfleet* from my bag and open it at the bookmark. "But that same day came Sam Tewkesbury to the Why Not…"

It doesn't matter what I read, Dad stares blindly ahead. I

could be anyone – nurse, care worker, volunteer. As I mouth the words, my sense of identity slips further and further away. Who am I when I'm no longer someone's daughter?

I feel guilty that he doesn't know about Si, but telling him would be no kindness. Even if the truth did manage to penetrate his muddled mind, then what? Inside, he might be screaming with grief at the untimely death of his son and no one would know. How cruel that would be. Bloody Wendy. She always has to be right.

Cinta brings me a cup of tea and a slice of cake, but the tea's milky and I don't drink it. Instead, I feed Dad tiny morsels of cake from a teaspoon. As he obediently opens his mouth, I realise our roles have reversed – I'm now the parent feeding a helpless baby. Every other mouthful, I hold the feeder cup to his lips, trying not to gag as tea and crummy sludge oozes from his lips.

When I can stand it no longer, I wipe his stubbly chin with a tissue and reposition his wheelchair to face the garden. I don't know if he sees the garden, but it makes me feel better. 'Well, I'd better be heading off.' I kiss him on the forehead, squeeze his shoulder and whisper the words he used to say to me when I was a little girl. 'Love you, darling.'

In the car park, I take a few moments to compose myself. Pulling my mobile from my pocket, I scroll through until I locate Si's blog.

Trigger Warning: Suicide and mental health

It started in my late twenties. I was married, working in a call centre and generally enjoying a good life. Until the day it hit me.

I got up and went to work like any other day. There was maintenance going on in the office next door – a guy banging away with a hammer – and suddenly the sound was inside my head. I found myself sweating, physically shaking and struggling to breathe. My mind flipped and I swept everything off my desk. Next thing I was on the floor bawling my eyes out.

My manager took me into his office and, when I'd calmed down, he drove me home.

My GP told me I'd had some sort of psychotic episode and prescribed anti-depressants.

A few days later my wife found me in bed with a cereal bowl full of tablets. I don't remember that. It's as if I've blotted it out, like it happened to someone else.

Over a period of months, I gradually re-emerged and returned to 'normal'. There were ups and a lot of downs, but I progressed.

I've had 'episodes' since. I don't think I'll ever be totally free. It's something I live with and, although the 'black dog' is better behaved than he used to be, I don't entirely trust him not to bite me.

I knew Si suffered from depression. He was open about it and said he knew it was coming. This sounds like more than that. I always suspected a suicide attempt, but he never confided in me, never opened-up about his feelings. Where was I? Busy, I suppose, with my life, my career, my son. I assume Wendy knew nothing either. I re-read the first two blog posts and weep. Who was my brother? How did I fail him so badly?

CHAPTER THIRTEEN

Frances Wilson's flier had stood out among the leaflets the funeral director gave me – wild, wacky and Brighton-esque. Now, as she stands on my doorstep, I'm unable to tear my eyes from her bright orange hair and psychedelic clothes. She looks like she's stepped off the album cover for *Sgt. Pepper's.*

'I'm such a muppet,' are her first words. 'I've left my briefcase somewhere.'

'Come in,' I say, showing her into the sitting room and equipping her with paper and a pen.

'I like to get a real feel of the person.' She waves her hands in front of her eyes as if channelling Mystic Meg. 'Just talk about Simon and I'll make notes.'

'Well, he was my twin…'

'That must make this particularly hard for you. Such a special bond.'

I'm touched by her perceptiveness. Frances is right, Si and I had more than a sibling bond. She prompts me for stories about growing up together, but when she asks about hobbies and interests, I find myself giggling.

'That's good.' She claps her hands in glee. 'Tell me what you're thinking right now. That's what I need to share.'

But of course, I can't. 'There were things none of us knew about Si…'

Frances nods. Now she'll label me as a bigot. *'Poor man was gay,'* I imagine her telling her colleagues. *'The sister couldn't handle it.'*

'Tell me anecdotes about the Simon you knew,' she says.

I talk about our childhood, confessing I was the more dominant twin. I share how Wendy and I dressed Si up like a doll. I tell her about when Si and Tina got married and how they went to Monaco for their honeymoon as he was obsessed with motor racing. 'As to his work life, I don't know much,' I say.

'Well, perhaps something will come to you. Or, if you get cards of condolence from work colleagues, I could read them out. Now, what about readings?'

'My sister will read a poem.' Wendy would prefer to say a prayer, but like me she'll honour Si's wishes to give him a humanist ceremony. 'Perhaps I could read something too? Although I'm not sure what…'

'And music?'

'Si loved Madness and Coldplay. I'll go through his CDs. I'm sure we can find something suitable.'

'It all sounds perfect,' says Frances. 'Now, have you chosen the venue yet?'

'I'm still ringing around. It's hard to decide. I don't know how many people will come.'

Frances bundles up her notes. 'Well, I'm going to type this up and email it to you. Anything you want changed, just let me know. It's an honour and a privilege to do this for Simon.'

After parking near Lewes Brewery, I cut through to Cliffe High Street. With a couple of hours before my appointment at Lewes Registry Office, there's something I need to do. The office for Robson-Taylor is located at the bottom of the high street – a green wooden door sandwiched between two shops. I press the buzzer, give my name and I'm let in.

The narrow wooden stairs and drab yellowed paintwork conjure up a shabby detective agency rather than a solicitor's office, but, as I reach the top, alighting on a newly carpeted landing, I'm greeted by a smiling receptionist.

'Mrs Edwards? Take a seat. I'll let Mrs Taylor know you're here.'

Moments later, a door opens and a striking young woman in a white blouse and smart pencil skirt steps out. 'Mrs Edwards?' Her handshake is firm. 'Please, come in.'

Her office, although compact, is orderly and presentable, with mahogany filing cabinets and abundant bookcases. She gestures for me to take a seat as she slides behind an enormous leather-topped desk occupying most of the room. 'Would you like coffee?'

'No, I'm fine, thanks.'

She smiles politely. 'You've come to collect your brother's will.' She taps a buff folder on the otherwise clear desk. 'I'm sorry for your loss.'

'Thank you.' I pull the copy will from my bag. 'I brought this. Do you want to see some ID?' I slide my driving licence from my purse.

'That's fine,' she says, after a cursory glance. Opening the folder, she extracts a document and hands it to me. Apart from the cream parchment cover and red ribbon binding, it looks identical to the copy in my hand.

'Thanks.' Stalling, I glance about the room, wondering how the potted plants thrive on such little light from the small Velux window.

'Was there something else?' she asks.

I swallow. 'Yes. You may not be aware, but the beneficiary is a person unknown to the family.'

She nods. 'Yes. After you rang, I dug out my notes.' She opens the folder again. 'I make a point, when the beneficiary is other than family, of asking the testator if they might elaborate as to their relationship. It never hurts under such circumstances.'

She pulls a piece of A4 paper from the folder and glances at it. I can tell she's already refreshed her memory of the words. 'I remember your brother. It wasn't so long ago when he made his will. I asked him outright about his relationship with Angela Bentley-Bell.' She gives an apologetic smile. 'He sat where you're sitting now, smiled and said – and I quote – "She's the woman who saved my life".'

The registrar is helpful and kind. She has all the necessary documentation from the coroner and I gratefully hand over the money for six copies of the death certificate, having been warned the world and his wife will demand copies.

The sun's shining as I step outside and I'm unusually optimistic. Perhaps things will go smoothly from here on in? Reluctant to get straight back into my car, I head for Lewes Railway Land Wildlife Trust, and wander along the river path enjoying the warmth of the day. Bees hum and damselflies skitter at the edge of the water. Suddenly everything feels wrong. Shouldn't it be raining? A grey day at least?

I head back to Tranquillity Funeral Home with the death certificate.

'We don't need that, just the green slip,' says the funeral director.

I rummage through the paperwork, but it's nowhere to be found. 'It must be here.' As panic mounts, I tip everything out of my bag. 'Everything they gave me went straight into this folder. Look – receipt, death certificates…'

'Don't worry. I'll call them. Was it Lewes Registry Office?'

'Yes.' The contents of my bag – tissues, make-up, keys, driving licence – litter the floor. I sink down in the middle of everything, trying to hold back tears.

The funeral director is speaking into the phone. 'So, we don't need it? Okay, thanks very much.'

I look up hopefully.

'Apparently we don't need a green slip when it's gone through the coroner,' she says. 'They email it directly to the morgue.'

'So, you'll be able to collect him?'

'Yes.'

I shove everything back in my bag. 'Thank you. I don't think I could bear it if I had to go back.'

I cross the gravel driveway and climb into my car. As I slam the door, tears flow.

My mobile beeps with a text.

> How did it go?

Angel, checking up on me. The only one to have expressed concern about me doing this on my own.

CHAPTER FOURTEEN

'Hello, Mrs Edwards? This is Tranquillity Funeral Home. I'm calling to let you know your brother is with us now.'

I exhale with relief. At least he's no longer in that cold morgue. 'Thank you. I'll drop his suit in.'

'Do you think anyone might want to visit Simon in the Chapel of Rest?'

'I'm not sure. Can I let you know?'

Tom glances up expectantly.

'That was the Funeral Home. They've got Si.'

He shovels the last spoonful of Weetabix into his mouth.

'She asked if anyone wants to see him.'

He moves across to the draining board with the breakfast bowl. 'I did wonder if someone would need to identify him.'

'Michael did that, but perhaps I should see Si for a final farewell.'

'Might be better to remember him the way he was.'

'Someone in the family should see him.'

Tom picks up his briefcase. 'I, for one, prefer to remember him mixing cocktails and clowning around over a beer.' He kisses my forehead. 'But it's up to you.'

The back door slams and I take a seat at the breakfast bar. Up to me? Of course, it is! Why did I even imagine Tom might come? I'm not scared of seeing a dead body. I'd seen Mum and I was only thirteen at the time. I feel like I need to finish things off. But do I want to go on my own?

A call to Wendy proves equally unfruitful. 'I don't need to see him. I'm happier remembering Simon the way he was.'

I hang up and scroll through my contacts, pausing at the last person I should be considering…

'Are you sure you should visit?' Angel asks.

'I think someone should see him one last time.'

'Perhaps it's best to remember him as he was?'

'My mind's made up.'

'Who will go with you? Your sister?'

'No.'

'Your husband?'

'He won't come.'

'You can't go alone.' She exhales. 'I'll come. You need someone with you. It's too much doing everything on your own.'

I meet Angel at the station. The funeral home is only half a mile away and I could have met her there. But she's taken the trouble to come, the least I can do is offer her a lift.

As she climbs into the Citroën, hints of orange blossom and patchouli fill the car. She pulls the seat belt across a designer dress that wouldn't look out of place on Princess Kate. Am I underdressed in jeans and T-shirt?

'Are you ready for this?' she asks.

'I think so.'

The funeral director greets us in the foyer.

'This is Simon's friend, Angel,' I explain.

'Nice to meet you.' The funeral director and Angel shake hands. 'This way, please.' She shows us into the consulting room. 'If you'd like to take a seat, I'll make sure everything is ready. Would you like a cup of tea? Or coffee?'

'No thanks,' I say.

Angel gestures towards the water jug on the coffee table. 'Water's fine.'

'Help yourself,' says the funeral director. 'I shan't be long.' She disappears through a door at the back of the room.

Angel and I sit on the two-seater couch. I'm strangely grateful for her company.

'Do you want some water?' she asks.

'No.' I chew my lip.

'It's okay, you know. If you're having second thoughts.'

'I know.'

She takes my hand. 'You don't have to do this.'

'But you've given up time.'

She shakes her head. 'That doesn't matter.'

Her empathy almost breaks me. I grab a tissue from the box on the table and ball it in my fist.

The funeral director re-emerges. 'Right, all ready for you. I've left the lighting on low. When you go in, the coffin will be in front of you with Simon's head to your right.' She studies my face. 'Look, there's absolutely no pressure. Lots of people prefer to remember loved ones as they were.'

I blow my nose. 'I just need a minute.'

The funeral director nods. 'If you decide after all that you'd rather not, that's perfectly fine. Take as long as you need. You don't have to tell me when you're leaving.' She returns to the outer office, closing the consulting room door softly behind her.

'Okay.' Leaving my handbag on the couch, I stand up, move towards the door and grasp the handle.

'Simon's head is on your right,' says Angel.

I hesitate. Soft music plays within. Mum's hands were crossed over her chest like a medieval saint. God, I hope Si isn't laid out like that. Letting go of the door handle, I turn around. 'Perhaps I will have some water after all.'

Angel pours us both a glass.

I sit down, cradling the glass in my hands. I'm grateful not to be sitting here alone. As I gaze about, I spot a folder on the shelf. From my previous visit, I know it's full of coffin options. I visualise the coffin – satin finish handles and purple lining. Si always liked bold colours…

Angel appears to read my mind. 'I guess this is the only chance to see the casket open.' She touches my arm. 'Are you all right? You've gone quite pale.'

I nod. Tom and Wendy told me not to come. 'Remember him the way he was,' they'd said. I wonder if the funeral director managed to get his suit on. It must be hard putting a suit on a dead body. I hope Si's tie doesn't clash with the coffin lining. I chose a bright one, but can't remember for the life of me what colour it was.

'We can leave if you like,' says Angel.

'I know.'

I stare at the door. Si's in there. Mum's skin was a grey-blue colour. She'd been embalmed. They'd parted her hair the wrong side and used too much make-up – rose red lips and rouged cheeks. Have they put make-up on Si? He'd hate that. Or perhaps he wouldn't… I exhale, recalling how I'd bent forward to kiss Mum's forehead. It was cold, like marble. And that terrible smell. Formaldehyde? I shudder.

'What are you thinking?' Angel asks.

'I'm wondering if this is a bad idea.'

'There's no pressure.'

I turn to look at her. 'But you've come specially.'

'To be here for you, whatever you decide.'

'Do you want to see him?' I ask.

She shrugs.

'You could go in alone?'

'It doesn't seem right. I'm not family.'

We sit a few moments longer.

'Come on.' Angel takes my hand. 'Let's go and find a decent coffee.'

CHAPTER FIFTEEN

The civil ceremony kicks off at two p.m. To avoid any hint of religiousness, it's held in the local Community Hall. Funny, I thought a civil ceremony was a wedding, but apparently the phrase applies to funerals, too. Ceremony is the wrong word, but service is worse. A chance for friends and family to come together to remember and celebrate Simon's life. But what life? There seem so many versions – my kind, modest, unassuming twin brother; the approachable and diligent work colleague; a man struggling with depression; and now this new Simon who gambled, used drugs, sex workers and indulged in erotica.

When I arrive, a quick calculation reveals the caretaker has arranged forty-eight chairs in a horseshoe shape. Is that enough? I've told the caterers to expect up to a hundred.

I move to the back of the hall, where two inept teenagers are slicing cakes. 'Why have you only set out twenty cups and saucers?'

The girls exchange a look before continuing to arrange food on doilies.

'Hi, Sarah.'

'Wendy.' My voice is a sob.

'Hey, it's okay.' She wraps her arms around me.

'They've not put out enough chairs.' I gesture towards the horseshoe. 'There'll be loads of work colleagues, and then there's family and friends…'

'Where's Tom?'

'Gone to fetch Auntie Vi from the station.'

'We can sort it. Bob, we need more chairs.'

'On it.' In seconds, my brother-in-law is in his element directing proceedings, while the caretaker kowtows, adding row upon row of additional chairs.

I look over her shoulder. 'Millie and Rosie not with you?'

'No, Rosie's out with a girlfriend – a long-standing arrangement – and Millie didn't want to come on her own. She's stayed home to keep Mary company.'

'Hmm.' Si was their only uncle. They might have made the effort…

'How are you doing, anyway?' asks Wendy, keen to change the subject.

'I'm okay.'

'It makes it real, doesn't it?' She pats my arm. 'Now, I've got this poem…' She pulls a slip of paper from her handbag. 'It's not religious, well, spiritual, but not strictly religious. Is that okay?'

I nod, past caring whether the poem is suitable.

She checks her watch. 'What time is everyone arriving?'

'Any time now. Parking's a nightmare. They've got another function in the room downstairs. A lunch for dementia patients and their carers.'

'We'll probably have them wandering in here then, poor loves,' Wendy chortles. 'Now, you're not to feel bad about Dad not being here. He wouldn't have understood.'

'I know.' But I do feel bad. It's wrong that Dad doesn't know about Si.

The double doors open as an elderly man shuffles into the room. The young woman holding his arm whispers encouragement. Spotting us, she does a double take, her expression momentarily as confused as his.

'If you're looking for the dementia lunch,' I explain, 'it's downstairs.'

She nods, steering the old boy around. Meanwhile, a gaggle of thirty-somethings try to come in and everyone becomes entangled.

Wendy strides over to sort them out. 'Hello, I'm Wendy. Simon's sister.'

'Hello,' says a woman who appears to be in charge. 'I'm Gayle Stevens, HR.'

I step forward. 'And I'm Sarah. Si's twin.'

Gayle takes Wendy's hand and mine. 'I'm sorry for your loss. Simon's work colleagues are so upset.'

'It's good of you to come,' I say.

'Oh, there are quite a few more,' she says. 'Twenty-five in total.'

'Then we definitely need more cups. Excuse me.' Leaving Wendy and Gayle chatting, I go in search of the serving girls.

When I return from the kitchen, hopefully having impressed upon the teenagers some sense of urgency, the room has filled up. Mercifully, thanks to Bob, there are plenty of seats.

Angel hurries across. 'Hi, Sarah. How are you doing?'

'I'm okay.' I'm surprised how pleased I am to see her.

She leans closer to whisper. 'Valentina might show up. I hope that's all right?'

Who the hell's Valentina, I wonder. 'The more the merrier,' I say, glancing at my watch. 'The celebrant said she'd be here early. If she doesn't arrive soon, I'll be reading the eulogy myself.'

Jamie's fiddling with the sound system when Tom and Auntie Vi arrive. With Dad not able to attend, she's the senior representative of our family. I'm about to go over to greet her when someone touches my shoulder and I spin round, staring into sad, hazel eyes.

'Sarah?'

The guy bears a strong resemblance to Aidan Turner and I find myself blushing. 'Yes?'

'Daniel.' He runs his fingers through dark, unruly hair. 'We spoke on the phone.'

'Hi Daniel. How are you doing?' What a stupid question, it's obvious he's in bits.

'Not great.' He gives a crooked smile. 'Simon was my best mate. I don't know what I'll do without him.'

A man not afraid to show emotion. His vulnerability works for me. Would it be inappropriate to give him a hug?

Just then, Frances arrives. 'Sorry,' I stammer. 'I've got to go.'

Daniel smiles. 'Of course. Catch you later.'

I move away and introduce Frances to Jamie. As they sort out microphones, I scan the guests. Where did Daniel go?

'It's well attended,' Wendy whispers in my ear.

'Yes.'

People congregate in informal clusters – family at the front; Gayle and Si's work colleagues to the right; friends, assorted old school mates and others I don't know to the left.

I raise a hand to acknowledge Tina and Jill sitting at the back. Ironically, not far from Angel. Beside her sits a very tall woman in a leopard skin coat, bouffant hair and face caked in make-up. She must be Valentina.

'Phew, made it.' Nicki rushes over, giving me an affectionate squeeze. 'Parking out there is impossible.'

Frances sidles up. 'Can we get everyone seated? The hearse has arrived.'

The journey from the funeral home to the Community Centre is less than a mile and I guess the traffic was light as they're right on time. I declined to have Si start his final journey from my house. It's not like he ever lived there.

I take my seat in the front row, with Tom to my left and Nicki to my right. Feeling flustered, I wave the Order of Service like a fan.

Frances steps onto the stage and nods to Jamie. He presses a button and Coldplay's "Yellow" accompanies the coffin into the hall.

Just thirty minutes, I tell myself. I can do this.

Frances clears her throat. 'My name is Frances, and I'm honoured to be with you today to celebrate the life of Simon Foster. I'd like to start by inviting Simon's sister, Wendy, to read a poem.'

Wendy's rendition is flawless and I smile approvingly as she re-joins Bob in the row behind me.

Frances moves back to the lectern and begins to read from the script we prepared together. 'Simon was well regarded at work…'

I look behind to where Si's work colleagues are nodding encouragingly. An older lady dabs her eyes with a tissue.

Frances continues, '…kind, patient, always at the end of a phone…'

As I wait for my cue, I think about how little any of us really knew about Si. Maybe I should tell them? Perhaps I should stand up right now and share his dirty little secrets. How, while they knew him as the diligent and helpful man in

IT, he was maintaining a double life that not even his closest family were aware of.

The congregation titter as Frances gets to the part about Wendy and I dressing Si up in a tutu. Was it our fault he turned out the way he did?

'And now Simon's twin, Sarah, will read an extract from Terry Pratchett.'

Like a dutiful sister, I take my place at the lectern and read. "Wen considered the nature of time…" I pause, wanting to howl, but Nicki's eyes will me on. Returning attention to the extract, I keep reading. "…the perfect moment is now.' Be glad of it."

As I step down from the stage, Jamie presses another button and "Wings of a Dove" by Madness plays as the coffin is carried out. Si always joked he wanted AC/DC's "Highway to Hell" as his funeral music, but Wendy was appalled. As a Christian, she's allowed one veto.

Frances, who's accompanying Si's body to the crematorium, follows the coffin out. The last chords of music fade away and everyone sits down.

'I think they're waiting for the family to move,' whispers Tom.

I stand up and walk sedately to the back of the hall. Tom, Wendy and Bob follow, and the rest of the congregation begin to chat.

Moving across to the refreshment table, I find it laden with enough food to feed an army, but there are no side plates or serviettes and those silly girls have still not brought up enough cups.

'I'll kill those girls,' I hiss at Tom. 'Hold the fort.' Down in the kitchen, the teenagers are giggling over their iPhones. 'For Christ's sake,' I yell. 'Do I have to make the bloody tea and coffee myself?'

They stare at me and the blonde girl rolls her eyes. I imagine them reporting back to their supervisor sarcastically: 'The sister was grief stricken'. Their boss hasn't bothered to show up. I hope she doesn't expect me to pay full whack.

Yanking open cupboard doors, I locate teabags and instant coffee. 'Find cups, mugs, anything, and bring hot water through in jugs. Do you have more milk?'

I know I'm being a cow, but I really don't care.

Back in the hall, my anger subsides when I spot Nicki passing around cakes and scones. She's such a good friend.

Tom and Valentina are deep in conversation when I pull him to one side. 'You're going to have to help serve the drinks.'

'I'm sure I can find someone to assist.' Tom winks at Valentina and she giggles back coquettishly.

Oh my God, they're flirting! 'She'll eat you for supper,' I hiss nastily.

'You okay?' asks Angel.

I smile in relief. 'I need help. Those stupid girls haven't made enough drinks.'

'I shouldn't worry. The guests seem perfectly happy chatting, and anyway, if they're that desperate, they can reconvene at the pub.'

Why did I even think she might risk chipping a nail? As I scan the room searching for assistance, an older woman catches my eye. It's the one who shed a tear during the eulogy.

Smiling sympathetically, she clasps my hands in hers. 'Your brother was such a wonderful man. His IT knowledge was second to none. If ever we had a problem, I'd say, "Well, I don't know, but I know a man who does".'

I'm momentarily transfixed by the lipstick on her teeth,

then, realising she's of no use, pointedly check my watch before extricating myself. 'Excuse me.'

The guests are leaving. 'There's loads of food,' I announce to the room. 'Please, take some with you.'

Wendy sidles up, her mouth full of sausage roll. 'There are no serviettes to wrap anything in.'

I take pleasure in pointing out the sausage roll is not vegan.

'We're off now.' Angel bestows air kisses.

We're down to the last few stragglers. As Tom and Bob stack chairs, I feel a tap on my shoulder.

'Gayle,' I say. 'I thought you'd gone.'

She slips me a business card. 'Call me on my direct line. Or pop in when you're passing. We need to have a chat.'

CHAPTER SIXTEEN

Less than a week to go before autumn term and so much to do – new schemes of work, examination analysis… and that's on top of the executor stuff. I used to be buzzing at the start of a new school year, but now everything's a chore. Why can't I get motivated?

'I'm just going to walk Brodie,' I call.

Tom looks up from *The Andrew Marr Show*. 'I thought we might drive out to Sheffield Park, walk around the estate, then stop for a pub lunch on the way back.'

I pull on ankle boots. 'I can't. I've too much to do.'

'You need to have some downtime. You'll make yourself ill.'

'I'm fine. Come on boy.' Opening the front door, I shoo Brodie through.

Back home, I make a cup of coffee and wander into the dining room, where I sit in front of my computer, log on and open Twitter.

When Tom sticks his head around the door, I slam the lid of my laptop.

'If you're engrossed with schoolwork all day, I think I'll pop into work. We've got a big auction on Tuesday.'

'Okay.' I momentarily wonder if Yvette will be there, but I'm more concerned whether Tom saw what I was doing. He thinks I'm obsessed and he's probably right. The thing is, what if Si's Facebook and Twitter sites get shut down? I need to find out everything I can while I still have access.

The front door slams and I open the laptop again, searching for Lady Layla. I'm surprised access to her site is so easy. Scrolling through, I find more videos. In one, an older, well-built man is entirely wrapped in cling film. With his legs bound together, he looks like a left-over chicken drumstick. The plastic distorts his features. Is it Si? I watch it three times but can't be certain. The squashed flesh could be anyone, but his voice doesn't sound like Si.

I click on another video and it's the most distressing I've seen so far – two dommes, Lady Layla and Delores the Divine – the photographer on the garage forecourt – working as a duo. Drinking champagne, they shriek with laughter as they slap a guy's bum. I really shouldn't watch, it's so undignified. I feel a sudden surge of loyalty towards Angel. Something tells me she doesn't treat her subs this way.

My coffee's gone cold. I'd like to make another cup, but I can't stop watching. No wonder my family are worried about me. Nicki thinks I'm at risk of getting sucked into this weird world, while Wendy believes the devil is at work. She says she's praying for me.

Scrolling further back, I find Lady Layla introducing two subs. The first has his back to the camera. "This is Hector doing the washing up, and over here is my butler, Spiro." The second sub is Si, on hands and knees, licking her feet and –

oh fuck, talk about inappropriate – wearing the suit I gave the funeral director to dress him in.

My mobile pings with a private message. Daniel.

> Hello Sarah. Sorry I rushed off after the funeral. It was all too much, you know?

Don't worry. I understand.

> You hang in there [kiss blowing emoji]

I close my laptop and turn to my "to do" list. At least now I have a solicitor taking care of the legal bits. She's already applied for probate and tomorrow I'm putting Si's flat on the market. I know I can't complete the sale until probate comes through, but I need to get things moving before term starts and the solicitor assured me there was no harm doing both simultaneously.

Picking up my cold coffee, I head for the kitchen. Brodie whimpers hopefully and I laugh. 'Sorry boy, you've already had a walk.'

Monday morning, I park in Si's parking space. Tom dealt with the sale of the Corsa. His mate Gary trades in second-hand vehicles and gave us a fair price – eighteen hundred pounds lodged in the executor bank account. I'd been worried that Si might have had outstanding hire purchase, but Tom reassured me.

'Gary checked. Did a search using the registration number.'

It takes three trips to lug all the empty boxes up to Si's flat. I unlock the door. It seems eerily quiet without Tom, but he can't take any more days off work. I don't mind. I need time here on my own. Today, I plan to make an inventory of furniture and personal possessions. I need to ask Angel if there's anything she wants to keep. Despite my earlier worries about her getting hold of personal stuff, she's been more than accommodating. She's told me if there's anything of sentimental value to me or the family, I'm welcome to take it.

We've kept the power and water turned on for now, so I put the pint of milk I brought with me in the fridge. Beginning in the sitting room, I work methodically, listing furniture and other items. I examine ornaments on shelves and open drawers, still convinced there might be something here I'm supposed to find. Something that will help me make sense of things. And, although I've begun to trust Angel, a tiny part of me still fears I might find a blackmail note.

I lift books from shelves and flick through them before boxing them up. 'Gwendoline Browning,' I read aloud from the frontispiece. Mum's maiden name. 'Okay Mum, I'll take that home.' I also find a copy of *Pride and Prejudice* presented to her as a school prize. Mum loved Jane Austen, so I keep that, too.

No signs, no clues. I move across to the sideboard and open the doors to find shelves filled with Ordnance Survey maps and travel guides. 'You certainly loved your walking tours, bro,' I say. 'I might be able to sell these on eBay.'

I yank all the stationery out of the cupboard below the stereo. There's also a huge box of assorted cables. I have no idea what they fit, but I box them up anyway. They'll probably end up in the garage with Tom's other redundant electrical leads.

I wander through the kitchen and flick the switch on the

kettle to make a cup of coffee. While the water comes to the boil, I look through a shelf of cookery books, pulling them down to read the titles: *Cooking for One, Quick Meals, Thirty-Minute Meals.* A wave of sadness engulfs me as I think of Si on his own. I spot a book with no dust jacket and open it. *Mrs Beeton*, one of Mum's old cookbooks. Fluttering between the pages are dozens of cut-out recipes from magazines, along with handwritten comments and adjustments on every recipe tried. I can hear her voice: "Add a spoonful of fresh herbs; Double the quantity to make 24 cup-cakes." She'd be pleased I'm helping Si.

I pour water into a mug and check the time. The estate agent should be arriving any minute. The doorbell rings.

'Hello, Mrs Edwards? I'm Marty.'

'Yes, come in.' I hold the door open.

Marty's tall and slim, and bounces into the flat like Tigger. 'I must say, this is an excellent location. Good train services to London and Brighton.' He wanders through to the sitting room. 'Good light. Two bedrooms, is it?'

'No, just the one. The other is only a box room.'

'You'd be surprised what's classed as a second bedroom nowadays. All right if I look around?' He's already opening doors, sizing the place up.

'Coffee?' I ask.

'No thanks. I've another three viewings this afternoon.' He stands in the middle of the sitting room. 'Did you know we handled the sale to your brother eighteen months ago?'

'Yes,' I say. 'That's partly why I chose you.'

'We have all the room measurements back in the office. Won't have any difficulty moving this on again. You do want to sell, I take it? The rental yield would be quite lucrative if you wanted to hang on to it as an investment.'

'It's not mine to keep.' I sip my coffee. 'And the beneficiary is keen to release the assets. There's a small matter of probate. Did the office tell you?'

'Yes.' He makes a few notes on his iPad. 'That shouldn't delay things too much.' He takes a brochure from his document case. 'This contains everything you need to know about our services. If it's all right with you, I'll get our photographer around tomorrow. She's a genius and will make the place look fabulous.'

'That's fine, but I won't be here myself. I'll leave a spare key with the downstairs neighbour.' I pick up the brochure and thumb through. 'Will you deal with viewings? I don't live in Lewes and…'

'It's all in there.' He taps the brochure. 'Right, I have everything I need.' He reaches out to shake my hand. 'Any questions, ring the office. It's a pleasure to do business with you.'

After loading the filled boxes into the car, I drive to the council offices. 'Would it be possible to see Gayle Stevens?' I ask the receptionist. 'She said I could pop in.'

She smiles. 'Take a seat. I'll see if she's available.'

I sit on a black leather sofa to wait. Moments later, the receptionist leaves her desk and walks towards me. 'Gayle says to come right up. I'm due a break, so I'll show you the way.'

I follow her to the lifts at the back of the reception area. The doors open on the fifth floor and she points along the corridor. 'HR is the first door on the left.'

As I step out of the lift, Gayle's approaching. 'Sarah.' We shake hands. 'Come in, come in.'

She shows me into her office, light and airy, with a well-tended yucca plant on the desk. We sit in comfy chairs. 'How are you doing?' Her face is full of concern.

'I'm okay. I've just put Simon's flat on the market.'

She nods. 'It's a difficult time. You're Simon's executor, I take it?'

'Yes, but not beneficiary.' I exhale. Gayle's well suited to HR, she's so easy to talk to. 'Actually, the beneficiary was someone we didn't know. It's all been quite difficult.'

Her face doesn't give anything away. 'I'm sure.' She hesitates as if making up her mind. 'I wanted to discuss the matter of Simon's Death in Service benefit.'

'Death in Service?'

'Yes. All employees who die whilst in the employ of the council are entitled to a death grant. It's a sizeable amount. About three times the annual salary.'

I blow out through my teeth. 'Wow. That's…'

'Approximately one hundred and fifty thousand. Often, employees name a beneficiary – husband or wife or other dependents. In Simon's case, no one was named.'

'Oh. What happens then?'

'Well, the Death in Service payment is normally separate to the deceased's estate but, when no beneficiary is named, the council can determine that it becomes part of the estate.'

'Right. I suppose it goes to the beneficiary then.'

Angel's inheritance just doubled.

CHAPTER SEVENTEEN

Friday night, Tom brings home Chinese takeaway and afterwards we share a bottle of wine while watching a film on *Netflix*. I can't concentrate on the plot. I know where Tom hopes the evening will lead. We haven't had sex in weeks. It's not unreasonable that he should crave a little attention. He's been patient, recognising how stressed I've been dealing with the aftermath of Si's death. Just a few weeks ago, I'd been complaining to Nicki that the intimacy was gone from our marriage. Now it's me who's lost my libido.

As the titles roll, Tom puts an arm around me. 'Early night?'

I jump up and begin stacking dirty plates. 'I need to clear away first.'

Tom switches off the TV while I carry the washing up into the kitchen. He follows me out and, as I load the dishwasher, puts his arms around me and kisses the back of my neck.

'You go on up,' I say.

I take my time wiping down the kitchen worktops and cleaning the sink. Then I open another bottle of wine, pour myself a glass and wander through to the dining room. If I give him an hour, he'll be asleep. I open my laptop and begin to scroll.

'How's it all going?' asks Nicki when I meet her in Browns for cocktails the following evening.

As I sip a Margarita, I feel my anxiety melting away. Nicki's the only one I can really relax with. 'Well, Si's not insolvent, but he certainly had a cash-flow problem.'

She chuckles. 'Well, you know Simon.'

'Sometimes I'm not sure I did.'

'You're his twin sister, Sarah.' She places a hand on my arm. 'You knew him better than anyone.'

'But we were so different. Si said I tried too hard.'

She muddles her cocktail. 'You do.'

'Thanks very much,' I retort.

'I'm not saying it's a bad thing, but Simon, well, he was a little more *laissez-faire*.'

'Meaning?'

'God, Sarah. I've known you both since we were kids. Si and I even dated a couple of times. Remember?'

I laugh. 'Yeah, we weren't destined to be sisters-in-law.'

She shakes her head. 'You should write a book about this.'

'Perhaps I will.' I smile contentedly.

She tastes her Sex on the Beach. 'Look, Sarah, you can tell me to mind my own business…'

'I'd never do that. You know we can say anything to each other.'

'I've been thinking about this woman and I'm not sure you should get too tight.'

'I have to communicate with Angel. She's beneficiary and I'm executor.'

'I know, but you could do that by email. You don't need to be so involved.'

I squirm. How can I make Nicki understand the connection I'm beginning to feel with Angel?

'Si was such a dark horse.' She chews her straw thoughtfully. 'You were never that way inclined?'

I snort. 'Sex hasn't featured in my life for some time.'

She nods sympathetically. 'Tom still not interested?'

'It's not Tom's fault. He was up for it last night. It was me who made excuses.'

'I'm not surprised. You've been so busy.'

I sigh. 'It's not just that.'

'What then?'

'I don't know. My world seems so dull and boring compared with Si's.'

'Poor Tom.'

I nudge her. 'Bet he wonders how come my brother got the sexy genes.'

'Hey, don't spill the alcohol.' She plays with a cocktail umbrella. 'You do seem intrigued by Simon's secret lifestyle.'

I shrug.

'Are you still looking at those online sites?'

'A bit.'

'I'm not sure it's good, seeing all that stuff about your brother. You'd be better remembering him the way he was.'

'That's what Tom says.'

'Well, for once, Tom's right.'

The paper bank statements finally arrive, and I spend hours poring through them and making costing sheets. 'As long as nothing else comes out of the woodwork, he's solvent,' I tell Tom.

He looks up from his newspaper. 'That's good news.'

'Yes.'

'No gambling debts then?'

'Nothing here. He paid his other debts back on a regular basis and there are no unaccountable cash withdrawals. I think the mortgage, loan and credit cards will be the end of it.'

'What about PayPal?'

'Payments show up on the bank statements and PayPal say there's nothing outstanding, but he was spending way beyond his means.'

'Really?'

'Yeah, probably two grand more than he earned each month. It was never sustainable.'

'Do you think he knew that?'

'For sure. When he sent that monthly expenditure spreadsheet to Angel, he clearly had a good idea what was going on and where this was leading.'

'Simon did suffer with depression. You don't think he deliberately…'

'Suicide? Oh God, I hope not!' I put my head in my hands. 'I don't know.'

Next morning, I sort through the books I brought home. Most will go to The Lion's Bookstore, but there are a few volumes I need to make room for, including Mum's books.

Sitting down at the dining room table, I thumb through

the 450-page *Mrs Beeton*. It's bulging with cuttings from *Woman's Realm* and, throughout the book, Mum's added personal reviews: "Double quantity and freeze"; "The children didn't enjoy this…"

I'm about fifty pages in when a scrap of paper falls from the book, fluttering to the floor. I pick it up, recognising not Mum's handwriting, but Si's spiky script:

> When I first saw you, Goddess, my heart skipped a beat. You are the most stunningly beautiful woman I have ever seen.
>
> I feel my whole life has led to your door. Before, life was a mess. Before, I lived a boring vanilla life, hiding my submissive side.
>
> I thank my lucky stars the day you came into my life and changed me for the better.

I'm sure he drafted this to Angel. His words sound honest and sincere. It's almost as if they were in a proper relationship. Is that how he felt? I clutch the note to my chest. I should trust her. This proves he loved her and believed she saved his life. I knew I'd find something. It's a sign I'm doing right by him. Okay Si, I've got this.

CHAPTER EIGHTEEN

'Excuse me.' Making my way to the front of the queue, I scan Zizzi's busy tables.

Nicki waves from the back of the restaurant. 'Sarah, over here.'

I hurry across and we air kiss before taking our seats.

'Why's it so packed?' I ask.

'End of the school holidays. Everyone's had the same idea.' She passes me a menu. 'We better get our order in before they start serving that lot.' She nods at a party of eight taking seats at a reserved table next to ours.

'What are you having?

'The special, crab and ricotta cannelloni.'

'Sounds good. I'll have the same.' I set the menu down. 'Sorry I'm late.' I slip off my cardigan and drape it over the back of the chair. 'I was going through Si's stuff and completely forgot the time.'

'It's fine.' Nicki catches the eye of a waitress moving a highchair into position at our neighbours' table. 'We're ready to order.'

The waitress smiles and pulls a handset from her apron pocket. 'What can I get you?'

'Two specials please, and...' Nicki raises an eyebrow in question. Without words, I nod agreement. 'A bottle of Sauvignon,' she adds.

The waitress taps in our order. 'Coming right up.'

Nicki leans back in her chair. 'I hope it's cold.'

'So' – I touch her hand – 'how did your date go the other night?'

She wrinkles her nose. 'Okay, but I won't be repeating it.'

'I'm sorry.'

'I always pick wrong uns.' She shrugs. 'Anyway, you ready for the off?'

'I suppose so. I just don't seem to have any enthusiasm.'

'You and me both!'

'And I've still got the bloody exam analysis to complete.'

'Want me to take a look?'

'No, it's just the usual. I'll get it done.'

'You sure you shouldn't be taking time off?'

'Si died four weeks ago. I'm fine.'

She shakes her head. 'You haven't even started to grieve. You should get signed off.'

'I can't. And anyway, I'll need to take the odd day off to sort things – solicitor's appointments and what not.'

The waitress returns with our wine.

'Perfect, thanks,' says Nicki.

'Food will be right out,' says the waitress.

Nicki raises her glass and chinks it against mine. 'Here's to a peaceful autumn term.'

I take a sip. The wine's so cold it makes me shiver. 'Damn, that's good.'

Nicki sets down her glass. 'You have talked to Brian

though? For a headteacher, he can be surprisingly compassionate.'

'I spoke to his PA. She said to let her know what I need and the school will work around it.'

'There you are then. Take some time off.'

'To be honest, it will do me good to get back to normal.'

The following day, sitting in the main hall listening to Brian's perennial 'State of the Nation' pep talk, I'm not sure normal cuts it. It's good that Si's death happened during the holiday, as it meant I didn't have to juggle work with all the other stuff I've been sorting out. But now, with just two INSET days before the kids return, I realise I've had no break.

Brian's PA has informed the leadership team of Si's death but, apart from a few sympathetic head tilts, no one acknowledges it. Only my faculty know what happened and I intend to keep it that way.

After coffee, I attend a meeting for heads of department. It's not until after lunch that Nicki and I get time to go through outline programmes of study.

'I'm sorry I didn't get to review the new schemes of work for Year Ten,' I say.

'It's okay. We'll run with what we've got until October, then evaluate. It's mostly 'learn to study' activities anyway, and we can do rewrites over half-term.'

'That's fine, as long as Ofsted don't decide to show up. You heard what Brian said this morning. We're due an inspection.'

'If it happens, it happens. We'll deal with it.'

I groan. 'Feels like I'm not keeping my eye on the ball.'

'Don't be silly. It's amazing you're here at all. If it gets too much, tell me. Or, better yet, take a few days off.'

'No, I need to be here.'

With Jamie back at university, I use his room to sort through Si's stuff. Starting with the largest box, I pull out a framed print of Michael Schumacher winning his sixth world championship. Perhaps Jamie would like this? He shares Si's love of Formula One.

Who am I kidding? I look around at the bare walls. Jamie's most treasured possessions have already been moved to his digs. It won't be long before Jamie himself is erased from the house. Who will I be when he no longer needs me?

I sigh as I dig into the box once more – ink drawings of Ferraris and pictures of volcanos. Si was a volcano junkie. He took evening classes in geology, planning holidays around the volcanos he most wanted to visit.

I lift out three framed photographs. Two were displayed on the wall in his sitting room – *Mount Vesuvius* and *El Misti* in Peru. The third was on his bedroom wall – a conical mountain with a lake in the foreground. The volcano's unfamiliar.

Taking out my mobile, I call Tina. 'Hiya.'

'How are you?'

'Just sorting through Si's stuff. Is there anything you want? Photos or anything? I know you shared quite a few holidays together.'

'I don't think so. I've got copies of all the holiday photographs.'

'There was a picture on the wall in Si's bedroom. A volcano, lush surroundings…'

'Probably Arenal. Simon was besotted with the Costa

Rican volcanos. There are five still active, you know? We were planning a trip, before we…'

'Costa Rica, of course. That's why he was learning Spanish. Okay, well if you think of anything else you want, let me know. Otherwise, it will end up in charity shops.'

Once I hang up, I open my phone and find Si's blog. He wrote something about volcanos:

Live long and prosper

Did I mention I'm an amateur volcanologist?

What is a volcanologist, I hear you ask? No connection to Spock and Star Trek, although I am a bit of a Trekkie on the quiet… but I digress.

A volcanologist is a person who studies volcanoes. How cool is that? Well, you might say, not particularly cool, perhaps rather hot… ha ha.

I think I'd have made a good volcanologist. Sadly, I wasn't much interested in geography or geology at school, so everything I've learned about volcanoes is self-taught.

Imagine being a volcanologist: having a job that has an impact on our planet – our very civilisation.

If I was a proper volcanologist, I'd be employed by the government or a research department in a university. I'd travel the world collecting physical samples and data; examine volcanic rock, ash and debris, seismic activity, atmospheric gases and land composition; be able to tell you how and why volcanoes erupt and even be able to predict them.

According to Greek and Roman mythology, Vulcan was the god of fire, the blacksmith of the Roman gods. When hot lava fragments and dust clouds erupted from the island of Vulcano in the Mediterranean Sea, they believed it was

Vulcan in his forge, beating out thunderbolts for other gods.

During the Middle Ages, many people thought volcanoes were entrances to the fiery underworld. They believed that human sacrifices to the gods would prevent volcanoes from erupting. Sometimes I wonder if I could become a sacrifice. Far more exciting to dive into an active volcano that to jump from a multistorey car park... but would I have the guts?

Was Si seriously considering a career change? Or was his love of volcanoes just a hobby? Pulling a box of oversized books towards me, I rifle through until I find what I'm looking for – an expensive-looking book entitled *Volcanos*. Thumbing through, I find the Costa Rican volcanos and compare the illustrations with the framed photograph. It's definitely Arenal. I slide the picture back in the box. Perhaps I can do a job lot on eBay?

My mobile rings. 'How are you, Sarah?' says Daniel.

I curl up on Jamie's bed, cradling the phone against my ear. 'Surviving. How about you?'

'I miss my old mate so much. I don't know what to do with myself.'

'I'm sorry.' I remember Daniel's sad eyes and wish I could comfort him.

'No, I'm sorry. You've been on my mind all day. It must be a million times worse for you.'

A thrill passes through me. I've been on his mind?

'I can't imagine what it's like to lose a twin,' he continues.

I love how he acknowledges the special bond between Si and me. 'It's tough.'

'Well, I'm here if you need me.'

'Thanks.'

'Look, I've been thinking about what you asked. Would you like to meet up to chat about Simon?'

My pulse quickens. 'I'd love that.'

'Okay. How about a meal? The four of us – you and your husband, me and Janice.'

'Sure.' Janice must be his wife. Why am I disappointed?

CHAPTER NINETEEN

Daniel suggests a Harvester on the outskirts of Brighton. Not the sort of place Tom and I usually frequent. As we approach the table, Daniel stands up and I notice he's a couple of inches taller than Tom. He's also older than I first thought – late thirties, perhaps?

The men shake hands and Daniel kisses me on the cheek. 'Good to see you both.' He turns to the attractive woman still seated. 'And this is Janice.'

'Nice to meet you,' I say.

She looks up from her mobile and, after a cursory nod, continues to scroll. Not overjoyed to be here, then.

We order at the bar, and Tom and Daniel attempt small talk. When the food arrives, Janice reluctantly sets aside her mobile to join in.

After we've finished the main course, Daniel gets up. 'I'm going for a quick fag.'

I throw a glance at Tom. I don't smoke, but can't miss the chance to get Daniel on his own. 'I'll come too.' As we leave the table, I hear Tom asking Janice about her job. Have to admit, he's a trooper!

Outside, Daniel offers me a cigarette.

I shake my head. 'I don't smoke actually.'

He lights up and exhales. 'I still can't believe he's gone.'

'Daniel, you said you and Si talked about everything. That you had no secrets.'

He scuffs his toe against an uneven paving slab.

'Did you know about his life in Brighton?'

He takes another drag. 'I'm not sure I'm ready to talk about that.'

'Look, I'm not asking for details, but do you know Angel? She was at the funeral.'

'I may have met her.'

'And Valentina?'

'Yeah, I know her. Not Si's type, if you know what I mean.' He grins. 'I've seen her Instagram pages. She was pretty tight with Harry.'

'Harry?'

'Simon's mate, Harry the Loner. He brought him along to a Madness concert once.'

'Why's he called Harry the Loner? Does he have no family?'

'I wouldn't know.'

This is going nowhere. 'Sorry,' I bite my lip. 'I'll stop grilling you. I know I'm putting you in an awkward situation.'

'No, it's okay.' He leans closer and wipes a tear from my cheek with his thumb. The gesture is intimate and my belly does a little flip. 'Hey, I get it.' His face is inches from mine. 'There's so much you don't know. Things you couldn't possibly understand.'

Staring into those hazel eyes, my voice grows husky. 'So… help me out.'

Daniel steps back, chucks his fag end onto the patio and grinds it under his shoe. 'Your brother was a chameleon.'

'In what way?'

'Different persona for different situations. Kept everything separate.'

'Sometimes I think I didn't know him at all.'

'You knew the Si he wanted you to know.'

'And the Si you knew?'

Daniel laughs. 'We had plans.'

'What sort of plans?'

'Oh, you know, pipe dreams. You seen that film *Cocktail*?'

'Yes.'

'The bar Tom Cruise works in... where was it, Jamaica? That's what me and Si dreamt about.'

'A bar on the beach?'

'Yeah. Bit of a cliché, right?'

'But how would Si fund that sort of lifestyle?'

'Oh, he had it all worked out. In a few years he'd take early retirement, sell his flat, cash in his pension and go for it while young enough to enjoy it.'

'And was it just a dream?'

'Yeah. Besides' – Daniel nods towards the restaurant door – 'what would I do with the missus? Speaking of which, we'd best go back inside.'

Tom glares at me as we join the others.

'Sorry,' I mouth.

Janice gets up. 'We really should get going.' She's clearly had enough of my husband's company.

'Don't you want dessert?' Daniel asks. Janice gives him a look and he raises his hands in submission. 'Well, thanks for a nice evening. Shall we split it?'

'The bill's already sorted,' says Tom.

'Cheers.' Daniel shakes Tom's hand again and gives me a hug. I can't meet Janice's eyes. I'm sure she thinks I'm making moves on her husband.

After they've gone, Tom sits back down. 'I've ordered a brandy.'

I notice he doesn't offer me one. I'm driving home then. A waiter delivers the drink.

'Sorry I was so long outside,' I say. 'It all got a bit emotional.'

Tom picks up the glass and swirls it around. 'Yes, well, I hope it was worth it.' His tone is snappy, and I wince. He knocks the brandy back in one. 'That Janice is bloody hard work.'

CHAPTER TWENTY

Next Saturday, blessed with an Indian Summer, Angel and I meet at The Level in Brighton. Meandering through the park with takeaway coffees, I note how men turn to give Angel a second look. It feels strangely thrilling to be walking alongside her; almost as though their admiration reflects well on me, too.

Mums amble along pushing strollers, while their children run ahead, keen to get to the play area.

Angel gazes at them and smiles. My God, she's stunning.

'Do you want a family some day?' I ask.

She laughs. 'What? And give up my highly lucrative lifestyle as a dominatrix?'

I find myself staring at her luscious lips. I've always been a lip gloss kind of girl myself, never daring enough to wear that shade. I imagine her applying a nude base, then outlining with lip liner before adding a layer of that succulent red and blotting them on a tissue… stop it! What the hell is wrong with me?

Trying to hide what feels suspiciously like a girl crush, I

gesture towards an empty bench. 'Shall we sit?' Regaining my composure, I continue. 'Sorry, I didn't mean to pry. Si never wanted children either.'

Her laughter is effervescent. 'He told me he didn't want to bring any more kids into such a fucked-up world. And besides, he wanted to travel.'

'That sounds like Si.' I take a sip of coffee. 'When we were trying to track you down, we found you listed as a legal advisor.'

'Yes, I was a lawyer, specialising in environmental law. I wanted to change the world.'

'That sounds noble.'

Her eyes twinkle. 'Perhaps, but the reality not so much. I got a job in environmental compliance – basically when a developer wanted to build, I ensured everything on the planning application was compliant in terms of energy, water and pollution.'

'Then why…'

'Why work in the sex industry?' Her mood flips like a switch. 'I didn't fall on hard times, you know. I became disillusioned. Becoming a dominatrix was a positive career choice.'

'Sorry, I didn't mean…'

'Yes, you did, but it's all right. It's what most vanillas assume.'

My cheeks flush. 'Vanillas?'

'People like you, living ordinary little lives.'

Is my life ordinary? I suppose it is, compared with Angel's. Before I can stop myself, I hit back. 'Not everyone has to have a Samantha Jones swing to enjoy a healthy sex life.'

Her eyes flash. 'You people…'

You people? Her words sting.

'You think dommes are glorified prostitutes. It's a complete misconception. We don't have sex with our clients. They don't even touch us.'

My heart's thumping. She's right. That is what I thought.

She sighs, expelling anger like air. 'Sorry, it's not you personally. It's just… I get this a lot.'

'It's okay.' My pulse rate slowly returns to normal. 'So' – my words are cautious – 'what attracted you to become a dominatrix?'

She shrugs. 'When life doesn't turn out the way you want, change it. Have you heard of Catherine Robbe-Grillet?'

'No.'

'She's a famous French dominatrix and a hero of mine. She has this power like no one else possesses. For her, control is everything.'

I scoff. 'Control is what people accuse me of holding on to.'

'Perhaps you'd make a good dominatrix, then.'

I stare at her. Is she teasing me, or what?

'Dommes are not just about sex,' Angel continues. 'We offer a valuable service, helping subs to fulfil their needs and desires.'

'Is that why Si said you saved his life?'

'Of course. What you probably don't realise is that I'm qualified in neuro-linguistic programming, counselling and financial management. I offer clients a complete package in terms of wellbeing.'

'I had no idea.' We sit in silence a long moment before I add, 'For what it's worth, I'm sorry. For stereotyping.'

She places a gentle hand on my arm and I shiver. It's a balm and feels like forgiveness.

'Come on.' Her tone is lighter, friendly once more. 'Tell me how you're getting on with sorting out the apartment.'

'Pretty good,' I say, pleased to change the subject. 'I've sent you the inventory. Are you sure there's nothing you want?'

She shakes her head. 'I didn't visit Simon, so there's nothing of sentimental value. Oh, except the gas masks. We used them in a photoshoot, so it would be kind of cool to keep those.'

'Okay, they're at home for safe keeping. I've been through all Si's personal stuff. If you don't want anything else, I'll sell any items of value and do a house clearance on what's left.'

'That sounds fine. Any offers on the apartment yet?'

I shake my head. 'Nothing firm, although there's quite a bit of interest. Marty at the estate agents thinks we should hold out for the top end of the valuation.'

Angel studies her nails. 'Whatever you think is a fair price. It would be good to get things settled sooner rather than later. I don't want the place standing empty as the weather turns cold.'

'Okay. Have you finished?' I drop our coffee cups into a nearby bin and pull a notepad from my bag. 'Right, Death in Service benefit. This is proving a little tricky. The solicitor says she won't get involved as it's not technically part of the estate, but Si didn't name a separate beneficiary, so Lewes Council say it *is* part of the estate.' I sigh. 'Everyone's dragging their heels, but I'm sure I'll get to the bottom of it.'

'You're so good, doing all this for him. If you need any help…'

'It's a bit awkward, what with you being beneficiary.'

'Yes, I see.' She smiles and I bask in the warmth. 'You're

doing a wonderful job, Sarah. Simon would be so proud of you.'

It's late afternoon before we go our separate ways. On impulse, I stop at Marks & Spencer to pick up one of their dine-in deals and a bottle of Merlot.

Tom's watching football when I get home, so I pop upstairs to take a shower. Vanilla indeed, I think, as I shave my legs. Tom and I don't need a drawer full of sex toys to have fun. I put on a lace bra with matching knickers and slip into a floaty dress from Monsoon that Tom always likes me in. Finishing off with lip gloss and a good spritz of Valentino Donna Eau de Parfum, I hurry downstairs.

I'm setting the dining room table with the best china when Tom catches sight of me and whistles. 'Wow! Special occasion?'

'No, just thought I'd treat us.'

He turns off the TV. 'Perhaps I should get changed, too.'

'No, you're all right, but could you find some music please?'

Moving across to the Sony music system, he selects a CD. Soulful jazz from Grover Washington Jr's saxophone fills the room as I carry in the main course.

'Gastropub moussaka served with buttered French beans,' I announce, as if I've spent hours in the kitchen.

'Looks great.' He pours the wine. 'How did you get on with Ms Bentley-Bell?'

'Good. It was glorious in Brighton, so we walked and talked.' Why do I feel like I've been cheating? 'She doesn't want any of Si's personal effects. Well, apart from the gas masks.'

Tom raises an eyebrow. 'Did you tell her about the interest in the flat?'

'Yes. She says to accept any reasonable offer. I think she wants things settled as soon as possible.'

'I bet she does.' He tucks into moussaka. 'This is good.'

'I mentioned the Death in Service benefit too.'

Tom sucks air through his teeth. 'I wouldn't have said anything about that yet. You don't want to raise expectations.'

'She's being perfectly reasonable about everything.' I load my own fork. 'She's very grateful for all my efforts.'

'So she should be.'

The silence is uncomfortable. This could so easily turn into an argument. I bite my tongue. I don't want to spoil the mood.

When we've finished the main course, I fetch dessert.

'Chocolate.' Tom grins. 'I might have known.'

I relax. It's going to be all right. 'You like chocolate too,' I retort. The melt-in-the-middle pudding is delicious but, as I pop the last spoonful into my mouth, I wonder if I should have chosen something lighter?

Tom stands to clear the dishes.

'Leave them,' I say, reaching across to touch his hand.

As if on cue, Bill Withers launches into "Just the Two of Us". Tom moves around the table and, for a moment I think we're going to dance, but he has other ideas. Taking me into his arms, kisses come fast and urgent as his hands reach to my neck, fumbling for my zipper.

'Easy tiger,' I laugh, turning to make things easier.

He slides down the zipper and slips the dress over my hips, leaving me in bra and knickers. Taking a step back, he appraises my body. Feeling strangely self-conscious, I hold in my tummy, wishing I hadn't eaten so much. Reaching for his belt, I tug him towards me.

Tom grins as I unbutton his fly and unzip him. He's already hard. It crosses my mind to perch on the table but, mindful of the best china, I smile invitingly and lower myself to the floor. As I lay down, I bash my head on a chair leg. 'Ouch.'

'Wait.' Laughing, Tom moves the dining chairs away. Kneeling beside me, he kisses my neck, then my cleavage, while fondling my breasts.

The corner of the rug jabs into my bum cheek. 'Ow.'

He pulls back. 'What?'

'Nothing, it's okay.' I shift my buttocks.

Taking the movement as a sign I'm aroused, Tom yanks at my lace knickers.

'Wait,' I say, 'you'll tear them.'

I remove them myself while he pushes his trousers and boxers down to his knees. I can't help thinking he looks a little ridiculous; he might have taken them off.

His kisses grow fierce as he moves his hand to probe down there with his fingers, making rapid circular movements. God, why are his moves so predictable? I might as well be a "paint by numbers" set – neck, boobs, down there… Was his repertoire always this limited?

I put my hand over his. 'Let's take it slow.'

'I'm not sure I can,' he growls.

He must know I'm not ready. Regardless, he climbs on top, fumbling to push himself inside me.

I close my eyes, wincing as he presses his groin against mine. Penetration really hurts. I'm dry and tight as a virgin. What is it Nicki says? *'Use it or lose it'*. It's been a while – maybe I've lost it? Perhaps my vagina's closed up, like a pierced ear when you forget to wear earrings for a few weeks.

None of this bothers Tom, grinding away for all he's

worth. This is really hurting; I have to relax. Slipping my hands inside his T-shirt, I stroke his back.

The pain slowly subsides and I open my eyes. Tom's lids are squeezed tightly shut and his face is all creased up. I resist the urge to giggle. My bum's getting friction burns from the rug, I wonder if it will leave marks…

Stop it! Be in the moment. But as I watch his head move back and forth, I notice how hairy his nostrils are. His jaw's tight, like he's grimacing – it's not attractive. I close my eyes again. Perhaps if I imagine he's someone else? Ryan Gosling would be nice. Is it bad to be fucking one man and thinking of another? It's not adultery… or is it? Perhaps it's worse. It's certainly deceitful…

Stop it! I'm with my husband and he's perfectly nice, thank you very much, Mr Gosling. I love Tom. Or at least I used to love him. I know his body as well as I know my own – the smell, the taste…

I snuggle into his neck and suck his ear lobe, which always turns him on. Spreading my knees a little wider, I attempt a modified "happy baby" pose.

His breathing is fast now. 'Oh Sarah… come on, come on…' he murmurs.

Obligingly, I breathe in and out a little quicker, my right knee banging repeatedly against the table leg as he thrusts. I hope the best china isn't working its way to the edge…

'That's it, that's it!' His voice is husky and I know he's close.

I throw in a few gasps and lift my hips to meet his.

'Oh God, oh God,' he cries.

Panting in small quick breaths, I fake an orgasm.

With a deep exhale and a shudder, he comes. I pat his back. Should I tell him well done?

Moments later he relaxes and his full weight drops on me.

'Tom, you're crushing me.'

He doesn't move.

'I can't breathe,' I complain, shoving him gently.

'Sorry.' He moves off and lays on his back. His eyes are closed and there's a stupid smug expression on his face. 'Worth the wait,' he murmurs.

'Yes,' I lie, getting to my feet.

He opens his eyes. 'Got any tissues?'

I toss him a paper napkin and begin to clear the dishes.

CHAPTER TWENTY-ONE

Angel sounds upbeat when I call her with an update. 'Hi Sarah. How's everything going?'

'Well, I think. We've had the money for the car and the bike, and I've sorted through Si's clothes and books. Last chance on the inventory.'

'I don't think there's anything that I want. Oh, perhaps the camera gear might be nice to keep.'

'Sure. I'll box it up with the other stuff. We've had an offer on the flat, too.'

'That's great.'

'I wondered if we could meet up on Saturday to discuss it?'

'I'd love to meet as friends, but regarding the offer on the apartment, just go ahead and do whatever you think is right. You know I trust you.'

Friends. There's a lump in my throat. It doesn't seem enough somehow. But it's good that Angel trusts my judgement. 'Let's meet anyway. I'd love to hear more about Si's life. There's so much I wasn't aware of.'

'Sure. Meet you at KitKat's in Kemptown? Two o'clock.'

'Fancy lunch on Saturday?' asks Nicki.

'Sorry, I can't. Executor stuff…' I feel my cheeks burn. She's my best friend and I hate deceiving her, but I know she won't approve of me meeting Angel.

'Okay, your loss. I had a deal for that new Italian restaurant in Burgess Hill and was going to treat you, but if you're too busy…'

Angel's there when I arrive. Seated beside her is Valentina.

I try to conceal my disappointment. 'Sorry, I had trouble parking.'

Valentina throws me a withering look.

'Aren't you going to get a drink?' asks Angel.

'Yes. Anyone else need a top up?'

'No, ta.' Valentina tosses her pink, silky hair. Didn't she have a black bouffant at the funeral?

Angel checks her teapot. 'And I've another in here.'

As I queue for a cappuccino, I hear them giggling. Are they laughing at me? I pay for my drink and take the seat opposite. 'I didn't expect to see you today,' I say to Valentina.

'Work nearby, don't I?' Her voice is unusually low and I try not to stare at her Adam's apple.

'We both hire rooms at The Lair,' explains Angel. 'It's not far from here.'

'That's handy.' I stir my coffee, only now putting two and two together. Of course, Valentina's trans.

Angel glances from Valentina to me. 'I thought you two might like to meet properly. You didn't get a chance to talk at the funeral.'

'S'okay.' Valentina stares defiantly. 'I spent time with her old man instead.'

My cheeks flush. Did she overhear what I said to Tom? With that Amazonian frame, I wouldn't like to get on her wrong side.

'Sarah wants to know more about her brother's interactions in the Brighton scene,' Angel continues.

'I never knew Spiro that well,' says Valentina.

'Come on, Valentina,' says Angel.

Valentina sips her latte with nonchalance.

'I hear you know a friend of my brother,' I say. 'Harry the Loner?'

Shooting me a look, she sets down her glass. 'Yeah, I know Harry. I know him as Hector though.' Using a paper napkin, she dabs froth from the corner of her mouth. 'He and Spiro were close. Spiro became a regular at The Lair.' She nudges Angel. 'I used to see him around, but he never visited me.'

Her laughter, deep and throaty, cuts off suddenly like someone threw a switch. 'By all accounts, your brother liked a bit of variety. My style didn't tickle his fancy, but he had a few sessions with Lady Layla.'

'She works at The Lair?'

'Books herself a room a couple of days a week, same as me, but uses The Kama for group sessions.'

'The Kama?'

'Kama Sutra. You can hire rooms by the hour.'

'And Si went there?'

'You'd have to ask Layla.'

'Is there any way I can speak to her?'

'I ain't her keeper.' Valentina stands up, towering above us in huge stiletto heels. 'Well, I can't sit around gossiping all day. A girl's gotta work.' As she swaggers out of the coffee shop, hips swaying, several men turn to watch.

'Sorry.' Angel reaches across to touch my hand and a frisson of excitement shoots through me.

'S'okay.' How is it that just being with her makes me feel more alive?

Angel pouts cherry red lips. 'She didn't tell us much.'

'She confirmed she knew Harry.'

She nods thoughtfully.

'But you never met him,' I say.

'No. When Simon and I met up, it was only ever the two of us.'

'You said The Lair's close by?'

'Just a few doors away. This place' – she gestures with her hand – 'gets loads of business from their clientele. I'm ordering another green tea. You going to drink that coffee?'

CHAPTER TWENTY-TWO

It's mid-November when I next meet with my solicitor.

'How are you?' Fiona asks.

'Busy at work. Everyone's rushing to get appraisal reviews finished by the end of the month.'

'You've done well not to take any time off.'

I shrug. 'With eighteen years' teaching experience, I wing it a lot of the time.' It's not strictly true. I couldn't have managed without Nicki; she's carried me for weeks. I need to make more time for her. 'The sale of the flat went through,' I add.

'I'm not surprised.' Fiona shuffles through papers on her desk. 'It's a great location, commuter friendly and buyers can be in London in ninety minutes.'

'Nothing came back from the Section 27?'

'No, and it's too late now for anyone to make a charge against the estate.'

I sigh with relief. I'd been so worried Si had taken out more loans I wasn't aware of. 'So his debts are settled?'

'Yes.' She casts her eye over the ledger. 'With the Death

in Service benefit, the beneficiary will receive in excess of three hundred thousand pounds.'

'And I'm done?'

'I'll get the closing accounts sent out later today.'

'Fantastic. Fiona, I just wanted to say, I don't know how I'd have got through this without you.'

'You're very welcome. I just hope the beneficiary appreciates how much you've done for her.'

I arrive home to a beautiful bouquet of pink and white lilies on my doorstep. My heart flutters as I read the card:

Thank you, Sarah. Although Si's loss still stings, I am forever grateful that you and I have become friends. Angel xx

Pulling out my phone, I bang off a text in reply:

> Thank you for the gorgeous flowers. My solicitor has confirmed the executor account is closed and you should receive a copy of the final accounts in the next day or two. See you at the weekend.

The past few months have been tough, but finally a weight's lifted.

I'm preparing the evening meal when Tom looks up from his newspaper. 'I was thinking we should go for a meal at the weekend. How about Saturday?'

'What's the occasion?'

He folds his paper. 'Finishing executorship.'

'My brother's dead,' I snap. 'I hardly think it cause to celebrate.'

'I didn't mean it like that, but you've been working nonstop. You're through now and you've done Simon proud.'

'I don't have time. I've a million and one things to catch up with.'

'Okay.' Tom sighs. 'It was just a thought.'

I'm bubbling with anticipation as I drive down to Brighton. Angel and I are celebrating with cocktails, raising a margarita or three to Si. I've packed an overnight bag just in case. Now I've finished my role as executer, we can be proper friends.

After parking near The Lanes, I stroll along the promenade. Down on the beach, a bunch of kids skim pebbles, making the most of the unseasonably pleasant weather. Out at sea, waves ripple in the late afternoon sun. As I near the pier, the sugary aroma of donuts and candy floss brings memories flooding back of family days in Eastbourne. Almost reluctantly, I tear myself away to cross the road, head past Sea Life and along Madeira Drive.

I trot up the steps of Coco Beach Club, past the doorman and over to reception. The receptionist, business-like in a white blouse with spotty neckerchief, looks up with a smile. 'Can I help you?'

'Hi.' I grin back. 'I'm Sarah Edwards. I'm meeting my friend, Angela Bentley-Bell. She's a member.'

'Have you got your guest confirmation email?'

'Er… no, but Angela should already be here.'

The receptionist consults her screen. 'I'm not seeing any record…'

Sensing someone behind me, I spin around to see the

doorman standing on the threshold and acknowledge him with an apologetic smile. I turn to the receptionist once more. 'Should I ring her? Ask her to come down?'

She frowns. 'Members are not allowed mobile phones whilst on the premises.'

'Okay. Perhaps I'll wait outside then.'

Moving away from the reception desk, I step out onto the terrace. The doorman watches me as I pull out my phone and send a text.

> Hi Angel. I'm outside. Can you come down?

I glance at the doorman, standing with his feet apart as if anticipating a rugby tackle.

When Angel doesn't reply, I walk back down the steps and turn right. Perhaps she's delayed? I wander along the pier where the cloying sweet smell, so enticing minutes earlier, now seems nauseous rather than nostalgic.

Half an hour later, there's still no response from Angel. I try ringing, but it goes to voicemail. I leave a message asking her to call me back urgently. What should I do? Is it possible the receptionist made a mistake and Angel's sitting upstairs waiting for me?

With trepidation, I approach the club again.

The doorman regards me with suspicion.

'I just need a quick word…' I gesture towards the reception desk.

He folds his hefty arms, but allows me to pass.

On reception, the young girl has been joined by a man in a shiny grey suit.

'Sorry,' I say, 'but would you mind checking again? I'm supposed to be meeting my friend, Angela Bentley-Bell.

She's a member and said she'd arrange a guest pass for me. Could you please check if she's inside?'

The man's smile displays cosmetically whitened teeth. 'My colleague and I have both checked. We have no record of a guest pass for Sarah Edwards and no current membership for Angela Bentley-Bell.'

'There must be some mistake. She comes here all the time. Sits on the terrace, swims in the infinity pool…'

He bends forward, lowering his voice. 'Your friend may well have visited our establishment as a guest, but I can assure you she's not a current member of Coco Beach Club.'

Back on the pavement, I consider my options. I could go Christmas shopping, but I'm not in the mood. I could drive home, but Tom will be there and I'll have to explain what happened, giving him more ammunition to support his low opinion of Angel. I pull out my phone and search through my documents. Angel's address was on the will, but I've never visited her home. We've always met in town.

Leaving my car where it is, I set out along Marine Parade. Reaching Royal Crescent, I turn left, towards Kemptown, and use Google Maps to locate Forsdyke Road. The three-storey Georgian terraced houses have been mostly converted to flats. Hardly surprising. Angel wouldn't own a whole house.

Outside number 67 is a "To Let" sign. Heart thumping, I march up to the front door and press the buzzer for Flat 3.

No reply. I don't know what else to do. Angel mentioned she and Valentina hire rooms at The Lair but does she operate from anywhere else in Brighton? Could she have forgotten we were meeting? Gone shopping? But we've had this planned for ages. Crossing the road, I lean against a wall and wait.

Twenty minutes later, a woman emerges from number 67. As she bumps a buggy down the front steps, I run across to help her.

'Thank you,' she says, as I lower my end of the buggy safely onto the pavement.

'You're welcome.' I peer at her fair-haired toddler. 'Hello.' The child smiles shyly. The child's mother is smiling too, waiting for me to move out of the way.

'Actually,' I say, 'I wonder if you can help me? I saw the "To Let" sign.'

'Yes, number three.' She brushes her fringe back from her face. 'Tenant moved out suddenly a few days ago. It's quite spacious, although I don't know what sort of state it's been left in.'

'Oh.' My cheeks burn. 'I wasn't looking to rent. I'm trying to find the person who lives there. Angela Bentley-Bell?'

The young woman shakes her head. 'Sorry, although we live in the flat below, I don't really know her. Saw her from time to time and she always said hello, but we never started up a conversation. I was always afraid she might complain about the noise.' She gestures to her golden-haired child. 'He's not a good sleeper.'

'Okay, well thanks anyway.' I walk back along the road. What the hell's going on? Has Angel moved? But she'd have told me, wouldn't she?

'She's gone,' I tell Tom. 'Just up and left.'

'Who can blame her? Three hundred grand in her pocket. She can do a lot with that.'

'But I've still got Si's camera,' I say.

'She'll buy a new one.'

'I need to speak to her.'

'Why?' says Tom. 'It's not like you're friends. You only stayed on good terms while sorting out Simon's estate.'

His words stab my heart. It takes all my willpower not to double up with pain.

'It's over.' Tom puts an arm around me and gives me an affectionate squeeze. 'You need to let go. You've done your best. It's time to accept he's gone.'

'No.' I stand still as a statue. It can't be over.

Tom flicks the switch on the kettle. 'I'll make us a coffee.'

I pull out my phone and scroll back through texts and emails from Angel. Nowhere does she mention plans for after Si's estate is finalised. My stomach lurches. I'm going to be sick. I run to the bathroom.

Minutes later, Tom knocks on the door. 'You all right in there?'

'Yes, just give me a minute.' Nothing I say will make sense to him. How can I explain? Why didn't I ask Angel about her intentions? I thought she might buy property, make a career change. I'd imagined us as close friends, meeting up to reminisce about Si. She was my only link to my brother. Now she's gone, his loss is real.

'Your coffee's on the breakfast bar,' Tom calls through the door.

Pulling myself up, I clutch the sink, staring at my reflection in the mirror. I feel betrayed. And yet Angel's done nothing wrong. Si left her everything fair and square. I wipe vomit from my chin, brush my teeth and go out to play happy families.

. . .

That night, Tom orders in a curry. We watch a film on TV, but I couldn't say what it was about.

At nine, I make my excuses. 'I think I'll have an early night.' I yawn for effect.

'Okay. Mind if I watch a bit of footie?'

Upstairs, I undress and climb into bed. It's like sinking into a swamp of despondency. Is this what Si meant by the black dog? Pulling out my phone, I search for his blog.

Trigger Warning: Suicide

My mind was made up, I wanted out. Out of this life and away from pain.

This time wasn't a cry for help. I wanted to die.

My plan was to take pills. I had antidepressants, but you only get given a small supply and I needed more. I decided to walk to the multi-storey car park three miles away, stopping at every chemist to buy pills. Once there, I'd swallow the lot and jump off. Easy, cheap and relatively quick.

I don't remember much about the start of the day. I know it was a Sunday, because it was quieter than a weekday. I left my wife in bed, and vaguely recall stopping at various shops and buying paracetamol. About half a mile from the car park I knew I hadn't got the guts to jump, so I went into the park, sat under a tree and took 96 paracetamol tablets, washing them down with a litre of cola. After a while I thought about my dog. I couldn't remember if I'd fed him, so I got up and walked home.

My wife was waiting, took one look and drove me to A&E, where they pumped my stomach and gave me charcoal to drink.

One of the things I remember was the nursing staff not

believing I'd taken that many tablets. To me, it seemed perfectly reasonable. If you're going to do it, go big.

A day or two later, one of the nursing staff went into vivid detail about what it's like to die from a paracetamol overdose. Slow and lingering, so I don't recommend it to anyone. They told me I was close to being sectioned.

I haven't cried much since Si died, but now the floodgates open. I can't seem to stop. I'm consumed with guilt. Why didn't I see how troubled he was? I should have been a better sister. I should have done more. Through my tears, I continue to read.

That day was the lowest point in my life. I never want to feel like that again. Now I fight the black dog. I'm stronger than he is. I recognise the signs early and get help before getting to the point of wanting to end it.

Life is good and precious. If anyone's going through this, talk to someone. No matter how low you feel, how lonely, how much of a failure, your life is important. Don't give up.

I blow my nose. I hear you, Si. I won't give up.

CHAPTER TWENTY-THREE

'Angel's disappeared,' I tell Wendy.

'Well, what did you expect?' We're weaving in and out of Christmas shoppers, so she has to wait until we're back together to continue. 'She's got her money. No point in her sticking around.'

'But we were friends.'

'You weren't friends, Sarah. You were a means to an end. As was Simon. You have to let it go.' She clutches my arm. 'It's no good. I can't take another step until I've had a coffee.'

I gesture towards Costa. 'Let's go in there.'

Wendy grabs a table while I queue. It was ridiculous to come to Brighton on a Saturday, but working full time leaves me little option. Usually, I enjoy my annual festive shopping expedition with Wendy, but this year there seems little point. It will be our first Christmas without Si.

'What can I get you?' asks the girl on the till.

'Two lattes please.'

'Can I tempt you to one of our specials? Gingerbread, Pumpkin Spice or Peppermint Mocha?'

'No thanks. Just two lattes.'

'That will be £7.80.'

I scan my card and stand to one side as the barista prepares the drinks. Since his divorce, Si had been on his own at Christmas. Last year, I persuaded him to join us for lunch. He was on good form and, after working our way through a bottle of gin, agreed to stay over. Had he been texting Angel the whole time? Filling her in on our boring vanilla Christmas?

'Two lattes.'

'Thanks.' I pick up the tray and make my way to Wendy.

'Well done.' She takes our drinks and props the tray against the chair leg. 'Goodness, it's busy.'

I stir my coffee. 'We've a decision to make.'

'What's that?'

'The funeral home rang. They have Si's ashes.'

She takes a sip of latte and wipes her lips with a paper serviette. 'I suppose we need to decide what to do with them.'

'Yes.'

'Any thoughts?'

'Well, bearing in mind his love of *Star Trek*, I did think we might blast them into space.'

'You are joking?'

'Kind of… although there are companies that send ashes up on a weather balloon. Some even offer a rocket, but the thought of Si exploding and sprinkling back down who knows where doesn't seem quite right.'

'That's utterly ridiculous. Simon left nothing to cover such outlandish schemes.'

She's right. Both options are exorbitant, but I can't resist teasing her a little longer. 'I suppose if we were being really authentic, we'd send him to another planet and let his body regenerate like Spock.'

Wendy snorts. 'Now I know you're having me on.'

I grin. 'There's no mad rush to decide.'

A small child at the next table begins to wail and Wendy grimaces. 'I'm so thankful ours are almost grown up.'

I sigh. 'Sometimes I wish they weren't.'

Wendy pouts sympathetically. 'Is Jamie away for the whole of the holidays?'

'Yep. He and his mates will be in Phuket on Christmas Day.'

'You and Tom should come to us.'

I pull a face. 'I don't think we'd be very good company.' That's an understatement. Tom and I are barely speaking and when we do it's to take chunks out of each other. 'And anyway, there's Brodie.' That will put her off – my sister's no fan of animals in the house.

She stirs her latte vigorously. 'Remember when we were little? We wouldn't go to sleep Christmas Eve, convinced if we stayed awake long enough, we'd catch Father Christmas in the act.'

I grin. 'God knows what time Mum and Dad got to bed. They must have been saints.'

She reaches across and takes my hand. 'It's just us now, Sarah. Come to lunch Christmas Day.'

At morning break on Monday, I ring the solicitor's office. 'Have you got a change of address for Angela?'

There's a pause before Fiona responds. 'Sorry, Sarah. Even if I had, I wouldn't be able to share it. Why? Is there a problem?'

'Yes.' I swallow. 'I was supposed to meet her a week ago and she didn't show. I went to her home address and she'd gone. Just up and left.'

'Sarah.' Her tone is calm. 'If Angela hasn't shared her new address, I suspect she doesn't want to be contacted.'

I'm free next period, so go in search of Nicki. She's carried me for weeks and I've been taking her for granted. As I poke my head around the door of her classroom, thirty faces turn to stare at me.

'Can I help you?' asks the supply teacher in front of the whiteboard.

'No, sorry,' I mumble, closing the door softly. I head to admin to seek out Marjorie, the cover supervisor. 'Where's Nicki?' I ask.

She frowns. 'Didn't she call you?'

'No.'

'Her mum's very poorly. It sounds critical.'

'Oh no!' I put a hand to my mouth. 'I'll call in on the way home.'

The afternoon can't pass quickly enough. At four o'clock, I'm ringing the doorbell to Nicki's two up, two down, terrace cottage.

She opens the door. 'Oh, I thought you were my Uber.'

Behind her, at the foot of the stairs, stands a suitcase in readiness. 'You're going to France?' I ask.

'Yes.'

'I'm sorry. I didn't realise things had gotten so bad.'

'No, well…' She shrugs. 'You haven't exactly been around much lately.'

A wave of guilt washes over me. 'But I'm here now.'

'Yeah…' Nicki looks distracted as she stares at her hands, as if expecting to be holding something. 'What was I doing?'

I step inside. 'What time's the Uber booked?'

'Ten past. What time is it now?'

'You've a few minutes.' I place my hands on her shoulders. 'Take some deep breaths.' As she complies, I recite my go-to checklist. 'Tickets, money, passport.'

Grabbing her handbag from the banister, she checks the side pockets. 'I printed off my boarding card and my purse is here with my credit card.' Her eyes widen in panic. 'What the hell did I do with my passport?'

I step through to the kitchen where I spot her passport on the worktop. 'Here.'

Nicki stows it safely in her bag.

'Coat?'

She grabs a fleece jacket from the peg behind the door. 'This one will do.'

'Right.' I pull her into my arms. 'She'll be okay,' I whisper.

'But supposing she's not? She's really gone downhill lately.'

Outside, an Uber driver gives a beep of the horn.

'I've got to go.' Nicki picks up her suitcase and we both step out of her house.

'Call me,' I say, as she slams the front door.

I get in my car, but don't start the ignition. Angel's gone and Nicki has her own problems to deal with. What am I going to do?

I've been ghosted. Googling both Angela Bentley-Bell and Angelica Belle reveals nothing. I search Facebook and Instagram to no avail. It's as if she's vanished into thin air.

My calls to Daniel go straight to voicemail. So much for

being there. Did I say something wrong when we met for the meal? Has Janice put her foot down and told him to have no further contact with me?

Finally, he returns my call. 'Hi Sarah. How are you doing?'

'Not great.'

'Me neither. I miss my old drinking partner so much.'

'Daniel, I know you said you'd never had dealings with Angel, but do you have any idea where I might find her?'

I hear his intake of breath. 'She's gone?'

'Yep. As soon as the money was transferred into her account, she disappeared off the face of the earth.'

'Sorry Sarah. I don't have a clue. If it's to do with Si's estate, can't your solicitor track her down?'

'It's not that. I have some of Si's things she asked for.'

'Valuable?'

'Not particularly – camera stuff, a few personal items…'

'I dare say she can treat herself to new ones now.'

'Yes, that's what Tom said.'

'Sarah, I hope you don't think I'm overstepping but…'

'What?'

'Perhaps it's time you stopped delving into Si's secrets?'

'I have.'

'No, you haven't. I know it's not easy, but you've done him proud, sorting out his affairs. You need to move on.'

I snort. 'You're the last person I expected to be saying this. What happened to, "I don't know what I'm going to do without him," and, "I'm here for you"?'

'Sarah…'

'No, it's fine. Have a nice life.' I end the call.

I don't need anyone's help. I'll find Angel myself.

CHAPTER TWENTY-FOUR

The following Saturday, I drive down to Brighton. KitKat's is quiet as I order a cappuccino and settle myself at a table near the door. I sense the barista's eyes on me. I'm not his usual clientele and he expects me to finish my coffee and leave, but I make the coffee last for as long as I dare before ordering a second cup and pretending to be occupied on my phone.

He's still watching me. I feel my cheeks flush. What am I doing here? This is ridiculous. I'm about to leave when Valentina walks through the door.

'Valentina,' I say. 'Can I buy you a coffee?'

She tosses her long blonde tresses before joining me. I go to the counter and order her a latte which she accepts without thanks.

'I brought you something.' I retrieve a large carrier from beneath the table.

Valentina peeks into the bag and raises a quizzical eyebrow. 'Otto?'

'Size ten,' I whisper.

She lifts the lid of the shoe box and smiles. 'Pretty.'

Suddenly realisation dawns. 'Girl, you bringing me dead man's shoes?'

I squirm. 'Sorry, I didn't mean to offend you.'

I reach to take them back, but Valentina hugs the bag to her ample chest. 'Didn't say I was offended, did I?'

'Okay, good.'

Stowing the shoes at her feet, she sits forward and stirs her drink.

'Valentina.' I broach the matter cautiously. 'I need help.'

She sips coffee.

'Have you seen Angel lately?'

Crossing her legs, she sits back and throws me a smug smile. 'She's gone.'

'Gone where?'

'That girl done played you. Took the money and scarpered.'

'She didn't play me.' Why am I so defensive? 'My brother left Angel his money fair and square. It was all legit.'

'Not the first time,' she mutters.

'What?'

'I said' – slowly she annunciates the words – 'I – doubt – it's – the – first – time. Angelica was always flaunting Chanel handbags and Jimmy Choos. Weren't nobody's fool. I wouldn't be surprised if she ain't pulled this stunt before.'

'It wasn't a stunt.'

Valentina's nostrils flare and she makes to get up.

'Sorry.' I raise my hands in surrender. 'It wasn't a stunt though. My brother really cared about her.'

'More fool him.' She sits back down.

I have a strong urge to slap her. Resisting, I take a slow, deep breath. 'Look, I need to find Angel.'

'Why?'

'She knows stuff. Stuff about my brother.'

She huffs.

'My brother was part of the Brighton scene. Is there anyone you know who might be able to help me?'

'Nope.'

'When we met before, you mentioned another dominatrix. Lady Layla?'

She shrugs.

'Where can I find her?'

Valentina's phone beeps. She checks the message. 'I gotta go.' She gets up.

'Valentina, please.'

'For fuck's sake.' She expels an exaggerated sigh. 'Meet me here Tuesday morning and I'll introduce you.'

'But I'm working Tuesday…'

She's gone.

When I get home, I'm surprised to find the house empty. I pick up the post on the doormat and check my messages.

> Had a bit of an emergency and got to stay late to sort things out. I'll grab something to eat. Don't wait. Tom.

I stick a jacket potato in the oven. It's a relief not to have to cook Tom a meal. Not to have to pretend everything's all right between us. I turn to the mail. Two letters – one looks like junk mail, the other is from the Inland Revenue. My heart sinks. Oh no, they're not charging me tax on Si's estate…

Ripping open the envelope, I find a cheque made out to me for one thousand two hundred pounds. The enclosed letter explains it's a tax rebate for Si and made out to me as executor. Now I have a justifiable reason for getting in touch with Angel.

I throw together a small salad to go with my potato, pour myself a large glass of wine and open my laptop.

'For God's sake, Sarah.'

I slam down the lid. I hadn't heard Tom come in. 'I was just…'

'I know exactly what you were doing and it's got to stop.'

I hunch my shoulders. 'You don't understand.'

'You're right.' He sighs. 'I don't understand. I don't get it at all. I've been patient, considerate…'

'My brother died.'

'I know, and I've done my best, but this isn't normal.'

'Grieving isn't normal?'

'This isn't grief, Sarah, it's obsession. You're obsessed with finding out about Simon's secret life. It's not going to change anything. He'll still be dead.'

I gasp as if winded.

He sits down. 'I'm sorry. I shouldn't have said that. It's just…' He runs a hand through his hair. 'I don't recognise you anymore.'

CHAPTER TWENTY-FIVE

'Sorry, but I'm not at all well… yes, I appreciate it's difficult, what with Nicki off too. I'll let you know if I can make it in tomorrow.'

Marjorie sounded far from happy and I experience more than a twinge of guilt. And Nicki… I must message to ask how her mum is…

Brodie whines. He needs a walk. I'll catch up with Nicki later.

It's ten o'clock when I get to KitKat's and an hour later before Valentina pokes her head around the door. 'Come on then, if you're coming,' she hollers.

Leaving my cappuccino unfinished, I grab my bag and coat, and hurry after her. 'Where are we going?'

Her strides are enormous and she doesn't slow down. 'Layla's got a shift at The Lair.'

We head along the road and left into an alleyway. Halfway along, Valentina marches into Theresa's Hairdressers, where, after giving the receptionist a cursory nod, she goes straight through to the back of the salon.

I follow her down a spiral staircase to a suite of beauty treatment and massage rooms below. Valentina whispers something to a young girl manning a second reception desk. The girl presses a button and a panelled wall opens to reveal a hidden door.

Valentina leads the way into a small waiting area furnished with a couple of old couches, a water fountain, and tea and coffee making facilities. Several doors lead off and she heads towards one on the right. 'Come on.'

It's like stepping into a womb. Three walls are crimson red, as is the carpet, while the ceiling and one feature wall are mirrored, making the space appear larger than it is. On the wall hangs a gigantic crucifix with leather straps at wrist and ankle positions. There's also a tall, padded bench with a series of straps and buckles at floor level.

Valentina smiles. 'Coffee? I've got a while. My sub cancelled on me.'

While she's gone, I gaze about. To my right is a small unit kitted out with BDSM equipment – whips of all size and type, a selection of dog collars with heavy chain leads, and something that looks like a hairbrush but with pins instead of bristles. Gas masks and straps hang from various hooks, while below is a set of drawers. Heaven only knows what they contain.

Valentina returns with two black coffees. 'Hope you don't take sugar or milk, 'cause there ain't none.'

'Thanks.' I take the proffered mug.

'I checked the book. Layla's already here. She's using the water room.'

'The water room?'

Valentina laughs. 'She might be a while. Make yourself

comfortable.' Lifting one leg, she mounts the bench as though it were a horse.

I don't sit down. 'How long have you been renting a room here?' My tone, business-like and professional, seems surreal.

'About three years. It's all right. Cheaper than The Kama, although they've got better facilities – a cage and everything.' She winks.

I sip my coffee, not knowing where to look. 'Perhaps I should wait outside?'

Valentina shakes her head. 'Don't want you upsetting the clients. Stick out like a sore thumb, you do.'

'How long will Layla be?'

'Long as it takes. She'll be doing the talk-down.'

'Talk-down?'

'Yeah. Can't let clients go straight back out on the streets after a session, so we give them a cuppa and sit and chat. Let them unwind before they return to reality.'

'Did my brother come here?'

Valentina cracks a wicked smile as she climbs off the bench. 'I expect she's finished.' She nods towards the door. 'I need to set up for my next sub.'

It's my cue to leave. That business about me not sitting outside was clearly bullshit. She just wanted to shock me.

I step into the waiting area to find Layla, wearing a bright orange coat over fishnet tights, perched on one of the couches. Although I recognise her from the videos, in the flesh she reminds me of one of those exploited child models seen on American TV documentaries.

'Layla?' I say.

She nods.

'Are you okay?'

She shrugs.

'I want to talk to you about my brother, Simon Foster. You used to meet him sometimes.'

The kid looks petrified. She can't be more than eighteen.

'You're not in trouble,' I reassure.

'We can't talk here.' She glances at a clock on the wall. 'Look, I've a sub arriving any minute. There's a pub just around the corner, The Black Pig. Meet you there in an hour.'

A couple of guys glance up as I enter. One wears a trilby, the other sports a multi-coloured waistcoat matched with azure blue nail polish. I go to the bar and order a J2O. I could do with a G&T, but I've got to drive home. Although it's almost lunchtime, the pub's quiet. I take the table nearest the door. I don't want Layla to have any excuse not to see me. It's ninety minutes before she shows up, having swapped her working attire for black leggings and leather boots. She's still wearing the orange coat. Her clothes seem more chain store than Angel's, but she certainly has her own style.

Giving me a quick nod, she approaches the bar.

'Usual?' asks the landlord in a cheery voice.

The podgy faced guy in the trilby folds Layla into his arms. He whispers something and she glances my way before responding. As she walks towards me, he watches her in the bar mirror. Has she asked him to keep an eye on things?

I gaze at her as she sits down. Her eyeliner and mascara are caked, her eyes puffy as if she's been crying. As she sets down her glass, I notice her hand is shaking.

'Thank you for coming,' I say.

'You're Spiro's sister.'

Spiro. I can't get used to that name. 'Simon,' I say.

'Sorry. Must have been a shock.' She sips her wine, her lipstick leaving a mark on the rim of the glass.

'I'm getting there. Did you know Simon well?'

'Only recently. He started visiting about six months ago. He'd become quite a regular though.'

'At The Lair?'

'Yes, but not just there.' She lowers her eyes. 'Spiro liked to mix things up.'

'Drugs, you mean?' I whisper.

'That, and other things.'

'Other things?'

She exhales. 'You really want to know?'

'Yes.'

'I was helping him with breath training.'

I never did get around to researching that on Google. 'Breath training?'

'Helps calm you when you're stressed.'

'Is that what the gas masks were for?'

'A gas mask or choker enhances sexual arousal.'

I nod as if knowledgeable of such things. I've read about sex games in the papers – people dying with a tie around their neck. 'I found some gear at his place.'

'What sort of gear?'

'The usual paraphernalia for a session, I suppose.'

'Ah.'

'Where else did you meet him?'

She shrugs. 'There's another place...'

'In Brighton?'

'Yes. The Kama Sutra. I rent with a friend to share the cost.'

I try to sound casual. 'What, a threesome?'

'No, we invite four subs between two of us.'

'Group stuff?'

She smiles. 'Not the way you're imagining. We're not escorts.'

Angel told me professional dommes don't have sex with their subs. Now I wonder… I can't stop myself. I lean closer. 'So, the subs… do they have sex with each other?'

She holds my gaze. 'The subs do whatever we command them to do.'

'Did you ever meet Simon in Lewes?'

She glances towards the guy at the bar who's watching as if ready to pounce. 'Once or twice.'

'At his flat?'

She nods, her face pale.

Suddenly I guess the reason for her nervousness. 'Layla, were you there when…?'

'Everything all right here?'

I hadn't heard him approach. 'Yes,' I say.

'Layla?' The guy in the trilby waits for confirmation.

'Yes, thanks Quinn.' She turns to me. 'Hang on a mo.' She accompanies him to the bar, where they have an animated exchange. He gesticulates my way several times, but she seems to reassure him as, with one final hug, he lets her go.

'We can't talk here,' she whispers to me. 'You'd better come back to mine.'

'How far is your place?'

'Not far.'

We head along Eastern Road, veering left towards Queen's Park. Fifteen minutes later, Layla's pushing open the entrance to a block of flats. I follow her up a concrete staircase to the second floor, where she unlocks a door. It's a tiny bedsit. I see why she can't bring clients here.

Dropping her shoulder bag on the floor, she slips off her coat, revealing limbs even skinnier than I thought. Opening the fridge, she takes out a bottle of wine. 'Want some?'

'Sure.'

She grabs two glasses from a cupboard over the sink. 'Sit down.'

I take the loom weave chair, while she perches on the bed. She pours wine and hands me a glass. I take a sip. It's cheap plonk and I try not to wince.

Layla knocks hers back. 'He were all right, your brother. Treated me like a lady.'

'I gather he took you shopping?'

She grins. 'Got me a black latex dress. Even oiled it for me.'

I don't tell her I've watched the video.

After refilling her glass, she offers me the bottle.

'No thanks.' I've barely touched mine. 'Layla, tell me the truth. Were you there the night Simon died?'

'No.' She tucks a strand of greasy blonde hair behind her ear. 'I was supposed to be. It was me set it up with Delores, one of the dommes I work with.'

'What happened?'

'I wasn't well. Tonsillitis. The doctor put me on antibiotics. I rang Delores to see if we could reschedule, but she was keen to go ahead. Spiro was bringing a mate and she couldn't do the session alone, so she said she'd get someone to cover for me.'

'Would that have been acceptable to Simon? He and you had gotten pretty close, hadn't you?'

She wipes her eyes with the back of her hand. 'When Delores called Spiro, he said it was fine.'

'So, it was Delores and…?'

'Krystal.'

'Krystal's another domme?'

'Yes.'

'And Si's mate?'

She shakes her head. 'I don't know who he was.'

'Could it have been Harry?'

Her face reveals nothing. 'Harry?'

'You might know him as Hector.'

She shrugs. 'I don't know.'

'Go on.' I nod encouragingly.

'Delores said Spiro and his mate were up for some play. They had poppers and ket, too.'

'Did she tell you what happened?'

'She said Spiro had a fancy bottle of champagne. We don't usually drink much when we're working, like to keep a straight head, but Krystal really rated the fizz. They got the guys doing all the usual stuff – pouring drinks, massages…' She hesitates. 'You sure you want to hear this?'

'Yes.'

'That's when Spiro had a funny turn.' She lowers her eyes. 'I'm sorry.'

I swallow. 'What happened then?'

'His mate sobered up real quick, and told Delores and Krystal to get out. A few days later, Valentina told me Spiro was dead. I didn't let on I already knew.'

'And what does Quinn know?'

'He knows your brother died and that you were looking for me. That's it. You won't say anything about them being there, will you?' She puts a hand on my arm. 'They'll be in deep shit if you do.'

Unable to guarantee this, I simply say, 'Thanks for

sharing with me,' then, unsure whether to push my luck, add, 'Layla, could you introduce me to Delores?'

Layla gets up. 'She won't speak to you.'

I place a hand on her arm. 'But you could ask?'

She pulls away. 'I said too much already.'

CHAPTER TWENTY-SIX

I stay behind after school to catch up on Year 11 marking. I used to enjoy teaching religious education. Not the marking – that was always a chore – but the teaching itself was stimulating. I loved planning lessons, making them contemporary and relevant for the teenagers passing through my classroom. Some even chose to continue the subject to A Level. Now, after delivering the same specification for the past six years, I'm bored. I've got Nicki's papers to fit in now, too. The latest from Marjorie is her mum could pop her clogs any day. Three scripts in on "The Freewill Defence" and my mind's wandering. Why did Harry cover up what happened? Perhaps he didn't want anyone to know he was there?

Half an hour later, I decide to finish the essays at home. Dropping the scripts into my bag, I retrieve my jacket from the back of the classroom door. As I'm putting it on, my mobile vibrates in the pocket. I frown as I read the caller ID. 'Hi Daniel.'

'Hi Sarah. How are you?'

'I'm okay.'

The silence between us is palpable. 'Look,' he says, 'I

didn't like the way we left things last time we spoke. I wondered if you want to grab a drink? Perhaps just the two of us this time?'

'I'd like that.' I swallow. 'Actually, what are you doing this evening?'

We meet at The New Moon near Plumpton, and I blush profusely when he greets me with a peck on the cheek. He's wearing glasses and really rocking the nerdy professor look. What am I doing?

'Sit down,' he says. 'I'll get the drinks in.'

I make myself comfortable in front of the open fire, surreptitiously watching Daniel chatting amiably with the bartender. As he turns in my direction, I look away, busying myself with my mobile.

'Malbec okay?' Daniel sets two glasses on the low beer-stained table and plonks down beside me.

'Malbec's great.' I tuck the phone in my handbag. The couch is saggy, and I adjust my posture to avoid rolling into him.

He hands me a glass.

'Thanks.' I take a sip. It's deliciously warm and smooth.

'So, how have you been?' he asks.

'Not great.'

'Me neither. I miss Simon like mad. Feels like I've lost a limb or something.'

I nod. 'I know what you mean.'

'He was such a good mate.' Daniel stares at me. 'I recognise a bit of him in you, you know.'

I feel my cheeks colour as he studies me. Our faces are so close, we could almost kiss…

Breaking eye contact, he pulls away. 'Look, I don't know how much you know.'

I take a slow breath and put down my glass. 'Why don't we just be completely honest?'

'All right.' He takes a sip of wine.

'I found out that Si was part of the Brighton scene.'

He nods.

'And by that, I mean the Brighton sex scene.'

'Must have come as a shock.'

I smile. 'You could say that.' I take another sip before continuing. 'You and Si were close?'

He runs fingers through his Harry Styles hair. 'Each to his own. I didn't indulge the same way Si did.'

'So, you didn't visit… dominatrix?' I whisper the last word.

'No, but I'm not judging.'

'But you knew about Angel?'

Daniel nods. 'I'd seen her photo. Here,' – pulling out his mobile phone, he scrolls through – 'Simon sent me this. Looks dead chuffed, doesn't he?'

I gaze at the image and catch my breath. It's a selfie of my brother and Angel. Not Angelica, but Angel. Just a pretty girl and her boyfriend out on a date. They look happy.

'Could you send me that?'

'Sure.' Daniel forwards the photo.

'I tracked down another of Si's dominatrix,' I continue.

'Who's that then?'

'Lady Layla. Valentina helped me.'

'And did you find out anything interesting?'

'Si wasn't alone the night he died.' To my chagrin, I dissolve into tears. 'I'm sorry, I…' Abandoning my bag and jacket, I make a dash for the loo.

I sit on the toilet seat, waiting for my sobs to subside. God, he'll think I'm such a wuss.

Taking a few deep breaths, I leave the cubicle and wash my hands at the sink. My mascara has run, so I use a paper towel to tidy myself up before heading back out to the bar.

Daniel glances up, his brow furrowed with concern. 'You okay?'

'Yes.' The word comes out as a shudder.

He gestures to a glass on the table. 'I thought you might need something stronger.'

'Thanks.' The brandy burns my throat. 'I suppose it's good that Si wasn't on his own.'

He reaches across to touch my hand. 'What exactly did this Layla say?'

'She wasn't there herself. It was two other dommes, Delores and Krystal. A mate of Si's was there too. Must have been him who called the ambulance. I wonder if it was Harry?'

'Christ,' says Daniel. 'If it was, why didn't he stay with Simon?'

'I suppose he didn't want anyone to know he was there.' I grab Daniel's arm. 'I have to track Harry down. He might be able to tell me more.'

'How are you going to do that? No-one seems to know who Harry is or where he came from.'

I give a small smile. 'I was hoping you might help.'

Daniel stands up. 'I'm getting a beer. Want something else?'

'No, I'm all right.'

I watch him saunter to the bar. While he's waiting, a man puts a hand on his shoulder and whispers something. My pulse quickens. That's Quinn. Does Daniel know him?

'What did that man say?' I ask when Daniel returns with a bottle of Peroni.

He smiles. 'He asked if we were together.'

My cheeks flush. Why's he lying to me?

He laughs. 'Sometimes you remind me so much of Simon.' He swigs his beer. 'So, what do you want from me?'

'I need to contact these other dommes. Apparently, Delores rents a room in a place called The Kama Sutra.'

'I thought it was Angel that Si was into?'

'Si had recently taken up with Layla and was spending loads of money on her. Angel and Si fell out after she saw a video Layla posted of the two of them out shopping with a wad of cash.'

Daniel winces. 'Simon didn't have that sort of money.'

'I know. He was spending way beyond his means. Did you ever go gambling together?'

'We'd have a flutter on the horses now and then, and the dogs. I didn't do much more than that. Oh, and fruit machines in pubs of course. Simon never could leave them alone.'

'So, you don't know if he'd got into trouble? Borrowed money to get out of debt?'

Daniel shakes his head. He's quiet, as if trying to decide something.

Suddenly I'm unsure about him. I stand up. 'I'd better be going.'

'Could you meet me in Brighton tomorrow night?'

My heart thumps. Can I trust him? 'Why?'

'I'll escort you to The Kama. Although I don't know if they'll let you in.'

We walk along Kings Road towards Hove. Turning right, Daniel stops outside a cream-coloured regency house with black iron railings.

I stare in astonishment. 'This is it?'

He shrugs. 'What did you expect? Giant pink handcuffs? A six-foot dildo draped across the entrance?' He takes my arm. 'Come on.'

Inside is a small and unremarkable reception area where a middle-aged woman with a bright pink fringe sits behind a desk. She doesn't lift her eyes from her magazine. 'Can I help?'

'Is Shane on tonight?' asks Daniel.

The woman picks up a phone and hits a button. 'Shane? Some people here asking for you.' She hangs up and returns to her reading.

I nudge Daniel as a haggard-looking guy approaches.

'Shane?' says Daniel.

The man nods. 'Follow me.' He leads us along the corridor and into a small office no larger than a broom cupboard.

Daniel turns to me.

I take a breath. 'I'm looking for someone. Delores the Divine. I understand she rents a room here.'

He looks me up and down, chewing gum noisily. 'What business you got with Delores? You the law?'

'No, I need to ask her about my brother.'

'All business here is private. If your brother engages in certain activities and wants to keep it quiet from his sister, that's up to him.'

'Her brother's dead,' says Daniel.

'I don't want no trouble,' says Shane.

'You won't get trouble from us. Look, she just wants to ask Delores a few questions.'

Shane thumbs through a diary on his desk. 'Delores works Tuesdays and Thursdays. I can make you an appointment if you like?'

I blush. 'I don't want an appointment.'

'Time is money. You want to speak to Delores, you pay for her time.'

'How much?' I ask.

'I can book you an introductory session for £200.'

'That's ridiculous. I only want to speak with her.'

Shane slams the diary closed. 'Please yourself.'

'Look, can't you just give her a message? Tell her I'd like to talk? She can ring me, my number's…'

'I ain't no message service. You wanna speak to Delores, you pay like everyone else.'

Tears prick my eyes.

Daniel looks from me to Shane. 'Look mate, this lady lost her brother very suddenly. She just wants a chat with Delores who may have seen him recently. That's all. Can't you give her a break?'

Shane sighs. 'Tell you what I'll do. I'll book you half an hour for £80. Can't say fairer than that now, can I?'

I pull out my purse and take out a credit card.

'Cash,' he grunts.

I check the side pocket of my purse. 'I've only got forty.'

He snatches the notes from my hand. 'Bring the other forty on Tuesday.' He opens the diary again. 'Delores has a booking at midday. Come around eleven-ish and she should be able to give you twenty minutes before her sub arrives.'

CHAPTER TWENTY-SEVEN

'Sorry' – although I'm speaking on the phone, I put a hand to my forehead – 'I've woken up with a terrible migraine.'

'Right…' Marjorie in admin makes no attempt to hide her sigh. 'I suppose I'll have to get a supply teacher in to cover you again.'

Is it my imagination, or is she weary of my excuses? If I'm not careful, Brian will make me an appointment with occupational health.

After parking in Regency Square, I meet Daniel outside the i360.

'You didn't need to come,' I say, as we make our way to The Kama Sutra. I'm still not sure whether to trust him, but he did help me get this meeting with Delores.

'I won't come in, but I don't think you should be doing this on your own.'

Shane's leaning on the railings outside. When he sees us

approaching, he discards his fag and grinds it into the pavement with his toe. 'Got my money?'

I fumble in my handbag for the forty pounds.

After checking the notes, he stuffs them in his back pocket. 'This way.'

We follow him into the hotel.

Daniel touches my arm. 'I'll wait here for you.'

'Okay.' My pulse races as I follow Shane past the reception desk and along the corridor. He presses a button for the lift, and we wait.

The lift arrives and Shane slides open the metal grille. 'After you.' He gestures for me to step inside.

We get out on the third floor and Shane leads the way along a corridor and knocks on a door. Without waiting, he turns on his heels and strides back towards the lift.

The door opens a crack and a woman in a black leather cap peeks out.

'Delores?' I say.

She nods, opening the door. Her style is military erotica, like a dancer from *Cabaret* – black leather biker jacket with cinched waist teamed with fishnet stockings and suspenders.

I blink as I step into the boudoir. Walls, curtains, carpet are all fuchsia, with a pink bed – circular and enormous, taking up half the floor space.

'Wow,' I say.

'Nice, innit?'

'If you like pink.'

'Sit down.'

I perch on a plush velour chair, while Delores sprawls across the bed, examining her manicured talons. 'I only got ten minutes.'

This half-hour appointment's getting shorter and shorter. 'Thanks for seeing me,' I say.

'Layla told you what happened that night.'

'She said you were there.'

'Yeah, me and Krystal.'

'With my brother and his mate. Was it Harry?'

'Well, I know him as Hector. Hector and Spiro.' She giggles. 'Krystal christened 'em Tweedledum and Tweedledee, on account of their matching goatees.'

'You'd met them before?'

'Only once. They came along to "A Day with the Dommes".'

I frown. 'What's that?'

'Nothing dodgy,' she snaps. 'They become slaves for the day. One'll be butler, serving drinks and washing up, the other might give us a foot massage, that kind of thing…'

'How much does that cost?'

'Going rate's £300.'

'And my brother attended these often?'

She shrugs. 'I guess so. Spiro was part of the scene.'

'How did Si know Hector?'

'No idea.'

'Do you know where Hector comes from? If he has family?'

She shakes her head. 'Far as I know he's a loner, down on his luck. Spiro was the one who paid.' She sits up. 'Look, Layla knew Spiro best. He were always buying her stuff. Why d'you wanna speak to me?'

'To see if you know any more.'

'Proper nightmare it was.' She shudders. 'Never seen anyone have a heart attack before. First off, we thought he was mucking about, but when he grabbed at the mask, trying to undo it…'

'Oh God.' I cover my face with my hands. 'He was struggling to get the gas mask off?'

'Went bright red and collapsed on the bed. His mate did mouth to mouth, but weren't no good. Poor bugger had gone. Then Hector starts yelling, "get your stuff and get out of here". Well, we don't need telling twice. We grabbed our coats and skedaddled.'

'What time was this?'

'Around midnight. I called Layla from a club in Brighton at one.'

'You went to a club?'

Delores' tone is defensive. 'Hector told us to get ourselves seen.'

'Why would you need to be seen?'

She shrugs again.

'Go on,' I say.

'I don't know what happened after that. Valentina told Layla that Spiro was dead and we all kept our mouths shut. Weren't going to do anything to draw attention.'

'Who else knows?'

'No one apart from Layla.' She sighs. 'Look, we shouldn't have left, but what else could we do?' She glances at her mobile. 'I'm sorry. Got a sub due in five.'

I get up to leave, but something's bugging me. I hesitate, hand on the door jamb. 'Would Krystal have told anyone else?'

Delores slides off the bed but doesn't reply.

'Delores?'

She exhales. 'She might.'

'Who? Who else knows?'

'Quinn. He looks out for us.'

Daniel stops pacing as I step out of the lift. 'Well?'

'Delores pretty much confirmed what Layla said. Harry was definitely there.'

He lays an arm across my shoulder and I'm glad he's here. 'Come on. Let's get out of here.'

'Harry and Si were mates,' he says, as we head along Sillwood Street. 'I don't understand why he didn't stay with Si until the paramedics arrived.'

'There's another thing. Delores says Si collapsed around midnight, but the coroner told me the 999 call came in at 01:05. I need to speak to Harry. Find out exactly what happened and why he covered things up.'

'That won't be easy. I've no idea how to get hold of him.' He links arms. 'Let's go to Kemptown for lunch.'

In Rupert's, I bag a table beneath the rainbow wall art while Daniel goes for drinks. When he doesn't come right back, I scan the bar and spot him talking to someone. As they finish their conversation, the guy picks up his trilby.

Daniel heads back with our drinks and the menu.

'Thanks.' I take my J2O and nod towards the bar. 'That was Quinn again, wasn't it?'

He shrugs. 'Was it?'

'You're a bad liar.'

'All right.' He takes a sip of beer. 'How do you know Quinn, anyway?'

'That doesn't matter. What did he want?'

'He was asking questions.'

'Like what?'

A muscle twitches in his cheek. 'Like who you are and why you're interrogating his girls.'

'I'm not interrogating them. I'm trying to find out what

happened to my brother. What's it to him anyway? Is he their pimp or something?'

Daniel takes another swig.

'Oh my God, he is. Was he Angel's pimp, too?'

'I told you, I don't really know him. I don't think dommes have pimps as such. It's probably more a matter of protection. Looking after girls working his patch.'

I scoff. 'Sounds like a pimp to me.'

'Please, Sarah.' His eyes are earnest. 'Stay away from him. Quinn's not someone to mess with.'

'Okay.' I hide a smile. Perhaps Daniel's just trying to protect me. 'Anyway, how am I going to track down Harry?'

Daniel shrugs. 'I don't know.' He opens his menu. 'I'm having The Full Hog. What about you?'

I peruse the brunch options. 'Poached eggs on toast, maybe…' A flurry of excitement by the doorway interrupts us and I spin round to see Valentina making an entrance in a red wig and a leopard print coat. Spotting us, she slides her Hermes handbag up her arm and makes a beeline for our table. 'Well, if it ain't my two favourite people.'

As Daniel gets up, she plants a smacker on his cheek and pats his chest. She's so bold and I realise I'm a little envious. I'd love to stroke his chest… my cheeks flush. I must be menopausal.

Slipping off her coat, she reveals a scarlet, body-hugging dress with white fur collar and cuffs. She plonks herself on Daniel's vacated chair, then looks me up and down. 'Girl, this is beginning to be a habit. You stalking me? What you doing in my neck of the woods?'

'I've been to see Delores.'

'Ha. Layla was helpful then. Told you I'd put you on the right track.' She pats my hand. 'I hope it's put your mind at rest.'

'Not really,' I mutter.

The barman delivers a martini to our table and Valentina spins round to blow a kiss to a middle-aged gentleman propping up the bar. She takes a sip before glancing my way. 'Just one of my adoring fans. Now, where's that handsome husband of yours?'

'Working,' I say.

Valentina looks at Daniel, then at me and raises an eyebrow. 'While the cat's away…'

'Excuse me,' says Daniel, 'I'm going to order some grub.'

Valentina leans close. 'I see you're still making eyes at our Daniel.'

'No, I…'

She throws back her head and laughs. 'Don't you go lying to me, girl. You'd better watch out, because Valentina has a soft spot for young Daniel herself.'

To my dismay, my eyes prick with tears.

'Oh, come on. Can't you take a little joke? We is sisters, ain't we? She turns towards the bar. 'Carlos?' she yells. 'Bring another martini for my little friend.' She pats my arm.

'It's clear to anyone with eyes in their head that there's chemistry between you two, but I'm gonna give you some advice. Life is short. Don't you waste no time. That's what your brother would tell you. Ain't that right? If you like our Daniel, you tell him so.'

Moments later, Carlos delivers another drink for me. Valentina snatches the cocktail stick from my glass and pops the olive into her mouth. 'Think you is dirty enough, girl.'

Daniel returns, pulling up a chair. 'What did I miss?'

I feel a stab of jealousy as Valentina strokes Daniel's cheek with her blue painted talons. 'Just girlie gossip,' she says, with a wink in my direction.

'Valentina,' I say, changing the subject. 'Do you know where I might find Harry?'

'Hector? Well, that's easy.' Valentina chuckles.

'Why?' I ask.

'He won't miss Erotica.'

'Erotica?'

She raises both eyebrows this time, as if she can't believe I don't know what she's referring to. 'Only the biggest Fetish Fashion Show of the season.'

'Really? And Harry will be there?'

'Sure.'

'When is it?'

'Wednesday night. Studio 69.'

'Do we need tickets?'

'Mention my name on the door. Don't say I don't look after my friends. And now you must excuse me.' She gestures towards a man setting up at a piano on a fluorescent checkerboard stage. 'That's my musical director.' She tosses her curly locks. 'Valentina's got rehearsing to do if she's gonna get these lovely people into the festive mood.'

Tom's working late again, so I walk Brodie before sitting down to eat. When he's not back by nine, I clingfilm his portion of Shepherd's Pie and put it in the fridge. By ten, I start to worry. His mobile goes straight to voicemail. Where the hell is he?

It's gone eleven when I hear his key in the latch.

'You're late.'

'I know, sorry.' He puts his keys down on the breakfast bar before opening the fridge and peering inside.

'Your dinner's there if you want it.'

'Think I'm past that now.' He grabs a beer.

'So, where were you?'

He sighs. 'At work. Where the fuck do you think I've been?'

'At the auction house?'

'Of course. We had a stock check to finish.' He yanks off the ring pull and slurps beer, staring at me with defiant eyes.

'So, how come Graham said you left hours ago?'

'Christ.' Tom slams the can down and beer bubbles out over the worktop. 'You've been checking up on me?' He shakes his head. 'You've got a bloody nerve.'

'Me?'

'Yes. You go gallivanting off to Brighton every chance you get and you're questioning me?'

I feel a sinking in my belly. 'I was worried…'

'Pah.' He scoffs. 'Worried? You don't give a toss. All you want to do is spend time with those weird friends of your brother.'

I wince.

'If you must know, I went for a drink. It's not like there's anything to come home to.'

'Who with?'

'What?' The vein in his temple throbs.

'Who did you go for a drink with?'

'No-one. Yvette might have been there for a while, but it wasn't like we were together.' Taking his beer, he heads into the sitting room. Moments later, I hear football on the TV.

CHAPTER TWENTY-EIGHT

'Come on, Daniel,' I mutter. We've arranged to meet on the seafront outside The Odeon and, although I'm bundled up in a big coat and scarf, the sea wind is biting. Finally, I spot him approaching along the promenade. 'Daniel,' I call, waving.

He crosses over, greeting me with a peck on the cheek. 'Sorry. Have you been waiting long?'

'No, but it's bloody freezing.' I shiver. 'Is the nightclub far?'

He grins, takes my hand and walks me around the corner of West Street where he promptly stops.

'What?' I say.

He points at the side wall. 'This is it.'

I gaze up at white-washed walls atop a black concrete base. Studio 69 is not what I'd imagined. Cinema and nightclub are housed in one giant cube, and the queue I'd passed earlier and thought to be a second entrance to the cinema is the line for the nightclub.

Rather than joining the back of the line, Daniel walks up to the bouncer on the door. 'We're here for the fashion show,' he says. 'We're guests of Valentina.'

The bouncer looks us up and down before unclipping the roped barrier. Murmurs of unrest stir among the people queuing and I sense disgruntled eyes boring into my back as we head inside.

After checking my coat, we follow signs for The Erotica Show, descending a steep narrow staircase to a large space below.

The disco-sized room is set out like a cabaret, with small, intimate tables. Waiters and waitresses bustle back and forth – girls dressed in bunny outfits and boys wearing little more than an apron. I'm reminded of the "butler in the buff" we hired for a colleague's hen do.

Daniel and I stand to survey the crowd.

'Yoo-hoo!' screeches a high-pitched voice. 'Over here.' Valentina beckons frantically from beside the catwalk. Hopes of sharing an intimate table with Daniel are dashed as we make our way to where three tables have been pushed together.

Valentina resembles a mermaid, with her purple flowing locks and figure-hugging gown of sequined teal. She's book-ended by two smartly dressed, middle-aged gents, who stand and shake hands with us.

'Dobryy vecher.'

'Nice to meet you,' I say, before turning to Daniel and mouthing the word, 'Russian?'

'We need more bubbly,' shrieks Valentina. One of the gents clicks his fingers. Immediately, a tanned and toned waiter shows up to take the order.

'You only just made it in time,' she hisses, as lights dim and the compere steps onto the catwalk. Dressed in a Michael Jackson military-style jacket and cap, he resembles Pray Tell from *Pose*. Valentina claps her hands in delight.

'Ladies and gentlemen.' He opens his arms in welcome

like a ringmaster. 'Thank you for coming along to our little show. I've had a sneaky preview' – he winks – 'and I can assure you that you are not going to be disappointed.'

The crowd whistle and hoot.

He's about to leave the stage when he spots Valentina. 'Well, well. If it isn't Valentina the Voluptuous. Now my evening is complete.' He blows an extravagant kiss while Valentina makes a show of catching it and holding it to her heart. 'And now, to begin…'

He steps off the stage as a rhythmic drumbeat commences and the first model appears. The young woman in a lilac and silver kimono struts her stuff, lowering the kimono from her shoulders to reveal nothing beneath but a pair of purple nipple pegs and the skimpiest G-string I've ever seen. Scowling she strides up the catwalk, stopping right by our table to pose before moving away.

'We seem to have the best seats in the house,' murmurs Daniel.

'But where's Harry?' I scan the audience trying to spot a guy with a goatee, but everyone's in darkness as spotlights pan across the models.

The waiter delivers a huge ice bucket with a magnum of champagne and a beer for Daniel. One of the gents pours the bubbly.

'*Nostrovia.*' He hands each of us a glass.

'*Nostrovia,*' I repeat, lifting the flute to my lips and taking a sip. It's delicious. Must have cost the earth.

Daniel chinks his beer against my glass. 'Cheers.'

Two young models on the catwalk are receiving lots of attention. The girls, barely in their teens, are dressed in pink latex miniskirts with skimpy bra tops. I glance at the two gents who are almost salivating. Disgusted by their *Lolita* fantasies, I shudder.

The drumbeat changes as two young men in flesh-coloured body stockings step onto the catwalk. One wears a crocheted helmet paired with a neatly trimmed beard, while the other sports a studded and chained dog collar. They dance and jive to rapturous applause and Valentina giggles coquettishly when they squat like witch doctors before her.

More models and more outrageous outfits follow. Macrame sequins, fishing nets in white and pink over black latex. A man in a white body stocking and impossibly high heels poses with a sultry pout, while a girl in a yellow-and-blue checked micro skirt and extra-long latex marigolds twirls like a cheerleader showing off black lacy knickers.

The penultimate design is worn by a man with a ponytail and plucked eyebrows. It's a full-length latex dress in sea green and the crowd go wild as he prances around as if he's Elsa in *Frozen*. The final offering is a man attired head-to-toe in black leather, including gimp mask. His outfit is topped with a tutu that looks as if it might be on loan from the National Ballet. Striding along the catwalk, he scowls menacingly down at us. At least I think he's scowling; I can't actually see his eyes, hidden beneath the mask.

Finally, a trio of young people in black take the stage. They must be the designers as, smiling and laughing, they accept the applause.

Valentina's beside herself. 'Marvellous, just marvellous,' she gushes.

One of the Russian gents tops up her glass, while his friend throws a hopeful glance in my direction.

I glare back, shuffling closer to Daniel who's taken off his jacket and rolled up his sleeves. I can't take my eyes off the sexy dark hair on his forearms.

The lights are turned up and disco music fills the room. Even the floor is gyrating, a checkerboard of flashing, multi-coloured tiles. I look around hopefully, although I wouldn't know Harry if I saw him.

'No sign,' says Daniel.

'Perhaps we should take a closer look around?'

Daniel nods and gets up.

Valentina glances across, a pout on her lips. 'You're not going?'

'No,' I reassure her. 'Just stretching our legs.'

Daniel works the room while I check the gender-neutral loos. They're out of this world – black and gold with Snow White-style ornate mirrors suspended above shiny stainless-steel basins, but no sign of anyone with a goatee.

I join Daniel at the bar. 'No luck?'

He shakes his head.

I check the time on my watch before nodding towards our table. 'I suppose we'd better stay a little longer.' As we approach, I see Valentina's been joined by a tall blonde in a stunning evening gown of shimmering gold.

'This is Krystal.' Valentina throws me a conspiratorial smile. 'Krystal, this is Spiro's sister.'

This is Krystal? She's gorgeous.

As we take our seats, she flashes a dazzling smile. 'Ah, yes. Delores said you were visiting.'

Visiting? She makes me sound like a maiden aunt.

The Russians are clearly spellbound, for another magnum of champagne arrives, and Daniel and I are plied with more drinks.

Krystal accepts a glass of bubbly and moves to sit next to me. 'I hear you spoke to Delores?'

'I did.'

She takes an elegant sip of her champagne. 'So, Spiro was your brother?'

Her attitude is condescending and I take pleasure in elaborating. 'Simon and I were twins.'

'Really?' She looks me up and down, as if assessing me. 'You don't look alike.'

I don't reply.

'He was quite a favourite with Layla,' she continues.

'I wouldn't know.' This feels like a grilling. It should be me asking the questions, but for some reason I'm wrong footed. 'I'm sorry' – I stand up – 'but it's time I got going. Nice to meet you.'

'Likewise.' Krystal moves closer as if to bestow air kisses. Instead, she whispers something I don't quite catch.

'Sorry?'

'I said, I'll be seeing you,' she repeats.

'Right.'

I collect my coat on the way out, puzzling over her words.

'You catching the train?' asks Daniel.

'Yes.'

'I'll walk you to the station.'

On the train, I check my phone. No message from Tom. There was a time when he'd ring to check I was okay. I spot a notification on Facebook and, when I check, it's a private message from Krystal.

> Hello Sarah. Meet me at The Duchess, Saturday night, eight p.m. We need to talk about your brother.

How the hell did she get my number?

CHAPTER TWENTY-NINE

Marjorie appears as I walk through the foyer. 'Morning, Sarah. Did Nicki manage to reach you?'

'No?'

'It's happened.' She tries unsuccessfully to disguise her satisfaction at being the bearer of news. 'Her mother passed away last night. I expect you'll be wanting to speak to her.'

'Yes, right, of course.'

I'm teaching first two periods, so it's break time before I get a chance to compose a message.

> So sorry to hear about your mum. Here if you want to chat.

I press send and turn my attention to a Google search for Krystal. She's easy to find – krystal_queen22. Both Facebook and Instagram accounts are set as private. What does she want to talk to me about? There's only one person who might help me understand what Krystal wants.

Saturday morning, I drive down to Brighton and make my way to Kemptown, where I spend two hours in KitKat's, hoping Valentina will drop by for coffee. When the café starts to fill up for brunch, I wander along to Theresa's Hairdressers and lurk across the road. I feel conspicuous and consider going in for a wash and blow dry, but supposing Valentina shows up while I'm at the basin? I check my watch. One-fifteen. This was a stupid idea.

At that moment, Valentina saunters out of the hairdressers and struts off along the road.

'Valentina!' I yell. 'Wait up.'

She spins round, clutching her heart. 'Oh my Christ! You nearly gave me a heart attack!' Tossing back her hair, today a blue wig, she appraises me. 'Girl, you lookin' shabby.'

'I wondered if you had time for lunch? My treat.'

'Hmm. Ain't no such thing as a free lunch.' She links arms with me. 'Come on then. I only got half an hour.'

We head back to KitKat's, now packed with lunchtime trade. The waiter who, earlier that morning, observed me making two lattes last an hour a piece, throws me a suspicious look.

Valentina puts an arm around his shoulder. 'Come on, Tony, you can find a little bitty spot for Valentina and her friend, can't you?'

He grunts. 'Give me a minute.' Disappearing into the garden, he returns with a small, rusty bistro table. Apologising profusely to the couple seated nearby, he shuffles their table along before retrieving a couple of vacant chairs and gesturing for us to sit down.

Valentina gives him a kiss. 'Thank you, Tony. You're a true gent.'

She tosses her hair again. 'Don't you go bothering with

no menus, we'll have paninis. Brie for me and an espresso.' She nods at me.

'Oh, and a tuna panini please.'

'And another latte, I'm guessing?' Tony mutters as he goes to fetch our order.

Valentina scans the room before reaching across and taking my hand. 'Now child. What is it you need?'

I swallow. 'I need to ask about Krystal.'

She purses her lips. 'Take my advice, you don't want dealings with that one.'

I lean forward. 'Did you give her my phone number?'

Valentina's eyes widen. 'What you suggesting, girl?'

I sigh, deflated. 'She private messaged me.'

Valentina holds out her palm. 'Let me see.'

I take out my mobile, scroll through and hand it over.

She sucks in breath. 'This ain't good.'

Tony arrives with our coffees and two glasses of tap water.

'Thank you, darling.' Valentina blows him another kiss before turning back to me. 'What does the witch have on your brother?'

'I don't know, but Quinn knows she was there when Si died.'

'You're shitting me.'

'No, she told him.'

'Stupid bitch.'

'Harry was there, too. He must have tidied up so it looked like Si was on his own.'

Tony arrives with our paninis. Valentina picks hers up and takes a huge bite.

I lift mine and nibble the corner. The tuna's piping hot and I wince as it burns my tongue. 'So' – I take a sip of water – 'Krystal?'

Valentina rolls bread around her mouth before swallowing. 'Now Angel's gone, Krystal's appointed herself head honcho.'

'I hadn't realised there was a hierarchy.'

'Oh yes. And Krystal's revelling at being top of the pecking order. What does she want?'

'I don't know.'

'Right. You leave everything to Valentina. I'll sort it.'

My heart leaps with gratitude. 'Thanks Valentina.'

I spend the afternoon wandering around stores heaving with Christmas shoppers. By five o'clock, Valentina hasn't called back. If I don't hear from her, I'll have to meet with Krystal. I need moral support. Pulling out my mobile, I call Daniel. 'What are you up to?'

'Why?'

'Krystal wants to speak to me. I'm meeting her at The Duchess.'

'What time?'

'Eight p.m.'

'I'll be there by seven.'

Although the interior's pretty tired, with yellowy brown paintwork and mismatched tables and chairs, The Duchess is packed with people getting an early start on the festive period. I've already necked a glass of wine when Daniel arrives.

'Want another?' he asks.

'No, I'd better pace myself.'

He heads off to get himself a drink, returning a few minutes later wearing a scowl.

'What's the matter?'

'I think that's one of Quinn's cronies.'

I crane my neck to peer through the scrum.

'Don't look.' Daniel sits down, his face ashen.

My heart thumps. 'This is my fault.'

'How come?'

'I told Valentina I was meeting Krystal.'

'Right.' He takes a swig of beer. 'And Valentina spoke to Quinn?'

'I guess so. What do you think he wants?'

Daniel shifts in his seat. 'Money, I should think.'

'Oh my God.' My hand flies to my mouth. 'Si owed him?'

He nods. 'It looks as if all Valentina's done is pique his interest.' He checks his watch. 'What are you going to tell Krystal?'

I pick up my glass before remembering it's empty. 'I don't know. Just hear her out I guess.'

Daniel nods. 'Well, you're not meeting her alone.'

I check the time – seven-fifty. 'I'm going to the loo.' When I come back, I shrug on my jacket. 'I think we should meet alone.'

'No.'

'You might scare her off. I want to hear what she's got to say.'

'Okay.' He glances around the room. 'The good news is Quinn's guy seems to have gone.' He nods towards a dark corner where a couple are vacating a table. 'I'll be over there.' Standing up, he winds his scarf around his neck. 'If you need me, just holler.'

He kisses my cheek and moves away. My hands are shaking, and I hold them in my lap to steady them. I shouldn't be doing this. I should call the police. And tell them what? A friend of my brother's has asked to meet me in a pub? I cross and uncross my legs, throwing surreptitious glances towards Daniel.

'Hello, Sarah.'

It's so busy I hadn't seen her come in. 'Hi.'

She runs slender fingers through her Elle Macpherson hair. Even in casual dress – skinny jeans and over-sized jumper – Krystal is stunning.

I gulp, gesturing my empty glass. 'Shall I get us a drink?'

She frowns. 'I hadn't realised how busy it would be. Let's find somewhere quieter.'

'Everywhere will be packed.'

She smiles. "Come on. Let's get some air.'

I glance across to where Daniel was seated, but there are too many people. I can't get a clear view. Hopefully he'll see us leave.

We head outside and along St James's Street into the heart of Kemptown. She links arms as we walk. I glance back a few times, but there's no sign of Daniel.

'How much do you know about your brother's lifestyle?' she asks.

My laughter sounds fake. 'Considerably more now than I did when he was alive.'

'I'm sure Valentina has filled you in on his... secret pastimes.'

We're walking along a badly lit street, scarcely more than an alley. I swallow. 'Yes.'

Coming to a halt, she rummages in her shoulder bag and pulls out a packet of cigarettes and a lighter. She places one between her lips and offers me the pack.

'No thanks.'

Shrugging, she lights her own before dropping the lighter back in her bag. She leans against a graffitied wall and takes a long drag. 'Such hobbies and interest don't come cheap.'

I'm standing in the middle of the narrow road. It doesn't feel safe. 'Look, Krystal. Why don't you get to the point?'

'You were Spiro's executor?'

'Yes.'

'And I'm sure you had to settle a number of debts. The legit ones at any rate.'

'Legit ones?'

'Banks, credit card companies and the like. But that wasn't the full extent of Spiro's creditors.'

I feel a chill prickle the back of my neck. 'I used a solicitor. We filed a Section 27 Notice. Anyone who had a claim on his estate should have contacted them in the allotted time.'

She takes another drag. 'Not everything works like that though, does it Sarah? When it comes to debts racked up through gambling or drug abuse, one can't always go through legal channels.'

'It's too late now. If Simon owed people money, they should have come forward. The estate's been finalised.'

She flicks her ash. 'Spiro had a nice flat. I dare say he didn't leave you out of pocket.'

Does she know Angel was his beneficiary? I raise my chin defiantly. 'I didn't get a penny.'

Her smile is saccharine. 'No?'

'No.'

'Well, how very mean of him.'

Footsteps approach. I glance up to see two men making their way towards me. My heart races. They're walking fast. I look at Krystal. She's grinning. They're close enough now for me to see they're broad shouldered and both wearing puffer jackets with caps pulled down low. What do they want? I should run but I'm paralysed with fear. Instead, I squeeze my eyes tightly shut and wait.

They brush past so close they almost knock me off balance. I get a waft of beer, sweat and stale tobacco.

'Mind out, love,' says a gruff voice while the other laughs.

I open my eyes. They've moved on, one whistling as they continue along the street and turn right.

I glare at Krystal. 'What was that about?'

'What? I didn't see anything.'

'I know you're trying to frighten me.'

'Is it working?' She stubs out her cigarette and takes my arm again as we retrace our steps. 'Poor thing, you're shaking like a leaf. Let me tell you about one of Spiro's creditors. His name's Quinn. You may have heard of him.'

I shrug her off. 'And those were his cronies, I'm guessing?'

She's tight lipped now. 'Your brother died owing Quinn quite a bit of money. He just wants the debt paid.'

'I told you. I wasn't Simon's beneficiary. I don't have any money.'

She taps her chin thoughtfully. 'What is it you do, Sarah? Oh yes, schoolteacher, right? Nice regular salary. Good credit rating, I expect.'

I feel sick. Does Quinn expect me to cover Si's debts? 'I can't go borrowing money. We have a mortgage to pay.'

'I see. Well, I'm sure Quinn would be open to other repayment terms.'

'What the hell are you inferring?'

'Oh Sarah!' She wags a finger. 'You do have a dirty mind.'

I'm relieved to see we're almost back to The Duchess when a BMW pulls up to the kerb. For a moment, I think I'm about to be bundled in. I open my mouth to scream, but no sound comes out. Krystal opens a rear door, slides in and closes it behind her. The window whirrs as it slides down.

'I've enjoyed our little chat, Sarah. I'll be in touch. *Ciao.*'

The car accelerates away.

Legs shaking, I stumble into the pub. 'Brandy please,' I croak. The bartender throws me a quizzical glance before pouring a measure into a glass and sliding it across the bar. I take a sip and cough.

The evening is in high swing with loud voices filling the air, but Daniel's nowhere to be seen. I take my glass and move across to a small table. Nearby, a group of lads are playing darts and I watch them, trying to distract myself. I'm just considering ordering another brandy when the door opens.

'Daniel,' I gasp.

Spotting me, he hurries over. 'I've been looking for you everywhere.'

I fling my arms around him, and he holds me close. It feels good and I don't want to let go.

Gently he releases me and lowers me onto the stool. 'I'll get you a drink.'

'Another brandy please.'

He goes to the bar while I pull a pack of tissues from my bag and blow my nose.

'What happened?' he asks, pushing the amber drink into my hands. 'One minute you were there and the next you'd gone. Oh my God, you're shaking.'

'I don't think I'm cut out for all this cloak-and-dagger stuff.'

'Tell me what happened.'

'Krystal said we'd go somewhere quiet to talk, then two of Quinn's thugs showed up.'

A muscle pulses in his jaw. 'Did they hurt you?'

'No, I'm just a little shaken.' I shudder when I consider how bad it might have been. 'I told Krystal I had no money, but I don't know if Quinn will come after me again.'

'We need to call the police.'

I grab his arm. 'No, Daniel. Whatever Si was mixed up in, I don't want Quinn coming after my family. You're right. I need to stop digging.'

CHAPTER THIRTY

It's gone midnight when I get home. Thank goodness Tom's away at an antiques fair. I'm exhausted but too wired to sleep. I keep turning everything over in my mind. In the early hours, I pick up the phone and call Daniel. 'What are you not telling me about Quinn?'

'Sarah, it's five in the bloody morning,' he hisses.

'I need the truth.'

I hear shuffling and imagine him slipping quietly out of bed so as not to wake Janice. When he speaks, the sound is echoey and I guess he's taken his mobile into the bathroom.

'Right, what do you want to know?' His tone is short, like I'm an inconvenience.

'Quinn. Tell me everything.'

He sighs. 'Simon and I met him at the races. Quinn was giving it large – hospitality suite, champagne and caviar, the works. At first things were great. All the time Simon was winning they were best buddies.'

'But Si stopped winning.'

'Big time. And Quinn didn't bat an eyelid. Bailed Simon out of what could have been a tricky situation.'

'So, Si was in his debt?'

'Yep. And Simon didn't like that, so he borrowed more and gambled more. He was convinced he'd have a big win and pay off his debts. Eventually Quinn closed the bank, so Simon borrowed from other sources.'

'Loan sharks?'

'Sort of... whoever they were, it wasn't legit.'

'And where did Harry fit into all this?'

'Simon kind of adopted him. He paid for him, even started a rumour that Harry was a reclusive millionaire. Perhaps that's why Quinn took the bait? All rubbish, of course, but as Simon got in deeper and deeper, I guess he thought there was no way out.'

'And then he had a heart attack.'

'Yes.'

'Caused by stress?'

'I don't know.'

'Will Quinn write Si's debt off?'

'I don't know. I can understand him being interested when you showed up asking questions. If you've convinced him you're a lost cause, he might go after bigger fish.'

'When you say bigger fish, you mean Harry?'

'Possibly.'

'Then we need to find Harry. If he was Si's friend, we have to warn him.'

'Sarah.'

'What?'

'We're not going to do that. You have to let it go.'

Sunday morning, I replay Daniel's words as I walk Brodie. *Let it go.* Like it's that easy. There's so much I don't know about Si. Why didn't he tell me he was in trouble? He knew better than to borrow from loan sharks. Was he too ashamed to tell me he had gambling problems? Perhaps the money didn't all go on gambling. What about the sex lines?

My mobile rings. I don't recognise the number.

'Hello?'

'Hello, Sarah? This is Krystal.'

Hackles rising, I stop in my tracks. 'You've got a bloody nerve.'

'Oh, come on. Don't be like that. I just wanted to say how impressed I was with the way you handled yourself last night.'

'Fuck off.'

'Don't hang up.'

I wait.

'Quinn and I have had a chat. He's prepared to write off Simon's debts.'

'What's he expecting in return?'

'You see, Sarah? I knew you'd understand. He just wonders if you might help us?'

Oh God. He wants to know who the beneficiary was. I can't give him Angel.

'Quinn's keen to get in touch with a guy called Hector,' she continues. 'You might know him as Harry the Loner.'

'I don't know him at all.'

'No, but I expect you'd like to speak to him. What with him being the last person to have seen your brother alive.'

'I'm hanging up now…'

'Okay, okay. Jeez. Just to say, Sarah, that if you did manage to track Hector down, and were kind enough to let us know, Quinn would see that you did all right out of it.'

'I'm not looking for Harry. In fact, I'm putting the whole thing behind me, so you can tell Quinn he can…'

'Okay. Thanks Sarah. Hope to speak soon.' With that, she hangs up.

'Bitch,' I yell into my phone. I look down to see Brodie sitting patiently, head cocked to one side. 'It's okay boy. Let's go home.'

I expect Tom home late afternoon but it's after seven when he walks through the door. Pulling on oven gloves, I retrieve his dinner plate from the oven. 'Well, this is ruined,' I snap.

'I'm not hungry, I ate at lunchtime.'

I scrape the dried-out meal into the bin. 'You might have told me you were delayed.'

'I called in at Ardingly on the way. Graham wanted an update.'

'Was Yvette there?'

'At the auction house? Not on a Sunday.'

'At the antiques fair.'

He moves to the sink to wash his hands.

'Well?'

'Well what?' he replies, lathering and rinsing like a surgeon scrubbing up for an op.

'I said' – I pause for effect – 'was Yvette with you in Newark?'

Grabbing a towel, he makes a show of drying every knuckle and joint. 'She's my assistant, what do you think?'

My pulse races. Did they drive up together? Did they spend the night in the same hotel? Perhaps it's my own guilty conscience making me antagonistic. 'You didn't call in at the auction house. When I couldn't get hold of you, I called Graham. He's been home all day.'

Tom throws the towel onto the worktop. 'Then why ask?'

'Oh, I don't know… to see if you'd tell me the truth?'

'For Christ's sake.'

'I just want to know where you've been.'

'I told you. The M1 was a nightmare.' Picking up his briefcase, he heads for the sitting room, pausing in the doorway. 'Oh, I nearly forgot.' Opening his case, he retrieves a USB from a side pocket. 'Steve managed to clear down the laptop. Most of the stuff was lost, but he managed to save this.'

'What is it?'

'Letters, I think.'

'Letters? Have you looked at them?'

'No, but Steve says they're rather explicit, so I'm not sure you should either.'

I reach for the USB. 'Okay, thanks.' He knows I won't be able to resist.

When I insert the memory stick, I find a folder entitled "personal" and open the first document.

22nd August 2018

Hello Goddess. This is my write-up of Sunday.

Goddess? That's what Si called Angel. Did he have to write up every session? Like homework?

I've trusted dominas in the past, but the level of trust I have with you is unique. You push me and I know I'll be tested, but I always try my best, taking or doing whatever you ask. There's nothing I would not do for you.

Being trained and guided by you is my destiny and I'm the happiest I've ever been in my life. With you, I'm still submissive the day after a session and the day after that.

So, this is the deal. To write ingratiating letters after each session. It's humiliating. But perhaps that's the point. Si sounds so grateful. I don't understand. I don't get any of this.

I open another.

18th November 2018

On Friday I sorted out my will...

Sorted out his will? What the fuck! Did Angel manipulate him into making her his beneficiary? Has she played the both of us? I check the date of the will – 16th November 2018.

I hope this demonstrates how much I want to please you, Goddess.

I love that you seem to enjoy our sessions as much as I do. There were moments last time when I feared I'd have to use my safe word...

Oh God, this is too intimate. I close it and open another:

5th April 2019

I don't understand, Goddess, why you haven't replied? I

keep reading back through our texts to see if I could have inadvertently upset you.

You gave me a task, which I set about wholeheartedly. I apologise if I failed you. I explained I'd hit a downwards spiral, but you told me to 'snap out of it and sort myself out'.

Calls herself a well-being counsellor and yet thinks someone suffering with mental health issues can simply snap out of it. What a bitch.

Your post on Twitter really hurt, Goddess.

You told me the amount I'm paying as tribute is not enough. Your exact words were 'the situation is unsustainable', but you know I'm paying as much as I can afford.

I've spent all day crying. I've tried my best, but I fear I've lost you. I don't want to go down the route of seeking another domme. I don't know where we go from here.

Your Heartbroken Spiro

Oh God. Poor Si.

The last letter is longer. Dated 5th May 2019 and addressed to "My Lady" it must be to Layla.

Tonight, I was higher than I've ever been, and it's all down to you, My Lady.

I've been submissive pretty much all my life, enjoying bondage for as long as I can remember. I have an addictive personality and know it's easy to fall off the rails. I've been into poppers since my late teens, but the other intox (nitrous and ket) are a more recent addition.

Tonight, with you, I went even deeper. It's the first time I've done coke…

I'm shocked by the drugs. Layla has a lot to answer for. Si says he's enjoyed this fetish for as long as he can remember. How did I not know any of this?

As you know, I had a previous contract with another domina. I paid her £800 a month and in return she trained me, kept me off nitrous and ket, and I was allowed to visit her for a session once a month.

I'd like to propose I make a monthly tribute to you of a similar amount. If I can see you once a month, I would feel truly blessed.

So much for Angel being Si's destiny. He's breaking up with one domme at almost the same time as negotiating a new deal with another. Was he playing them in the same way they were playing him? £800 a month for one session? God, Angel was raking it in.

There is no other domme I trust to take me to the places you took me tonight. I'd be honoured to escort you to a fetish club and be your public slave. I'm no longer in a relationship where I need to worry about marks, so if you'd like to leave them, I'm okay with that. Canes and whips are fine.

Thank you again for a wonderful session, My Lady. I truly believe I have found the domina of my dreams.
Your loyal slave, Spiro

I close the document. *The domina of my dreams?* What a load of crap. My brother's words are sycophantic and fickle. Arse-licking at best. And yet, perhaps that's all part of the game?

I wonder if Layla did leave marks? I feel sick. The post-mortem mentioned nothing. A sudden thought creeps into my head. He was seeing Layla when he suffered the heart attack and yet Angel was his final beneficiary. Did he intend to change his will again? In acting on her behalf, I believed I was carrying out Si's wishes. Could I have got it wrong?

If only I could see Angel one more time, I might clarify things. She said they'd had a falling out, but I hadn't realised it might be permanent. Or was it? I can't change things, but it would put my mind at rest to be reassured they cared about each other as much as she led me to believe.

CHAPTER THIRTY-ONE

Time drags over the rest of the term – lessons, meetings and coursework marking. I used to love my job; now I can't stand it. Life at home is miserable, too, with Tom and I barely speaking. It takes all my willpower not to scream at him. I'm sure he's keeping things from me, just like I've been keeping things from him. Since Angel disappeared, my life is a series of repetitive actions – get up, go to work, come home, prepare a meal, try to sleep – rinse and repeat.

Having declined Wendy's invitation to spend Christmas with her and Bob, the holiday is a non-event. With no energy or inclination to cook Christmas dinner for the two of us, I resort to plated meals from M&S, and the usual festive repeats on TV do little to fill the time. At least I manage to catch up on schoolwork and ready myself to face the spring term.

I still haven't managed to speak to Nicki. She's not taking my calls or returning my voice mails. As time passes, the gulf between us grows wide. Have I done something to upset her? I feel so guilty. She's always been there for me.

January 5th is an INSET day and Nicki's back. Over coffee in the staffroom, I extend an olive branch. 'Sorry about your mum.'

'Thanks.' Her tone is curt.

'I did try to ring you. Several times, actually.'

She rinses her cup in the sink. 'I'll be in my classroom if you need me for anything.' In the doorway she hesitates, looking back. 'I have to take a few days of leave this term to sort things out. Brian says it's fine. Sorry if it leaves you in the lurch, but you know what it's like.'

She's definitely pissed off with me. Feeling like the lowest of the low, I traipse back to my own classroom, but I can't concentrate. Nicki's my best friend and I've neglected her in her hour of need. I have to make things right between us.

As I plan lessons for the coming week, I hope she won't be away too many days. I've done a reasonable job keeping departmental things going, at least on the surface, but any day now Brian's going to look a little closer and the whole thing will implode.

Friday evening Tom staggers in after midnight, dropping his briefcase on the floor. Glancing my way, he gives an exaggerated sigh. 'Uh-oh. Guess I'm in trouble again.'

'Are you drunk?'

'What-if-I-am?' he slurs.

'I think we need a conversation.'

'Oh.' He attempts to stand upright. 'Now we need a conversation, do we?' He stumbles forward, stabbing a finger into my chest. 'Her ladyship wants a conversation, so everyone else must comply.'

I take a step back. 'Not right now, obviously.'

He blinks, his head jerking as if he's been struck. 'Good.' He spins on his heels, aiming his body towards the sitting room. 'Good.'

I watch from the doorway as he collapses headlong onto the couch.

Next morning I'm in the kitchen when Tom stumbles in, rubbing his forehead.

'There's fresh coffee.' I gesture towards the coffee percolator.

Tom lowers himself slowly onto a kitchen stool.

'Do you need paracetamol?' I take a packet of capsules from the cupboard, fill a glass with water and set them down in front of him with a mug of black coffee.

'Thanks,' he says.

I wait until he's swallowed the pills and taken a swig of water. 'What's going on, Tom?'

'You tell me.'

'Staying out late, getting drunk. This isn't you.'

His sigh is like air released from a tyre.

'Tom…'

'You wouldn't understand.'

'Try me.'

He puts his head in his hands, mumbling something I don't catch.

'What?'

He looks up. 'I said, I'm just so fucking lonely.'

'I'm sorry. It's my fault. I've been preoccupied dealing with all Si's stuff.'

Tom shakes his head. 'No.'

I wait.

'This began before you lost your brother.'

'What began?'

'Hard to say.' He sighs again. 'You're always so busy… with work… no.' He shakes a finger, as if scolding himself. 'Sorry, I'm not going to lay it all at your door.' Reaching out, he takes my hand. 'We need to face it, Sarah. We've been drifting apart for years.'

My pulse begins to race. 'No, it's just the Si thing…'

He hauls himself up, winces and puts a hand to his brow. 'I've been seeing someone.'

My heart sinks to my belly. 'Who? Not Yvette?'

His eyes seem to bore into my soul.

'Oh my God!' I clamp a hand over my mouth. I'm going to be sick.

'At first, we were friends. We have a lot in common.'

'Oh, come on' – I snort – 'that old cliché?'

'I was lonely, Sarah. You have no idea. And Yvette's a good listener.'

'I bet she is!'

'Don't be like that. She's a lovely person.'

'For Christ's sake.'

'Well, she's a little less complicated and a lot less controlling than you!'

'You bastard.'

We both recoil at the harsh words.

'How long?' I ask.

He winces again as he sinks back down. 'A little over a year.'

'Fuck.' My heart's pounding. I lean against the breakfast bar to steady myself. Am I having a heart attack? Like Si? I take deep breaths, trying to slow my pulse. 'Are you having an affair?'

He doesn't answer.

'Did you sleep with her?'

'Not yet.'

'Not yet?' I step away from the worktop.

He reaches out a hand. 'Sarah…'

'No.' I brush him away. 'No, this isn't happening. We're a team. You can't do this to me.'

Tom lowers his head. 'I want a divorce.'

CHAPTER THIRTY-TWO

I run upstairs, slamming the bedroom door. I half expect Tom to follow, but he doesn't. After a few moments, I throw myself onto the bed. This can't be happening. Angel's disappeared, Nicki's not speaking to me, Jamie doesn't need me anymore and my husband's halfway out the door. What's left? Darkness descends like a black cloud and for the first time I understand Si's depression. What's the point of living when everything has gone?

My phone's plugged into the wall charger. I sit up, unplug it and search for Si's blog.

Trigger Warning: Suicide

I can't talk about mental health without mentioning my suicide attempts. The first was during my first (diagnosed) depressive episode. My GP put me on antidepressants that had bad side effects. Basically, I wasn't getting better and the pills were making me worse. It culminated in my wife coming home from work to find me sitting in bed with that cereal bowl on my lap. Every pill I could find in the house was emptied into it. In all honesty, I don't remember much – it was literally a cry for help. Anyway, the doctor came out quick and changed my prescription.

Perhaps this doesn't count as attempted suicide as I didn't have the intention of following through. The attempt I'm talking about came a little while later. I'd been on antidepressants and, to most people, seemed to be coping. In reality, I was pretty disturbed and researching the internet for the best ways to commit suicide. There are lots of sites. Strange really, when you think about it, because anyone who's been successful isn't around to tell us how it felt. But such logic doesn't apply when you're considering it.

Gassing yourself is popular, but I ruled this out as I had a diesel car and there's some argument that diesel fumes don't kill you.

Hanging is reasonably cheap. The main problem is getting the right drop – too short and you strangle yourself slowly, too long and your head rips off. I had a good drop from my garage loft, but I was still worried about strangulation. I didn't want anything slow and painful.

Slashing your wrists? Messy and dramatic. Also, long and lingering.

Pills? Now this would be okay, but which to take? Unless you rob a chemist, most people don't have access to the sort of thing the internet suggests.

Drowning? No, couldn't bring myself to try that. I fear I'd fight for life at the end.

Guns? Yeah, great if you're American, but I'm in the UK. How the hell do you get hold of a gun over here?

Tall buildings. Now this was a possibility, but you need a certain number of storeys to be confident you'll die. Too few and you wind up crippled. Too many and you leave a hell of a mess. You also need access to the right building. Brighton has a couple of multi-storey car parks…

Tossing the phone aside, I crawl under the duvet. My husband's leaving me. I've been so caught up with all the Si stuff, while right under my nose my marriage has fallen apart.

I must have dozed because the ring tone wakes me. I reach out and read the caller ID. 'Wendy, I'm so pleased you've called, Tom and I…'

She interrupts. 'Sarah, it's Dad. He's had a massive stroke. I'm so sorry.'

Déjà vu. My sister ringing to tell me Si's dead. No, not my brother. This time it's my father. A wail begins in the pit of my stomach, climbs my oesophagus and emerges from my mouth.

Tom has his arms around me, holding me while I cry. Deep gut-wrenching sobs for the loss of Si, Dad, my marriage…

It's an age before I'm cried out. I don't want to stop. When I do, Tom will leave. Finally, I'm spent.

Tom eases me down on the bed. He brings me a cup of coffee and holds my hand. 'Talk about bad timing.'

I try to smile. 'Don't joke.'

He sighs. 'Well, I'm not going anywhere. Not right now. Let's get to the other side of this and then we can talk again.'

'Promise?' I hate how pathetic I sound.

'Promise.' He hesitates in the doorway. 'I'm not going anywhere right now, but Sarah. You do know this doesn't change anything?'

CHAPTER THIRTY-THREE

Wendy and Bob handle arrangements. There's not so much to do. Dad's house was sold when he moved into the nursing home and the three of us made joint executors and beneficiaries. As Si's no longer alive, the estate will be divided equally between Wendy and myself. At least Angel doesn't get a cut.

I don't have a lot of input into the funeral, apart from picking music for on the way out. I choose "Dance with My Father Again" by Luther Vandross, which always makes me cry. It's a Christian service in the small church in Eastbourne where Mum and Dad were married. Dad reserved a plot with Mum, so finally they're together again.

Tom's amazing. He's by my side throughout and I love him for it. But every moment brings me closer to the time when he'll be leaving. When did I become such a weak person? The loss of Si was hard – I always considered him to be my other half – but now, losing Dad, it's like the last person who really knows me has gone and, somehow, I've disappeared too.

After the funeral, Tom and I sit Jamie down to explain we're getting a divorce.

He nods.

'You don't seem surprised,' I say.

'I think you two were the only ones who didn't see it coming.' He stands up. 'Anyway, I'm back to uni and after that I'll probably stay on. Get a flat share around Leicester. I assume you'll be selling the house?'

Tom and I look at each other.

'We haven't discussed that yet,' says Tom.

'Okay, well, let me know. I'll have stuff to clear out.' Jamie runs upstairs.

I picture him, alone in his room. Although I don't think any of us think of it as Jamie's room since he went to university.

Tom flicks the switch on the kettle. 'Coffee?'

'No, I'm awash.'

He sits down opposite me.

I'm suddenly very weary. 'I suppose selling the house is inevitable?'

'I suppose.'

I trace a pattern on the tablecloth with my finger, sensing Tom watching me.

'There's something I want to talk to you about,' he says.

I sigh, not sure I can take any more.

'Yvette suggested…'

'Yvette?' I glare at Tom.

He swallows. 'Yvette thinks it might be a good idea for us to meet. The three of us. To talk about things going forward.'

'I'm not meeting with that bitch.'

'That's not fair. None of this is her fault.'

I leap to my feet. 'Not fair? My God! There's nothing fair

about any of this. You can tell your tart that I have no desire to discuss anything with her.'

'Wait, I…'

I'm already at the door. 'You think I'm going to let her rub my nose in it? Sell the bloody house. See if I care. At least I have Dad's legacy to live on.'

CHAPTER THIRTY-FOUR

I put my head in my hands. 'I can't bear all this.'

'You know what your trouble is,' says Daniel. 'You can't bear things being outside of your control.'

'What do you mean?'

'I've watched you. You like everything to be just so. You're the exact opposite of Simon.'

'We were twins,' I say. 'Si and I couldn't have been more alike.'

'But that's not true, is it? What makes someone become a sub? Nature or nurture? Simon was raised to be submissive. You said yourself you were always bossy.'

'You're saying it was my fault?'

'No, I'm saying take a *chill pill*. Relax.'

'Oh God, you sound like Tom.'

'Poor Tom. Can't be easy, living with a control freak.'

'I am not a control freak,' I yell.

Daniel sips his drink.

But it's true. I do like to have everything just so. That's why I'm good at my job and not so good at being married.

Tears roll down my cheeks. Daniel leans across and wipes

them away with his thumb. 'I could help you with that, you know,' he whispers.

'With what?' I sob.

'Always wanting to control things. I could teach you how to let go.'

'What do you mean?'

'You asked before, about the relationship between Janice and me.'

'You don't seem to have much in common.'

'After five years of marriage, we were both unsatisfied.'

'Did you go for counselling?'

'We tried that. It didn't work for us.'

'So, part company. Get a divorce if you're unhappy.'

He takes my hand. 'I'm not unhappy now. Not anymore. Not since we discovered the answer.'

I blow my nose. 'What's the answer?'

He leans forward to whisper. 'For us, it's swinging.'

'Swinging? You mean wife swapping? You and Janice?' I giggle.

'What's so funny?'

Now I've started laughing I can't seem to stop. 'Janice doesn't seem the type.'

'But I do?'

I ignore that comment. 'Tom found her hard work.'

'She didn't fancy Tom.'

I'm wounded on Tom's behalf.

'She was angry that night. Thought I'd set the evening up to get to know you. She realised from talking to Tom that swinging wasn't his thing, and she was angry because she thought I wanted sex with you.'

'That's ridiculous.'

'Is it?'

I swallow. 'You thought Tom and I would be up for swapping partners?'

'God no. I was drawn to you because you remind me so much of Simon. I knew you were vanilla.'

That word again. 'Thanks a lot.'

He grins. 'I did fancy you though. Still do.'

'Daniel, I…'

'What am I to do with you, Sarah?'

My pulse quickens. What does he have in mind?

He gets up.

'Where are you going?'

'To get you another drink.'

He returns from the bar with a tray of shots. 'Here.'

'I don't do shots.'

'You do now.'

I pick up a tequila. We chink glasses and knock them back.

I cough, eyes stinging and throat burning.

'You okay?'

'Yes. So are these supposed to help me let go?'

'No.' The grin begins at his lips and finishes with his eyes. 'I was about to suggest sex with a stranger.'

'Swinging, you mean?'

'Not necessarily. There are other options.'

'Such as?'

He shrugs. 'An escort, threesome, one-night stand…'

'That's not my thing either. Tell me more about you and Janice.'

'What about me and Janice?'

'About swinging.'

He sits forward. 'Why? Are you and Tom interested in giving it a go?'

I snort. 'Hardly. Anyway, Tom's doing his own version with Yvette.'

Daniel nods. 'The affair. Is it serious?'

'He wants a divorce.'

'I'm sorry Sarah.'

'So, distract me.' I neck another tequila. 'Tell me about the swinger scene.'

He grins.

'So, you and Janice… you get it on with another couple?'

'Sometimes.'

'I thought that was the whole point. Throw car keys in a bowl, take out a set, swap houses, cars and wives…'

'I dare say it used to be like that, if you lived in the Sixties.'

'So, what happens now?'

'Anything you want. Sometimes we get together with another couple. Janice and I have our regulars. Sometimes we invite someone to join us for a threesome.'

I guffaw. 'I'm not having sex with you and Janice!'

He shrugs. 'Sometimes it's a woman, sometimes a guy.'

'What else?'

'We watch each other have sex with someone else. Sometimes we engage in group sex.'

My cheeks burn.

'Am I turning you on?'

'God no. So, are there any ground rules?'

'It has to be consensual and, if one of us wants to veto, we do. Oh, and there's no kissing.'

'Aw, shame.'

He grins. 'You like kissing?'

I feel a shiver. 'Doesn't everyone?'

He moves closer until I can almost taste his minty breath.

'Tell me more,' I say.

'Sometimes we go to Fraternize. It's a club in Brighton.'

'What do you do there?'

'It's couples only – burlesque, dirty dancing, group sex. Janice and I treat it as foreplay.'

I feel a flush creeping up my neck.

'Sometimes we spend the night at a swingers' hotel in Southampton.' His voice is low and husky. 'They have locked rooms where two or more couples engage in group sex, and unlocked rooms where couples just turn up, watch for a while, mix it up… there's a hot tub too, but Janice and I avoid that. It tends to get a bit… milky.'

'Eww.' I wave my hand. 'Stop it. I've heard enough.'

'Can't tempt you, then?'

CHAPTER THIRTY-FIVE

I stop outside Shangri-La and check the message on my mobile for the umpteenth time.

> Go to reception and collect the key for Mrs Grey. Head up to the room and follow instructions.

Am I really doing this? I'd been so against it at first. It seemed so tacky. And yet, Tom's playing away… Perhaps no-one's monogamous anymore. Sex with a stranger. Could that really help me to loosen up? Stop my need to be constantly in control? I stifle a giggle. If nothing else, it's an adventure. Daniel's hardly a stranger and I fancy him like mad. But can I really become a submissive?

Quivering with excitement, I slip my phone into my pocket, shoulder my rucksack and stride confidently through the door. More seaside B&B than hotel, the reception area is small and tatty with once white paint yellowed by age and tacky prints lining the walls.

The man behind the desk, preoccupied with completing a sudoku puzzle, doesn't look up.

'Erm...I'm Mrs Grey. Please may I have the key to my room?'

Barely acknowledging me, he lifts a key from the rack and slides it across the desk.

'Thank you,' I say. So much for a welcome!

I head up the stairs as if I know where I'm going. Reaching the landing, I check the number on the key fob – 212. I guess that's second floor. The carpet is sticky under my feet as I take the second flight of stairs and move along the corridor, checking numbers on doors – 210... 211... 212. If the inside is as terrible as the rest of this place, I'm leaving.

Sliding the key in the door, I step inside. The room is surprisingly welcoming, with low lighting emitting a warming glow, but my eyes can't fail to be drawn to the bed. King size, it dominates the space with its wrought iron frame and high mattress, while a deep maroon bedspread does nothing to reduce its regal presence. I squeeze past it to check out the ensuite. Not bad. Clean and functional, with a large tub and a generous supply of pristine white towels on the heated rail.

Suddenly wobbly, I step back into the bedroom and sit on the bed. That's when I notice the note on the pillow.

Number one – open champagne.

I gaze about the room. In the corner stands a fridge and, on top, two fluted glasses. I smile as I turn back to the note.

Number two – open present.

Present? I notice a gift-wrapped parcel on a chair. Feeling like a kid on her birthday, I scoot across to retrieve it. My heart beats with excitement as I untie the silver ribbon and remove the turquoise wrapping paper. Inside, I find two smaller parcels and pick them up to examine them. *This one first,* reads the label on one. I tear open the tissue – two scented candles, matches and Verbena Foam Bath, along with another note. *Run a bath and use the whole bottle of bubbles. Enjoy a good soak before opening your second gift. I hope you're enjoying the champers.*

In the bathroom, I turn on both taps and tip most of the lemony bubbles into the flowing water. While the bath's filling, I retrieve the champagne from the fridge. The cork comes out with a massive pop, and I fill both glasses and take a sip. Gorgeous. Returning to the bathroom, I arrange the candles, one either side of the tub, and light them. The aroma of lilac and wild rose begins to fill the air.

Testing the water, I turn off the taps and strip before climbing into the tub and laying back to luxuriate in the warm water. Heaven. I reach for my glass and take a sip of champagne, giggling as I'm tickled both inside and out. Things are stirring down below. Will he arrive while I'm in the bath?

I stay in the water until it cools and my glass is empty. Wrapping myself in a fluffy towel, I go back into the bedroom. Time for my second gift. I top up my drink before tearing the tissue from the remaining parcel.

Put this on. I hope you're drinking the champagne! A red satin camisole and matching lace knickers. I've never worn anything as sexy as these in my life. Dropping the towel, I step into the knickers and slip the camisole over my head. The fabric feels wonderfully silky as it slides across my skin. Are you watching, Mr Grey? When will you arrive?

Throwing back the bedspread, I'm delighted to discover pure white linen sheets, fragrant and sweet smelling. I lay down and sip my champagne.

Half an hour later, I'm bored. No TV, no radio. I check my mobile. No messages from Mr Grey. I read back through the notes. Come on, Daniel. I've done everything you asked. *Drink the champagne.* I eye the bottle. All right. I was going to save you some, but you've asked for it… Halfway down the third glass I feel a little tipsy. If you don't hurry up, Mr Grey, you'll find me asleep.

These pillows are so soft and comfy… I put my glass on the bedside table, lay back and close my eyes.

I jolt awake. I'm not alone. My eyes fly open and I try to scream, but the sound is muffled by a hand over my mouth.

'Shhh, Sarah.'

Why can't I see anything? Did he turn off the lights?

'I'm going to take my hand away now and you're not going to scream. Nod if you understand.'

I nod and he removes his hand. 'Good girl.'

'Why's it so dark?' There's something over my eyes. 'Am I blindfolded?'

'Shhh,' he repeats. 'Don't thrash about so much. You'll make them tighter.'

Tighter? I can't move my hands.

'I said DON'T wriggle.' It's a command.

Flinching, I tug gently. My wrists are tied to the iron bedframe. I move my legs. Thank God, they're still free.

I take a gulp of air. 'I'm not sure I…'

'Sarah, you need to trust me.'

I want out, but I'm afraid to say.

'Good girl. I see you've done everything asked of you. Now, just relax.'

Relax? Like that's going to happen. I exhale slowly while plotting in my mind how to get out of this. What the hell was I thinking? I've let a man I don't really know tie me up. He can do whatever the hell he likes and no one knows where I am. Oh Sarah, you stupid little fool.

My voice is meek, compliant. 'Do I have to keep the blindfold on?'

'Yes.'

He's moved away. Where is he? Sounds as if he's sitting on the chair.

'Thank you for leaving me a little champagne,' he says.

Without sight, my other senses are enhanced. I hear the sip of champagne, smell his familiar musk aftershave.

'Did you enjoy your soak?'

'Yes.' My skin smells of lemon meringue.

'You're very beautiful Sarah.'

I twist my lower body away from him. I must look ridiculous stretched out on the bed like a crucifix. I shiver, realising there are no bedclothes. I'm vulnerable and exposed.

The chair creaks. He's coming closer. Fingers trace my cheekbones, my neck… Featherlike, they graze my breasts, flutter across my belly. I shiver.

Wordlessly he repeats the same motions. He's barely touching me, but my skin's alive, the tiny hairs on my body erect. A light touch on my neck, between my breasts and down to my waist. He moves no lower and gradually I feel myself untense.

'There,' he says. 'That's better.'

There's movement on the mattress. He's sitting down. Is he looking at me? Embarrassed I turn my head away.

He puts a finger under my chin to bring it back. 'I'm going to undress you now, Sarah.'

Undress me? I'm wearing next to nothing.

I feel something cold against my belly. Metal? A knife? What the hell's he doing? With competence, he slices through the silk as though it were butter. My breasts feel a draught of cool air and my nipples stand proud.

Those featherlike motions begin again, from the small of my neck, across the top of my breasts, down the inside of each arm and along each finger. Back to my throat again and down to my middle. His fingers travel to my left breast, then the right, small circular movements scarcely touching my skin. Is this what they call tantric sex? Oh my God, I'm so aroused. My nipples harden against his fingers. He comes close and runs the tip of his tongue around each one.

He still hasn't touched me down there. His fingers play with the delicate lace at the top of my knickers. I want him to take them off. He moves his hand lower, still on top of the silky fabric. Tiny, circular motions. I'm wet. My back arches, my buttocks lift from the bed.

'Shhh.' he says again.

Then he's gone and I lay there, feeling the loss, wondering what will happen next.

His hand touches my right foot, his voice low. 'You remember your safe word?'

I shiver and nod my head. 'Yes.'

I don't resist as he ties something around my right ankle. It's soft – a chiffon scarf perhaps? He repeats on the left before spreading my legs and fastening my ankles to the foot of the bed.

'But I've…'

'Shhh,' he says.

I giggle. 'But I've still got my knickers on.' How will he get them off now I'm spread eagled?

But he knows what he's doing. The mattress sinks as he kneels over me, both hands on the left of my hip. Suddenly he rips and the pretty knickers are no more. I shiver again.

Now he begins with my feet. Feathery touches all the way up the inside of my legs, always stopping before he gets to…

'Ohhh.' I groan. My body's a cello and he's the musician. He can play any tune. He's the master and I'm his slave. He can do whatever the fuck he likes.

My gasps are urgent and breathless, but still he's barely touched me.

'Please,' I say.

'What, Sarah? What do you want?'

'I want you inside,' I beg.

'Is that what you need?'

'Yes.'

He straddles me. He's so hard. When he thrusts himself deep inside, I push myself up from the mattress wishing I could dig my heels into the bed to push harder. He bears down, swift and fast, then he's gone, pulling out to ejaculate.

I feel warm liquid trickle down my legs and I'm left wanting.

He climbs off the bed. My arms and legs are released as he slices through the bindings. When I hear him turn on the shower, I pull the blindfold from my eyes. Seriously? Is that it? I experience waves of frustration and disappointment in equal measures. Most of all, I'm humiliated.

When he finally comes out of the bathroom, I'm curled into a ball and pretending to be asleep.

He moves about the room while I lay still. After a while there's a kiss on my shoulder; a whisper in my ear. 'I've got to go but you stay. The room's paid for. I'll call you tomorrow.'

As he closes the bedroom door, I burst into angry tears.

I wake, naked and alone. Was it a dream? No. I'm sore as hell down there and I can smell him. I stumble into the bathroom, step into the empty bath and douche with the shower head. As I let the water wash me clean, I cry again.

There's no trace of him in the bedroom. If it wasn't for the stickiness between my legs, I might believe it had never happened. Even the glasses and empty champagne bottle have gone, along with the tissue paper and remains of the sexy underwear.

I pull on my jeans and a T-shirt before making one final check of the bedroom. I don't want to leave anything of myself here. Last night, soft light from the bedside lamps hid stains on the bedspread and carpet. Now in the daylight, everything looks cheap and sordid. Sliding my rucksack over my shoulder, I make my way downstairs.

The woman on reception smiles as I drop the key on her desk. 'Have a nice day,' she says.

I take the walk of shame, feeling like a whore.

CHAPTER THIRTY-SIX

I've never thought of myself as an adulterer. I always believed Tom was "the one". When I took my marriage vows, forsaking others until death us do part, I really meant it.

And then Tom betrayed me. Not sexually, at least not yet, or so he says, but the emotional betrayal hurts. The thought that it's Yvette he turns to, talks to, shares his dreams with… in some ways, it's worse than them sleeping together.

It's my fault. If only I hadn't neglected him so much. All right, my brother died, and my father followed soon after, but I didn't need to shut him out. And yet, didn't Tom say it started before that? *'I'm so lonely in this marriage,'* he said. How terrible to think that's how I made him feel.

And now I've slept with someone else. Committed adultery. Is it less bad if it's just sex, rather than an emotional connection? It feels worse. Somehow, I talked myself into believing I felt something for Daniel, but how much of that was my brain trying to create emotional attachment? I don't love him. I don't even like him.

I think back to all that stuff with Quinn. Where was Daniel when I was all but abducted? Conveniently, he managed to stay out of trouble. He's not someone I can count on. I allowed him to brainwash me. How did he convince me that being in control was a bad thing? Letting go wasn't liberating or freeing. It left me vulnerable and weak. Now I feel violated, used and abused.

Later that morning, he calls. 'Hi, Sarah.'

'Hello.' My cheeks are hot. I'm so angry.

'I wanted to check that you're okay.'

'You didn't wait to see.'

'No, I had to get back.'

I exhale. 'Look, Daniel, what do you want?'

'I don't want anything, Sarah.'

'Right, well, I think it's best if we don't see each other again.'

'If that's what you want.'

He's not even going to fight for me. 'Is that all you've got to say?'

'You seem to have made up your mind.'

'For fuck's sake, Daniel. Is that what this was about? Getting your leg over?'

'Oh, come on, Sarah. You know it was never about me. Last night was for your benefit, not mine.'

'Bullshit. To think I betrayed my marriage vows to sleep with you.' I fight to hold back tears. 'I thought I could trust you.'

'You can trust me, Sarah.'

'No, I can't. You manipulated me. Sweet talked me into believing it was for me, when all the time it was for you. You clearly *get off* on being the master, my saviour, but I didn't enjoy it. In fact, the whole sordid episode disgusts me.'

'I'm sorry you feel like that.'

'I do. And I never want to see you again.' I end the call and sit back, gasping for air. God, that was terrible. I nearly jump out of my skin when the phone rings again. Is it him calling back? I check the caller ID. No.

'Hello, Valentina?' I say.

There's a pause before she speaks. 'Look, you said if I should ever hear from Angelica…'

My pulse races. 'She's been in touch?'

'Come see me tomorrow and I'll fill you in. Midday at KitKat's.'

Valentina strolls into the café in three-quarter length satin gloves, a black flick-up bob and, despite it being January, Jackie Onassis sunglasses. 'Hey, girl.'

'Want a latte?' I try to contain my excitement as I order our drinks.

She sits primly, knees together, handbag on her lap. 'I don't know if I should be telling you this, but that girl's living the high life. You don't need to worry about her no more.'

'Where is she?'

'Costa Rica.' She purses her lips. 'That girl's getting her fill of sun, sea and sex.'

'But how do you know?'

Opening her handbag, she pulls out a postcard. I take it and stare at the picture - a leopard up a tree. Why hasn't Angel sent me a postcard? Flipping it over, I scan the words:

Dear V. Saw this gorgeous creature and thought of you. Do me a favour? Hold my reservation at The Lair a few more weeks? I've sent funds to cover. Be in touch when I know my plans. Love A xx

'Funny, huh?' Valentina holds out her hand to take the card back. 'Don't you just love that girl?'

'Mind if I take a pic?' Before she can argue, I take out my phone and snap photos of each side.

Costa Rica. It makes sense. Angel and Si talked about going there before he died. He'd even been learning Spanish.

At home I open Si's blog.

<u>*Volcanoes*</u>

Volcanoes are amazing. Put simply, a volcano is an opening in the Earth's crust. Volcanoes are found where tectonic plates are moving apart or coming together, or where there's stretching and thinning of the crust's plates. The thing most people don't understand is that volcanoes also help the people living near them, bringing tourists (like me) to the area and improving the soil so crops can be grown.

Although Costa Rica is a small country, it has loads of active volcanoes and, Arenal, which last erupted in 1968, is one of the most active. This trip has been on my bucket list for quite some time. It's no easy option. The closest regular travellers can get to the Arenal volcano's top is a multi-hour strenuous hike up Cerro Chato, Arenal's mountainous neighbour to the south. But I shan't let that deter me…

. . .

Arenal. The last volcano on Si's list. He never did make it to Costa Rica. But wait. He could still go. I could go to Costa Rica, hike to the volcano's base and scatter his ashes. Si's final trip. What better resting place? Everyone keeps saying I need to let go. This will be my goodbye. One final act of kindness.

CHAPTER THIRTY-SEVEN

Wendy's tone is incredulous. 'You're sure Costa Rica is where he'd want his ashes scattered?'

'Yes, he was definitely planning a trip.'

'It couldn't be Eastbourne with Mum and Dad?'

'Hardly. Not after all we found out.' I grin. 'Mum would give him hell.'

'Do you realise what it will cost?'

'Yes, but I can use some of the money Dad left me. Seems only right, after Si missed out on his share.' A sudden thought pops into my mind. 'You should come.'

'Me?'

'Yes. We could make a little holiday of it. Spend a few days sight-seeing.'

'Costa Rica,' she muses. 'Bob and I have never been there.'

Bob? Shit. I didn't think this through. Bob's presence would ruin everything. I swallow. 'I meant the two of us. Si's sisters.'

'I couldn't possibly travel without Bob. No, that wouldn't do at all. When are you thinking of going?'

'Easter break,' I say, wondering how the hell I'm going to back-pedal out of this.

'Oh, we're hosting visiting elders from Canada in April. Sorry, Sarah. That's a definite no can do.'

Thank Christ for that. I might manage to pull the wool over Wendy's eyes, but Bob would see right through me. 'It's okay. I'll go on my own.'

'Won't Tom go?'

'You know he won't.'

'It's such a pity, the way things are between you two. Marriage is for life, Sarah. Not something to be tossed away lightly. Can't you find it in your heart to patch things up?'

'It's not me who's leaving.' But that's not strictly true. I've neglected my marriage, too.

'It sounds as though you're running away. Bob and I think you should sit down with Tom and really talk things through. There's a group at our church who deal with marital problems. Bob's had a word with our pastor, David, and he's going to give you a call.'

'Wendy, no.'

She sighs. 'It's been a tough few months. I suppose it might do you good to have a break.'

I exhale. 'It will. And the weather's perfect that time of year.'

Back at school, I approach each week with optimism, expecting the weekend to have cleared the air between Nicki and me. Instead, I find us skirting politely around one another as if we're colleagues who don't get on. This has to stop. Catching her in the photocopy room, I position myself between her and the door, effectively blocking her exit. 'Hi Nicki.'

She glances up from her copying, as if only just realising I'm there. 'Oh, hi.'

'Can we talk?'

She exhales. 'I guess.'

'Look, I'm sorry if I took our friendship for granted and I'm especially sorry for not being there for you when you needed me.'

She picks up her photocopying from the printer tray. 'You've had a lot on.'

'We both have.'

'I'm sorry about your dad.'

'Thanks. And I'm sorry about your mum.'

She gives me a rueful smile. 'We're both orphans now, aren't we?'

I lay a hand on her arm. 'I miss you, Nicki.'

She sighs. 'I miss you too.'

'Come to dinner. Friday night.'

'No, come to me. I've a new recipe I want to try out.'

I pour us both a glass of Muscadet while Nicki adds chunks of breaded fish to a pan of sizzling butter. 'I like watching you cook,' I say.

She snorts.

'What?'

'You don't need to try so hard.'

'Okay.' I sip my wine. 'Did you hear Tom's gone.'

She shoots me a look. 'Gone where?'

'He's left me.'

Her jaw drops. 'Bastard. Since when?'

'Everything fell apart just after Christmas, but he hung on until after Dad's funeral. He's been fantastic, really. The writing was on the wall for months, I just didn't see it. Even Jamie knew before me.'

'What are you going to do?'

I shrug. 'Well, for starters, I slept with Daniel.'

'Oh my God!'

'I suppose I wanted to get my own back. It was a huge mistake.'

'It didn't make you feel better?'

'No. I don't think I'm much of an adulterer.'

'It's not adultery if Tom left you first.' As each piece of fish reaches a perfect golden brown, she flips it over. 'Did you use protection?'

'I'm on the pill.'

'I don't mean that. It's just, Daniel…' She turns to face me. 'Well, sounds as if he's been around, you know?'

'Oh God!' My heart skips a beat. 'I hadn't even thought about that.'

'Get yourself checked out. There's a private clinic in Hurstwood Lane, just behind the Princess Royal. It'll cost, but they're very discreet.'

STIs. As if I haven't got enough to worry about. 'Anyway,' I continue, 'I don't suppose you want to come to Costa Rica at Easter?'

'What?'

'You and me. Girlie holiday.'

'Why Costa Rica?'

'Because that's where Si wanted his ashes scattered.'

'Oh, Sarah…'

'It's important.'

'I can't go swanning off to Costa Rica. I've got to sort out what I'm doing with Mum's house.'

'Can't you do that later?'

'No.' She turns down the heat under the skillet. 'I've got Zoom calls lined up with *agent immobiliers* and a scheduled Skype call with a *notaire*.'

'Please come. It'll be a laugh.'

She snorts. 'Scattering ashes, a laugh?'

'That will only take one day. I have to do this, Nicki. Please?'

Using a slotted spoon, she lifts out the fish goujons and sets them on a square of kitchen roll to drain. 'What about Wendy?'

'She won't come.'

'Oh, so I'm second choice?'

'Not really. I had to ask Wendy, she's my sister. I'd much rather go with you.'

'Hmm.'

'What can I do to help?'

'Check the French beans. They should be done. Should be asparagus really, but it's too early.'

Taking the lid off the steamer, I test the vegetables with the tip of a knife. 'Yep, perfect.'

'Plate up, then.' After transferring the fish, Nicki sprinkles it generously with herbs.

'It smells delicious,' I say, treated to the punchy aroma of lemon and parsley.

She tops up my glass. 'Crispy monkfish with capers. A new recipe I picked up in France.'

I slice off a small piece of fish and pop it in my mouth. Creamy and succulent, it melts on the tongue. 'Wow. Tastes amazing, too.'

'Thanks.' Her cheeks glow as she chinks her glass against mine. '*Santé.*'

'*Salud!*' I take a sip of wine before setting my glass down.

'How does one transport ashes, anyway?' she asks as we tuck in.

'I'm not sure. I'm worried about them going in the hold. It doesn't seem right to pack the urn between knickers and socks.'

'After what you found out about Simon, I'm sure travelling with a few undies wouldn't bother him.'

'I suppose not. If I put the urn in my hand luggage, it'll use up half the weight allowance.'

'How much does the urn weigh?'

'Just under four kilograms. I checked on the bathroom scales.' I gaze at her hopefully. 'If you came to Costa Rica, we could split the ashes between us.'

'Knowing our luck, they'd decide we were a couple of drug mules. I don't know about you, but I don't want to spend the next twenty years in a Costa Rican jail.' She places her knife and fork together on her plate. 'Sorry, Sarah. But if there's anything else…'

'How about minding Brodie while I'm away?'

CHAPTER THIRTY-EIGHT

Tom insists on driving me to the airport. 'You can't go by train. The journey will be a nightmare.'

'Don't come in,' I say, as we exit the M25.

'I thought we'd grab a coffee or lunch?'

'It's silly to pay for the car park. Anyway, I want to go straight through and look around the shops.'

'Okay.' At the drop-off point he gets out of the car and lifts my suitcase from the boot.

I extend the telescopic handle. 'Bye then.'

He gives me a crooked smile. 'You know I'm always here for you, Sarah.'

I shrug. 'Yeah, right.'

'I mean it. You don't erase twenty-five years overnight.'

'Okay.' What do we do now? Kiss? Hug?

Tom solves the dilemma by squeezing my shoulder. 'Hope it goes well. After you've done the deed, perhaps you'll get to relax for a few days. You deserve a break.'

. . .

I check-in and deposit my hold baggage with no problems before approaching security.

'Hello.' I offer the uniformed official a smile. 'I'm travelling to Costa Rica with my brother's ashes.'

'Passport and death certificate, please.'

Having accessed an online site called *Everlasting Memories,* I'm confident as I pull the paperwork from the side pocket of my carry-on bag. 'I have everything in accordance with Transportation Security Administration guidelines. Death certificate and a certificate of cremation from the crematorium, plus a letter from the funeral home confirming what's in the urn.'

The official peruses the death certificate. It takes a while and my heart begins to race. 'I've got both of our birth certificates, too,' I stammer. 'Belt and braces I know…'

He waves away the additional documentation. 'The ashes need to be x-rayed.'

'That's fine. They're still in the plastic container supplied by the funeral director.' I continue to babble as the green urn disappears through the plastic flaps on the conveyor belt. 'I was told either plastic or cardboard is fine.'

My mouth is dry. Although legally security aren't allowed to tamper with the contents of a funeral urn, they could ask me to tip the ashes into a tray for inspection. I'm not sure I can cope with seeing Si's remains being scrutinised in a plastic tray.

The urn emerges on the other side and the official gives a brisk nod. Breathing a sigh of relief, I stow it safely in my bag.

After wandering around the departure lounge, I take a seat and pull out my copy of *Lonely Planet Guide to Costa Rica*. I'm familiarising myself with the section on local food and drink when I'm distracted by a family – the kids noisy and boisterous, excited to be going on an aeroplane. I feel a lump in my throat. If only I was off on a regular holiday.

We land at Juan Santamaría International Airport at ten minutes past six. It's weird I've been travelling for eleven hours and yet only three hours have elapsed. After collecting my suitcase from the baggage carousel, I approach security feigning a confident air. It seems scarier this time.

A blue-shirted guard raises a hand, indicating I should stop. 'Papers?'

I hand them over, my heart thumping in my chest. 'You should find everything is in order.'

After perusing the documentation, he signals for me to lift my bags onto a table. 'Open these, please.'

I flip open my suitcase and loosen the fastenings of my carry-on bag.

The guard rummages through my neatly folded clothes before turning to the rucksack. Spotting the green canister, he lifts his radio and mumbles some words in Spanish. Within seconds, another official is striding towards us.

The first slides his hands into the rucksack, extracting the canister as though it's a bomb. The second, dressed in black and carrying a gun, scrutinises the urn from every angle, paying particular attention to the seal.

I swallow. I'd used masking tape in the hope they'd think it had never been opened since leaving the crematorium. In fact, it had been opened and the contents sniffed by both Tom and Jamie.

Sweat trickles down my back. They're going to make me open it and tip the contents into a tray. I've read that sometimes it's not just ash. There can be pieces of bone. I swallow down a mouthful of vomit.

Other passengers file past, whispering and rubber necking. I bet they think I'm a drugs mule.

The two officials exchange words in Spanish while I stare wide-eyed, like a rabbit caught in the headlights. I have no idea what they're saying. I'm alone in a South American country. Any moment, I expect sniffer dogs to arrive and four Costa Rican policemen with machine guns to surround me. Will they confiscate Si's ashes? Has this all been in vain? Tears of frustration trickle down my cheeks.

The official with a gun barks a final order before walking away. The first official sets the canister down on the table and waves his hand.

Is he dismissing me? 'I can go?'

Already dealing with another passenger, he fails to reply.

I slide the canister into the rucksack, close the suitcase and lift my baggage down from the table. Moving away from the busy flow of passengers, I find space against a wall and crouch down, shaking and emotionally drained.

After a few deep breaths to compose myself, I haul myself up. I have to find the bus to La Fortuna. With the rucksack on my back and the suitcase bumping along behind me, I hurry swiftly across the concourse following signs for *Salida*. With every step I expect to hear rapid footsteps and someone shouting, 'Stop that woman!'

Safely on the bus, I text Wendy, Nicki and Jamie to say I've landed. According to the guidebook, La Fortuna is a little over one hundred kilometres from San José and the journey takes around three hours. Retrieving a neck cushion from my rucksack, I attempt sleep.

Despite two lanes, Route 702 is winding, and I'm kept awake by a small child seated opposite. Tired and fretful, she maintains a constant grizzle. I know how she feels.

My mobile bleeps with a message from Wendy.

> Glad to hear you've arrived safely. Hope you're not too exhausted. Speak tomorrow x.

As we near the rainforest, the bus stops to drop passengers at various accommodations. I watch enviously from the window as they collect bags and rucksacks from the hold and stagger away to their beds.

La Fortuna is the final destination. Stiff legged, I clamber down the steps and wait for my suitcase to be unloaded.

Most of the other passengers have dispersed when I hear a voice. 'Senora Edwards?'

I spin around to see an olive-skinned man in a tatty jeep. 'Yes?'

He offers me a white-toothed grin as he jumps from the vehicle. 'My name is Pedro. I drive you to Finca Cacao.'

I glance about. The coach driver is preparing to pull away. I'm standing in the middle of a Costa Rican town with a guy who might be about to abduct me, but what choice do I have?

Pedro lifts my suitcase into the back of the jeep and gets into the cab. With trepidation, I climb up beside him.

In moments, we're traversing potholed roads. The rocking motion of the jeep is strangely stultifying and I stifle a yawn.

Pedro glances at me. 'Long flight, huh?'

'Yes.'

'Not far now.'

I feel my eyelids droop. Suddenly we make a sharp turn and I'm jolted awake. We're on an unmade track, but the sign saying Finca Cacao reassures me.

Pedro pulls up in front of a ranch-like building and I peer out of the window as a dark-haired woman of about my age comes down the steps to greet me.

'Sarah?' She smiles. 'I'm Maria. You must be exhausted. Come. I show you the way.' I slide down from the cab and she takes my arm, leading me along a narrow twisting path. Her torch lights the way as we're serenaded by a whirring, clicking sound.

I stop in my tracks. 'What's that?'

Maria laughs. 'Frogs. You'll get used to them.'

After a couple of hundred metres, we round a bend and, in front of us, nestled among giant vegetation, is a wooden hut.

'So.' Maria pauses to let me take it in. 'This is the cabana.'

'It's orange,' I say, admiring how the tiny building almost glows in the dark.

'Sienna,' she says, opening the door. The décor is dated, with mahogany furniture that's clearly seen better days, but it's clean and the double bed welcoming, with floral sheets in cheerful sunflower yellow.

Pedro places my case at the foot of the bed. '*Buenas noches*,' he says, stepping back outside.

Maria opens another door. 'And here is the bathroom.'

I poke my head in. It's basic but adequate. 'Great.'

She gestures towards a tray set on top of a chest of drawers. 'There's a kettle, but for tonight I have prepared you a flask and a snack.'

'Thank you.' I raise my hand to conceal another yawn.

Maria laughs. 'It is late, and you've had a long day. Sleep well, Sarah. I will see you in the morning.'

'*Buenas noches*,' I say.

'*Buenas noches*.' She closes the door and the murmur of their voices fades as Maria and Pedro retrace their steps.

After using the loo, I check out my supper. The flask contains hot chocolate and I pour myself a cup. On a plate are two small pasties. I pick one up and bite into it. The pastry is flaky and sweet, drenched in a sticky honey topping and filled with a succulent pineapple puree. Alternating mouthfuls of pastry with sips of chocolate, I roll my eyes appreciatively. Yum.

I undo my rucksack and lift out Si's urn. After giving it a once-over to ensure it's not damaged, I stow it in the bottom of the wardrobe. I really should unpack, but instead I open the suitcase and retrieve my wash bag. After brushing my teeth, I kick off my trainers, slip off my jeans and bra, and climb into bed.

CHAPTER THIRTY-NINE

The room is pitch black and I have the strangest feeling I'm not alone. Grabbing my phone, I click on the torch and scan the room. On the wall beside the bed, a gecko blinks lazy eyes, before raising his head and scuttling away. I shudder. I guess he's my roomy for the next few days. Throwing back the sheet, I check the floor carefully before popping into the bathroom to use the loo. I wash my hands and, still sleepy, hop back into bed.

I'm woken again by a knock at the door. '*Buenos dias.*'

'Come in,' I call, pulling the sheet up to my neck.

Maria bustles into the room, setting a tray down on a dark wood sideboard. 'Did you sleep well?'

'Yes, thank you.'

She opens the patio doors, allowing the yellow muslin curtains to billow gently in the breeze before retrieving the tray and carrying it outside.

Throwing back the sheet again, I tug on jeans and follow her onto the terrace. The cabin's nestled among the treetops while, all around, like a huge green counterpane, lays the plantation. Beyond the cacao trees stands Arenal, dominant and imposing.

'Wow! The view is amazing. I hadn't realised how far up we are.'

The trees are alive with birds, the air filled with their chorus. I jump as a creature leaps around amongst the branches just metres from where we're standing.

Maria chuckles at my reaction. 'Monkeys,' she explains. 'Don't leave food out here or they will steal it. Enjoy your breakfast. Come and find me over at the house when you're ready to check out the plantation.'

'Thank you.' After she's gone, I seat myself on a wooden chair. Although I can hardly tear my eyes from the vista, my stomach disagrees and grumbles impatiently at the delay. I turn to the breakfast tray. Maria has prepared fresh fruit and coffee, as well as some sort of savoury egg dish – a cross between an omelette and scrambled, dotted with chunks of red and green peppers.

The alarm on my phone vibrates and I check the time. Eight a.m. Thank goodness I allowed myself a day to acclimatise before the challenge of the volcano hike.

After breakfast, I linger on the terrace a while before making my way into the bathroom. I undress and pull back the plastic floral curtain to step into the shower. The water is a shock – low pressure and freezing cold. I suppose I should have expected it. Feeling grubby from the journey, I force myself to stay under the intermittent flow. As soon as I step out, my skin dries instantly. I add moisturising products and run fingers through my wet hair. It will dry in no time in this heat.

Pulling on jeans and a fresh T-shirt, I spend a little time unpacking before retrieving my trainers from beside the bed, grabbing a floppy sunhat and sunglasses, and heading outside. The humidity hits me as soon as I emerge.

I make my way down the path towards the ranch, where Maria is pegging washing to a line.

'*Buenos dias,*' she calls.

'*Buenos dias,*' I reply.

'Did you enjoy your breakfast?'

'Yes, it was delicious. Thank you.'

She steps towards me. 'What are your plans today? If you want to go to town, I can call an Uber? Or if you'd prefer a quiet day' – she waves an arm expansively – 'you're welcome to explore. I can ask Pedro to give you a tour if you like?'

I shake my head. 'I think I'll just chill and get my bearings. Is there somewhere to eat locally?'

'There are a number of sodas – small eateries – on the road into town where you can get a good meal for 1500 colon.'

'1500 colon? That's about three quid, right? Wow.'

She smiles. 'You can borrow a bike,' she nods towards a lean-to on the side of the building, 'or, if you want to go into La Fortuna after dark, Pedro will drive you. Of course, if you just want snacks, come to the house.'

'You're very kind.'

I stroll off along the driveway. I'd expected a cacao plantation to smell of chocolate, but disappointingly it doesn't smell of anything other than vegetation. After a few metres, I stop and fan myself. It's so hot. I manage another twenty minutes before turning back.

While I've been gone, Maria's cleared the breakfast tray and left a jug of water beside my bed. I pour a glass and carry it out to the terrace with my rucksack. Pulling the paperwork from the side pocket, I read through the itinerary. I'm to be picked up in La Fortuna at nine in the morning. Hopefully Pedro will drive me into town. I read the description of the hike:

After a twenty-minute walk through lush rainforest, we follow a trail cut through the rocks. Steep steps lead to the huge mass of lava rocks. Reaching the highest viewpoint, we will absorb the most spectacular panoramic views.

I sit forward. Highest viewpoint? It doesn't mention anything about the crater. Why did I not notice this before? My heart starts to race. Grabbing the itinerary, I head down the track to the ranch and knock on the door.

'Come in,' calls Maria.

I find her in the kitchen. A small child playing on a colourful rug nearby stares up at me with huge, dark eyes.

'Hello,' I say.

'Say hello, Gabriela,' says Maria.

The child smiles.

Maria laughs. 'Her English is non-existent. I'd hoped she might pick up a little from our visitors, but I fear she's content to sit and smile.'

'She's gorgeous.'

'Is there something I can get for you? A sandwich perhaps?'

'No, I'm fine, but I wanted to ask you about a hike I've booked for tomorrow.' I hand Maria the itinerary.

She scans the paper. 'Eco Adventures. Yes, they're very good.'

'I booked the longer option, The 1968 Bosque trail?'

'Yes, it is a little challenging.' She glances at me as if assessing my fitness. 'You should be fine. It takes you past Lago Los Patos.' Noting my confusion, she translates. 'The Duck Lake. It's beautiful.'

'But only to the highest viewpoint?'

She nods.

'But I want to go to the crater.'

She laughs. 'The lava plains are the closest you can get.'

My heart sinks. Si would have found a way. 'There must be someone who will take me up the volcano?'

She shakes her head. 'In town you'll find guides offering this, but it's illegal. And very dangerous.'

How could I have been so stupid? There's no way I'm going to scatter Si's ashes in the volcano.

I take up the offer of Pedro driving me into La Fortuna, where I enjoy a chicken and rice dish at La Cascada, a thatched palm-leafed café recommended in my guidebook. It's packed, obviously a favourite with tourists, and I'm glad I chose to eat early. I'm back in the cabin by nine and, once in bed, settle down to reread Si's account of an earlier volcano visit.

<u>*Mount Vesuvius*</u>

Just five miles east of Naples, Vesuvius is one of the most famous volcanoes in the world. It's not the biggest, but classed as one of the most dangerous, being the only one to erupt on European mainland in the last 100 years.

My wife (now my ex) was keen to take a trip to Italy and, with Vesuvius as the icing on the cake, who was I to disagree? I persuaded her to include Pompeii in our itinerary, but a hike up the mountain was a step too far. She stayed below, sightseeing, while those of us made of hardier stuff trudged up the long stony dirt track winding up the side of the volcano.

The track gave way to a single path, several times disappearing entirely to leave us clambering over rocks like goats.

Our guide was knowledgeable. He'd been climbing for the past twelve years and pointed out security measures taken to keep the local population safe. There are sensors around the crater detecting movement or changes in temperature. Thanks to this monitoring, volcanologists can predict a potential eruption and clear the area.

As we made our way up, I noticed the ground was composed of ash and slivers of rock. Up here, you're reminded that this is still an active volcano. There were signs of past eruptions all around – lava trails of grey and red and steam escaping from under rocks. Once we reached the edge of the crater, the smell of sulphur pervaded. Here you feel real heat and we clambered inside, taking turns to stick our hands into a steaming vent.

Reaching the highest point, you get a view of the city of Naples, along to Sorrento and across to the island of Capri. While others 'oohed' and 'aahed', all I wanted to do was climb back inside the crater and explore. All too soon, we were heading back down.

'You're literally covered in dust,' said my wife as I joined her for coffee.

I wore that ash like a badge of honour.

CHAPTER FORTY

I slide the urn into the rucksack, the words of a song by The Righteous Brothers running through my head – "He Ain't Heavy…"

Maria gives me more sweet pastries for my journey – apparently, they're called *empanadas* – and Pedro drops me off outside a church with a tall clocktower in La Fortuna in plenty of time.

The minibus is already half full when it arrives, and I climb aboard and find a seat. The bus makes one more stop at a hotel on the outskirts of town before the driver picks up his microphone. 'Good morning, ladies and gentlemen. I'm Jorge and I'll be your driver and guide for the day. We're heading now for the National Park. We'll be on the road about fifteen minutes.'

The other passengers chat while I stare out of the window at banana trees, low buildings, stores and a few broken-down vehicles. All the while, Arenal looms large beside us. Am I doing the right thing? Si didn't specifically say this was where he wanted his ashes scattered. Wendy and I would never be able to come and visit him like we would if we'd scattered them at Eastbourne. Tom and Wendy think I'm bonkers bringing Si's ashes all the way out here. It wasn't exactly cheap, and I should probably have saved the money for when I set up on my own, but there's something about Arenal. It was on Si's bucket list. I have to carry out this last act for him.

The voice of the driver interrupts my thoughts. 'Here we are. Make sure you have water and anything essential for the hike. Don't carry more than you need.'

The other passengers grab bags and jackets and clamber off, mostly heading for the toilet block. A couple have stopped to ask Jorge a question, but he breaks off when he sees me lugging my rucksack down the steps. 'That looks heavy. You can leave it onboard if you like? It will be perfectly safe.'

I shake my head as I haul it onto my shoulders. 'No, it's fine thanks.'

As I move across to join the others, I spot a couple with a young child. I hadn't noticed her on the minibus. How the hell is a little kid going to make it on a five-kilometre hike? The issue is soon resolved as the mother slides the toddler into a metal framed papoose on her father's back. She ain't heavy either, I suppose.

We set out through the forest, passing giant grasses three metres tall and I feel like Alice in Wonderland. I stare down at my feet – black lava trodden by thousands of sightseers who've made this trek.

Jorge points out giant boulders lining our way. 'These big rocks were hurled into the air by the volcano.'

'When was the last eruption?' someone asks.

'Arenal was active until 2010,' replies Jorge.

I lengthen my strides until I'm level with the young couple and toddler. The child's asleep, her head nodding in rhythm with her father's steps. I'm already out of breath and wish someone could carry me.

'I hope the bloody thing doesn't decide to spew its guts today,' says the mother, puffing along beside me as the path widens.

We head uphill through trees and Jorge points out glimpses of the volcano. Soon, the path narrows again and we navigate steep steps in single file, like a trail of ants. It's hard going, and I wonder if Si's looking down on me. Ahead, Jorge is regaled with question after question by keen volcanologists. That's where you'd be Si, up the front. Or perhaps you know it all already? Perhaps you'd be arguing with Jorge, offering counter evidence as to cause and effect.

It occurs to me that for most of my fellow hikers this trail is a once-in-a-lifetime experience. Pity I'm in no mood to enjoy it. I trudge on, rucksack straps slicing into my shoulder blades. Oh Si, why couldn't you have been passionate about something other than bloody volcanoes?

As we reach a grassy meadow, Jorge comes to a halt. 'This is where the trail divides. We take the forest walk – it's a little longer, but rewarding.'

Longer? Great! I swig from my water bottle. Mind you, Si would love this.

Following a dirt path, we head into dense rainforest once more. I traipse after the others, gazing at the lush vegetation – mosses, ferns and grasses. A bird makes a strange noise that sounds like a smoke alarm and everyone laughs.

We emerge by a small lake.

'This is Lago los Patos,' says Jorge. 'Formed by the eruption.'

Duck Lake. Despite my mood, I catch my breath. It's as beautiful as Maria promised. I glug down water while others take photos and pose for selfies.

Twenty minutes later, the trails merge once more.

'This is the lava plain and as far as we go,' says Jorge. 'From here, you have the best view of the volcano and, over to the west' – he points – 'Lake Arenal. In 1979, they constructed a hydroelectric dam, tripling the size. It's Costa Rica's largest lake.'

My fellow hikers, 'ooh' and 'aah', taking panoramic photos with cameras and iPhones.

'We have lunch here.' Jorge squats down and unpacks the picnic – sandwiches, water, fruit and energy bars.

'Excuse me.' I point to my watch. 'How long do we stay here?'

'Fifteen to twenty minutes,' he replies.

'Thanks.' I move away from the others, heading along a narrow path. The rocks are dark and jagged, and I have to concentrate to avoid falling and twisting an ankle. With a quick glance at Jorge, I clamber over a boulder and squat down low. Peering back, I see the others have found suitable spots to sit, supplementing lunch with biscuits and crisps from their rucksacks. They're all gazing in the opposite direction, admiring the view.

I stifle a giggle, feeling like a kid playing truant. I don't have long. Sliding my rucksack from my back, I unfasten the buckles and retrieve the urn. I cradle it in my arms. I should say something…

Unscrewing the lid, I peer inside. 'This is goodbye then, Si.'

It's sheltered here, but I move around so I'm the right side of the wind. I don't want to carry bits of my brother all the way back down on my clothes.

I begin to tip out the ashes. They're much lighter in colour than the volcanic lava ash surrounding me. I'd intended scattering it all, but there's so much – a huge heap of grey ashes, as if someone's had a barbecue. I stop pouring and screw the top back on the urn. With the toe of my walking boot, I move the ash around, trying to blend it in. The different shades of grey swirl like an abstract painting. Should I take a photo? No, that seems disrespectful. I stand for a moment, looking down. Si and Arenal, mixed together. It feels right.

I recite the words I've chosen: 'Live now; make now always the most precious time. Now will never come again.' Picard's words. Not the most famous of *Star Trek*'s quotes, but 'Live long and prosper' didn't seem right, and anyway, he was always Si's favourite.

I'm stowing the urn back in my rucksack when I hear a shout. Slipping my arms through the straps, I step back onto the path.

Jorge is approaching, waving both arms frantically. 'You must stay in sight. This area is dangerous,' he scolds.

'Sorry,' I say.

My face is flushed as I join the others, feeling like I've been caught smoking behind the bike sheds.

We head back to where the trails cross and Jorge leads us on another detour, stopping beside an enormous tree. The trunk is as broad as a dinosaur and, as I gaze up into the canopy, it seems to go as high as Jack's beanstalk.

'How tall is it?' someone asks.

'Thirty metres,' says Jorge. 'This is the Ceiba tree. One of a few trees that survived the eruption.'

On the way down, Jorge is in a hurry. 'We need to pick up the pace,' he says.

As I'm bringing up the rear, he's probably aiming his remark at me. Several times he looks back to check that I haven't absconded. I wonder if anyone does? Perhaps they go as far as the guide will take them before venturing off on their own. I chuckle. Si might have been one of those. Although I didn't scatter all his ashes, I feel a little lighter. As if I've achieved something. At least I've made a start.

The others are dawdling too, staring up into trees, trying to catch sight of the birds and beasts that live here. There's great excitement when Jorge points out a hummingbird.

When we get back to the entrance, there's a rush for the toilets. Jorge spots another driver, a colleague I guess, and they share a joke while we queue for the facilities.

We pile back onto the minibus and Jorge does a headcount, seeming relieved he hasn't lost anyone.

'Right,' he says, 'now the best bit – the waterfall.'

Weary after our hike, we're subdued on the thirty-minute journey. Jorge puts on the radio and a few passengers sing along to Abba. Abba? Even all the way over here?

We disembark and head for the waterfall. Most people are prepared with swimming costumes under their clothes, but a swimsuit hadn't seemed appropriate attire for an ash-scattering mission. Instead, I perch on a rock, watching the others whoop and squeal as they run under the falls.

'Mind if I join you?' The mother and toddler sit beside me, the little girl curled into a ball on her mother's lap.

I wonder at the wisdom of bringing such a small child on a nine-hour excursion. 'She looks done in.'

'Yes, it's a long day.' The woman glances at me. 'You're not going in?'

'No.'

We sit in silence. The little girl has her eyes closed and sucks fiercely at her thumb.

'Are you enjoying your trip?' asks the woman.

'Yes thanks.'

'The scenery is amazing and the people so welcoming. We head for the ocean tomorrow.'

'Me too,' I say. 'Well, in a few days' time.'

Back on the coach, Jorge does his best to stoke up enthusiasm for the last visit of the day. 'It's the best bit,' he says again. 'Right up in the clouds with all the sights and sounds…'

The woman with the toddler taps my shoulder. 'Long as you're okay with heights.' She winks.

'This part is self-guided,' says Jorge, as we pull into Mistico Hanging Bridges. 'Be sure to pay special attention to the different layers of the rainforest – treetops, understory and forest floor. That way, you'll be able to appreciate many of the species housed by this spectacular biological corridor.'

I lag behind, determined to lose the others. As I pass an archway framing Arenal, I pause to admire the view. 'See, Si? Not so far away.' It's surprisingly quiet here. Perhaps because it's after noon. Slowly, I meander along the sixteen bridges, pausing to enjoy the peace.

Finding myself alone, I set down my rucksack and lift out the urn. Glancing quickly back and forth to check no one's coming, I unscrew the lid. 'Okay Si, this is as good as it gets.' Reaching out, I scatter more of Si's ashes onto the treetops below. 'I hope you approve… argh!' A monkey swings from a branch to land inches away from me and I almost drop the urn.

'Hello, you.' I cradle the urn as I recover from the shock.

The monkey stares back with big round eyes. For a moment it's as if we're communicating.

I feel a shiver run down my spine. Could it be? No, that's ridiculous. Tentatively I reach out a hand. 'Simon?'

'Mummy, look, a monkey!' A small child hurtles towards me, eager feet making the bridge sway.

The monkey's on full alert. Giving me a knowing glance,

he swings back into the trees as the little boy comes to a halt beside me.

'He's gone.' While the child gazes, crestfallen, after the departing monkey, I lower the urn to my feet.

'Robert!' The boy's mother hurries across the bridge. As she reaches us, she grabs the boy's hand. 'You mustn't run off like that.'

'But we saw a monkey.'

His mother offers me an apologetic look. 'Sorry,' she mouths, as they move across the bridge. The boy's father brings up the rear and, as they disappear from earshot, I hear him distracting the child with the promise of an ice cream.

I crouch down and stow the remaining ashes in my rucksack.

CHAPTER FORTY-ONE

I've flown halfway across the world to scatter Si's ashes, but I've still got half an urn left. What the hell am I going to do with them? Whatever I do, I need to get on with it. The clock's ticking. Surely there must be a way to get up to the crater? If only I'd been brave enough to do a runner when we were at the lava plains, but it was such a vast expanse and I'd have had no clue how to navigate.

After breakfast, I head down to the ranch. Pedro's on the driveway with his head under the bonnet of the jeep.

'*Hola, Pedro.*'

He looks up. '*Buenas dias, senora.*'

'Thanks for picking me up last night.'

'You're welcome. It was a long day, no?'

'It was.' I shuffle from foot to foot. 'Maria said I might be able to borrow a bike?'

'Sure. Give me five minutes.'

After selecting a mountain bike from a number hanging in the lean-to, Pedro checks the tyres before providing me with a map and pointing me in the direction of town.

. . .

Spotting an internet café in the main street, I prop up the bike and head inside. I gesture to the bank of three computers. 'Wi-Fi?'

'Two dollars,' says the guy behind the counter.

I pay him and settle myself at a table near the window. Signing into Zoom, I check the time – ten-thirty. Teatime at home. A good time to catch Wendy. The fan whirs as the computer attempts to connect.

Suddenly Wendy's on the screen, frowning as she adjusts the audio. 'Hello? Sarah? Can you hear me?'

'Yes.' I grin. 'It's good to see a familiar face.'

Behind her, the bifolds are open. Hearing bird song from her garden, I'm suddenly homesick.

'Well, it's about time you got in touch. I've been worried.'

'I texted when I landed. The Wi-Fi and phone signal out here is rubbish.'

She nods, sliding onto a kitchen stool. 'What time is it there?'

'Mid-morning.'

'The day's almost gone here. How have you been getting on?'

I swallow. 'It's not been as easy as I'd hoped.'

'Oh Sarah. Has it been dreadful? You shouldn't have gone all that way on your own.'

I laugh. 'It's not dreadful. The country is beautiful, the people are friendly and I'm staying in a cabin on a chocolate farm.'

'Oh well, you can bring me some of that back.'

I shake my head. 'It's just cacao beans.'

She leans forward, lowering her voice. "Did you manage to *scatter the ashes*?'

The last three words are mouthed as if someone might be listening.

'Not entirely. It's not possible to get up to the crater.' Now it's my turn to whisper. 'I'm having to scatter them in smaller amounts and be a little *creative*.'

Wendy scoffs. 'Oh, for goodness' sake! All that way…'

'It's fine. I'm finding suitable spots. I think Si would be pleased.'

'Well, hurry up and…' The screen freezes.

When the connection returns, I've missed what she said. 'What?'

'I said, when do you go to the coast?'

'I've got two more days here, then five in Playa Esterillos.'

Wendy nods. 'Try and relax…' the signal drops out again, '…a few days on a sun lounger somewhere nice.'

'I will. I'm losing you, Wendy. I'll call again in a few days.'

I check my emails and I'm surprised to find one from Valentina.

Hey girl. Haven't seen you in a while. Just to let you know that Krystal hasn't mentioned your name again, so hopefully Quinn got the message.

Thought you might like to see this.

Underneath is a forwarded email from Angel.

Dear V.
Sitting on a Caribbean beach sipping Guaro Sour. You can let my Lair reservations go. At last, I've found my Eden. Thanks

for taking me under your wing when I first moved to Brighton.
Love A xx

Guaro Sour? I remember reading in *Lonely Planet* that Guaro is the national drink of Costa Rica. Attached is a selfie taken on a tropical beach. At first the beach appears to be shadowed by palm trees but, when I zoom in, I realise the sand is black. Do all beaches in Costa Rica have volcanic sand? I Google "black sandy beaches Costa Rica". The top result is "Playa Negra– a surfers' paradise". If Angel's still in Costa Rica, perhaps I can track her down? Further searches reveal two beaches named Playa Negra, located on opposite coasts. My heart sinks. I'm booked into a hotel on the Pacific coast, but I do have free cancellation…

I spend another thirty minutes exploring options before I lose Wi-Fi completely.

'It's stopped working,' I tell the guy behind the counter.

He shrugs. 'Try again later.'

Back outside, I leave the bike where it is and stroll along the road. Three doors away is a café and I head inside.

'Diet Coke, *por favor.*'

'Six-fifty,' says the woman serving.

I take the can, and I'm about to sit down when I spot a peg board displaying various advertisements. I scan the posters. *Extreme hikes to Cerro Chato.* That rings a bell… the flyer shows a picture of an emerald-green lagoon.

'Where is this?' I ask the woman.

'Cerro Chato, the crater lake.'

The neighbouring crater mentioned in Si's blog.

Pulling my mobile from my bag, I tap in the phone number on the flyer. '*Hola.* Do you speak English?'

'Yep.' His accent is North American.

'I see you offer private tours to Cerro Chato?'

'We do.'

'I'm looking for a guide to take me to the Arenal crater.'

'We don't do that. It's illegal.'

Shit, this conversation would be better in person. 'Do you have an office where I could come and speak to someone about private tours?'

'Avenue 321.'

'Thanks.'

I finish my Coke and head back out into the sun. It doesn't take long to locate Extreme Hiking – a small wooden hut with a rusty jeep parked outside. A tattooed guy, more Hell's Angel than tour guide, mans the desk.

'*Buenos dias,*' I say. 'I spoke to you on the phone.'

He glances up. 'The lady who wants to go to the crater.'

'Yes. Can I ask how much?'

He raises an eyebrow. 'How old are you?'

I stick out my chin. 'I hardly think that's…'

'The climb to Cerro Chato is serious hiking – steep slopes, muddy ravines.'

'But it goes to the crater? The one with the green lake?'

'You catch glimpses of the lake, but the last part of the trail is closed. Folks venture further at their own risk.'

'I'm prepared to take that risk. I'm reasonably fit.'

He snorts. 'No way I'm taking you up there. It's tough as an army assault course.'

'Well, actually, it was the Arenal crater I really wanted to get to.'

He throws back his head and roars with laughter. 'Man, you're a hoot!'

'I have money.' I tap my shoulder bag.

He glances over his shoulder before lowering his voice. 'I'll tell you something for nothing. Don't go telling strangers you're carrying money. There are cowboys who would take it from you in a heartbeat, leaving you stranded.' He sighs. 'Look, you seem like a nice lady, but you're a tourist, not a hiker. Why don't you take one of the rainforest and lava plains tours? Your hotel will help you out with that.'

'It's the crater I need to get to. In memory of my brother.' Tears prick the back of my eyes. 'I've come so far…'

He shrugs. 'Hundred and fifty dollars. And don't say I didn't warn you.'

On the way back to Finca Cacao I stop at a soda with free Wi-Fi where I feast on *gallo pinto* and chicken. After using my phone to make alternative hotel and travel arrangements, I'm feeling smug as I linger over a platter of fresh fruit.

By the time a second delicious cup of coffee arrives, doubts are creeping in. Am I about to embark on a fools errand? Costa Rica's a big place. What possible chance do I have of tracking Angel down?

CHAPTER FORTY-TWO

Pedro drops me at Extreme Hiking, where Tattoo Guy's loading up the jeep with supplies.

He glances at me. 'Punctual, I like that.'

I wait patiently while he checks the contents of his rucksack. Five minutes later, two guys wander up in shorts and hiking boots.

Tattoo Guy straightens up. 'Right, it's just the three of us. Let's get introductions out of the way. I'm Raul.'

The guy with a beard has an Australian accent. 'Hi. I'm Pete and this is Stewie.' He claps his companion on the back.

They turn to me.

'Sarah,' I say.

'Chuck your things in the back and climb aboard,' says Raul. 'We've got a long day ahead.'

'Give me that,' says Pete.

My sky-blue rucksack looks ridiculously girlie beside the guys' serious backpacks, and I feel my cheeks flush with embarrassment.

Pete rides shotgun, leaving Stewie and I to clamber into

the back. The jeep heads off at speed and I hang onto the roof strap to prevent myself rolling about.

At The National Park, Raul pulls up beside the Observatory Lodge and we pile out.

Pete shields his eyes, surveying Arenal in the clouds above us. 'How far is the lake?'

'Two-and-a half-kilometres,' says Raul.

'That's not so bad,' says Stewie.

'Bad enough.' Raul turns to address me. 'Water and lunch is included' – he pats his backpack – 'you want to leave your bag here?'

'No thanks.' I slide my rucksack onto my back and step out determinedly. I'm pleased I decided not to bring the heavy urn. Instead, I decanted some of Si's ashes into an old juice bottle, funnelling it in with a cone made from the A4 plastic wallet that had contained my travel documents.

Even from the start, the trail through the rain forest is steep. We've only gone a few hundred metres and I'm already puffing.

'Okay?' asks Raul.

I catch my breath. 'Fine.'

We pass giant ferns and cross dry lava beds, and soon I'm bringing up the rear. Everything is green – trees, plants, moss. In places, our way is blocked by fallen boughs covered in creepers, while all around, water trickles and wind whispers through the leaves.

'All right?' calls Raul. 'We're just coming to the hard part.'

'Great,' I mutter through gritted teeth. God, Si, I hope you appreciate this.

We pass through gullies of clay so hard it could be rock. On we go, clambering over boulders and navigating ankle-deep mud. Pete and Stewie leap across like giants, but for me, much shorter, the steps are higher and the stretches further. Trees tower above and unfamiliar birds mock me from high in the canopy.

'Almost there,' calls Raul, for perhaps the twentieth time since we started out. 'We'll take a break in a minute.'

Arriving in a clearing, I'm reassured to see Pete and Stewie panting too. Raul rifles around in his backpack for water bottles and hands them out.

I swig mine back and wipe my mouth. 'Water never tasted so good,' I quip.

After an energy bar and ten-minute break, we're off again. This time I do my best to keep up, ignoring grazed knees and trying not to freak out at the size of the ants. It's just an obstacle course, I tell myself, grateful for the grip on my hiking shoes. But it's harder than the Tough Mudder Nicki and I did for charity last summer.

'Almost there,' calls Raul. If I was closer, I'd slap him. All I want to do is curl into a ball. Perhaps they could collect me on the way down?

As I haul myself up to join the others on a rocky promontory, Raul points through the trees. 'There, you can see the crater.'

'A guy at our hostel told us the trail is closed at the top,' says Stewie.

Raul nods. 'There's a way through though, if you're happy to take it at your own risk.'

'Sure thing,' says Pete. 'Haven't come all this way not to swim in the bloody crater.' He slaps Stewie on the back and they laugh.

We gulp down more water and I examine the worst of my insect bites and abrasions.

Raul stows the bottles in his rucksack. 'The next bit is tougher.'

Tougher? My God, I'll never make it.

Up we go. Now we're essentially climbing, seeking footholds between roots and ledges. Thirty minutes later, we come to a halt.

I stare at the sign ahead. *Trail closed. No access to Cerro Chato. Do not pass this point.*

Pete and Stewie turn to Raul. He moves forward and steps over the fence. The other guys follow. I stare in dismay. The barrier's as high as my chest.

'If you work your way to your left, there's an easier place to cross,' says Raul. 'You guys go on up to the ridge. When you get to the top, make your way down the ravine as best you can.'

'Hope the swim is worth it,' calls Pete, already disappearing up the overgrown track ahead.

Raul points to my left. 'This way,' he says, moving in the same direction on his side of the fence.

Sure enough, a little further down, a fallen branch aids access. He offers his hand, but I brush it away. 'I'm okay.'

It takes another twenty minutes to ascend to the rim of the crater. I stand on the ridge and look down. 'Christ, it's a sheer drop.'

'Two hundred metres,' says Raul.

Through the trees I glimpse green and, down below, Pete and Stewie are whooping and yelling as they splash about in the water.

Raul searches for a cut down to the lake. 'There's no elegant way to do this,' he says. 'I suggest sliding on your bum.'

He goes first, presumably to break my fall if I should slip.

By the time we get to the tiny beach, I'm scratched to pieces. The lake ripples gently, a silent green lagoon. Pete and Stewie have stopped larking about and are floating in the water.

'It's got a high mineral content and it's damn cold, but I guess this is what you came for?' Raul shakes his head. 'I have to say, there were times when I didn't think you'd make it.'

'Me neither.' I allow myself a laugh. Crouching down, I cup water in my hands and pour it over my battered limbs. It's icy cold but feels delicious.

Raul moves away to set out our lunch on a large rock.

'Come on in,' yells Pete. 'The water's lovely.' Stewie ducks him and he shrieks.

'Well, I have come all this way…' I unlace my boots, take off my socks and step into the water. It's bloody freezing! It takes a few moments to get used to it enough to lower myself in but, when I do, Pete and Stewie whoop in congratulation.

I swim a few strokes before glancing back at the shingle beach. Raul is watching me.

The water is too cold to stay in long, so I work my way to the edge and clamber up on the rocks. Pete and Stewie are still goofing around.

'Aren't you going to swim?' I ask Raul.

'In a minute. I like to have at least one person on dry land in case there's a problem.' He gestures to the picnic – sandwiches, fruit and water. 'Have some lunch.'

I help myself to a sandwich and sit on the rock watching Pete and Stewie. They're like a couple of kids and I can't help smiling. Si would love this.

When they come out for their food, Raul jumps in for a quick dip. This is my chance. Grabbing my rucksack, I move away from the lads. Hopefully they'll think I've gone for a pee.

Concealed behind the undergrowth, I retrieve the juice bottle with Si's ashes, squat down between the rocks and unscrew the cap. 'Well Si, I didn't think I'd make it, but I have. This is a pretty good spot.' As I pour, clumps clog the neck of the bottle and several times I bang it against the edge of a rock. Empty at last, I stow it away.

When I get back to the others, Raul is out of the water and shaking himself like a dog.

'We'd better be heading back,' he says, packing away the remains of our picnic.

I gaze up at the steep slope. How the hell am I going to get back up?

Luckily, Raul knows the lay of the land and picks a trail which is challenging but not impossible. We clamber over the ridge and head back down. I stick close to Raul while Pete and Stewie dawdle behind. I guess the adrenaline that got them up is waning on the way back down.

'You did good,' says Raul as we near the bottom. 'You proved me wrong.'

'Thanks.' I smile.

We're heading for the jeep when Raul points to the hotel. 'You can grab an outdoor shower over there if you like.'

'Nah,' says Pete. 'The mud is a badge of honour.'

Badge of honour… that's what Si said. I feel a warm glow.

The guys are in high spirits as we head back to town.

'Come and have a beer,' says Pete.

I stumble wearily out of the jeep. My legs seem to have seized up on the short drive. 'Oh, I don't know…' I check my watch. Pedro's not due to pick me up for thirty minutes. 'Okay, sure.'

The four of us head for the nearest bar.

'Cheers.' Stewie clinks his beer glass against mine. 'You did good today.'

'For a Sheila,' quips Pete, with a wink.

I sip my beer contentedly. Tomorrow, I head for the ocean and begin my search for Angel. But tonight, I bask in a sense of achievement. Si, I did you proud.

CHAPTER FORTY-THREE

I'm woken by a knock and for a moment I'm disorientated. Where am I?

The key turns and a cleaning woman peeks around the door. '*Servicio de muscama.*'

'No, no,' I wave her away. 'No *gracias*. Come back later.'

I'm exhausted. On little more than a whim, I exchanged a two-bus journey from La Fortuna to Playa Esterillos, for a bus, domestic flight and second bus to Puerto Viejo de Talamanca. The journey of 350 kilometres had taken the entire day. Thankfully I hadn't lost money on accommodation.

I lay on my back watching the fan spin slowly around. At least this apartment has a fan. Unlike the cabin. I sigh. I'd said goodbye to Maria with a heavy heart. We hugged like old friends. I already miss her.

Dragging myself out of bed, I shower and root around in my suitcase for clean underwear, shorts and a T-shirt.

When I open the door, heat hits me like an oven. I thought the ocean breeze would cool the air, but it's hot. Children's shrieks suggest a pool nearby. Shielding my eyes, I glance around to get my bearings before heading for the main building.

'Breakfast?' I ask the guy on reception.

He points to the clock and waves his hands. '*Esta terminado.*'

'Okay,' I say. 'In town?'

He nods, dismissing me to attend to another guest.

I wander outside where a cacophony of noise and colour invades my senses. Restaurants and small souvenir shops sprawl onto a street, lined both sides by haphazardly parked vehicles. Bicycles of all type weave between potholes at breakneck speed.

Ding, ding. I leap back to avoid being mown down by a cyclist with a surfboard tucked under his arm. Finding myself outside a colourful Caribbean café, I retreat inside to order coffee.

'Breakfast?' I ask hopefully. The waiter places a menu on my table.

I order *gallo pinto*, with a side of eggs.

The phone signal's rubbish, so I compose a quick text to Jamie.

> Sorry love. Got here really late last night and slept in this morning. Anyway, arrived safely at the coast and just enjoying a late breakfast – or is it brunch? Speak later. xx

I stare out of the window, watching couples stroll arm in arm and families laden with beach paraphernalia. I'm in paradise and yet I've never felt so alone.

The waiter returns with my food.

'*Gracias.*' I'm getting used to this traditional Costa Rican breakfast but it's filling, and I only manage half before pushing my plate away.

I've not managed to speak to Nicki. I wonder what she's doing back home. Is she regretting not coming? I gesture for the bill. I can't sit around here all day. I've got the last of Si's ashes to scatter, and I need to concentrate on finding Angel.

On heading down to the beach, I'm disappointed to find not black sand, but yellow sand streaked with mud. 'More like Littlestone,' I grumble to myself, but at least it's not as boggy. I wander past small wooden boats, where a couple of huge birds squabble over fish remains. They're too big for seagulls… my God, are they vultures?

The beach stretches ahead, sandwiched between ocean one side and jungle the other. A brown-and-white dog bounds up, wagging his tail and I bend to pet him. 'Hello, where did you come from?' Glancing around, I spot his owner walking my way. She whistles and the dog hurtles back to her. Brodie would love it here.

I pass the wreck of a ship, its flat wooden deck protruding above the waves. It must have been here years, as a tree has grown up through one end. Two figures kitted out with snorkels and flippers waddle down the beach. I pause to watch as they reach the water, wade in and swim towards the hulk.

Every few hundred metres, a hand-painted sign advertises accommodation or surfing lessons. The signs coincide with more heavily populated areas, where sun worshippers too hot or lazy to make their way to a less crowded spot lounge on sun beds beneath palm leaf canopies.

I slow down, surreptitiously scouring the oiled bodies. Could Angel be here? As I plod on, the sand becomes grainier and more consistently black. Heat radiates up, scorching my legs, and I'm grateful I wore socks and trainers rather than flipflops. Good job Wendy didn't come. She'd be moaning like mad.

My mouth is parched, and I cast around for a beach bar. Shading my eyes from the glaring sun, I spot a young man sitting cross-legged under a tree.

He grins at me. *'Pipa fria?'*

The cooler beside him looks promising. Is he selling ice cream?

Opening the lid of the cooler box, he extracts a coconut.

'Oh, okay. How much?' I ask.

'One dollar.'

I pull a coin from my shorts pocket.

With practised dexterity he swings a machete, hacks off the top of the coconut and inserts a straw.

'Gracias.' I take the coconut and sip. I've never had fresh coconut water before. It's deliciously refreshing. My attention is drawn by a flurry of activity under the trees where a gaggle of small children point excitedly into the branches.

'What is it?' I ask the vendor.

He shrugs. 'Monkey? Sloth?'

After finishing my drink, I check the time on my mobile. Two-fifteen. I've been out for hours. This is hopeless – like searching for a needle in a haystack. There must be a better way to track down Angel.

I'm flagging as I stagger up the beach to my hotel. A beach bar is open and a dark-haired waiter with Latino good looks turns to smile. 'What can I get you, *senorita*?'

'Diet Coke please.'

He fills a glass with ice and adds a slice of lemon.

'Thanks.' The glass drips with condensation as I lift it to my lips. So good.

The bartender gestures along the beach. 'A little hot for walking.'

'Too hot. I walked to Playa Negra.'

He nods. 'Many tourists like to see the black sands.'

'Yes.' Nearby, a couple are vacating a small table with a sunshade. I signal to the barman that I'm not doing a runner and move across to claim it. Slowly I sip my drink while looking out to sea.

Two boys are making their way along the beach. They must be selling something as they're getting short shrift from the families they approach. As they get closer, their words reach my ears. 'Beautiful waterfalls…'

Perhaps I need to look further afield for Angel? I lift a hand. 'Wait. Are you selling excursions?'

'Yes, lady,' says the tallest boy, who can't be more than twelve. 'I make you good deal.'

'Where to?'

'Amazing day. Country park, waterfall and kayak. You like chocolate, lady? I do special deal. One hundred dollar, including tax.'

The younger boy hands me a scrappy piece of paper.

I scan the poster, type-written and amateurish. 'This includes transport? From the hotel?' I point to the apartment complex.

'Yes, lady. Everything included. You wanna book?'

'I'll think about it.'

'You book now, lady, and I give you special deal. Lunch included.'

'She said she'll think about it.'

I turn my head to see the handsome barman glaring at the lads.

'I come back later, lady,' says the older boy, and the two lads scamper away.

'Rip off merchants,' says the bartender. 'Take your money and don't turn up.'

'Thanks.'

'You want a top up?'

'No, I think I'll head back to my room.' I move towards the bar. 'What do I owe you?'

'You're a guest here? Give me your room number and I'll open you a tab.'

'Apartment 35. Cheers.' I step away, then turn back. 'So, if I did want to book an excursion, where's the best place to do that?'

He nods towards the hotel. 'Reception will sort you out.'

There's been a shift change and a young woman now mans the desk. As I approach, she offers me a welcoming smile. 'Can I help you?'

'I hope so. I'm interested in booking an excursion to local places of interest.'

'Certainly.' She reaches below the desk and takes out a folder. 'There are several options. We offer full and half-day excursions. I recommend a visit to Cahuita National Park. It's on offer at the moment. Fifty dollars.' She hands me a bundle of fliers.

'Great, thanks. I'll take a look.'

I head back to my room. After emptying my trainers of black sand, I lay down on the bed and thumb through the fliers.

Cahuita National Park is one of the oldest national parks of Costa Rica founded in 1970 to protect the coral reef. Because of its white sand beaches, large number of coconut palms, turquoise sea and coral reef, this is a spot you do not want to miss. You will meet white faced monkeys, sloths, snakes, raccoons and numerous other different types of species that you will be able to observe and learn about. After the hiking in Cahuita, you will go to an amazing waterfall where you will be able to swim.

It sounds gorgeous. Surely Angel would have made a visit there? I flick through the other leaflets, then stop abruptly. A leopard up a tree. Just like the one on the postcard. The flier advertises an animal rescue centre. It's not a leopard, but a jaguar. I scan through the history of the place. They're proud of their animal conservation credentials. With her environmental background, that would appeal to Angel.

Slipping on flip-flops, I hurry back to reception. 'I'd like to visit this place.'

The receptionist takes the flier. 'Ah yes. Good choice. But you can purchase tickets for the Animal Rescue Centre for twenty-five dollars at the gate.'

'How far away is it?'

'About five kilometres. We can order you an Uber.'

'Great.'

'When did you want to go?'

'Tomorrow?'

'Sure. Guided tours are nine-thirty and eleven-thirty. You need to arrive at least fifteen minutes before.'

I shower and change before heading to the restaurant for dinner. When the waiter realises I'm dining alone, he discreetly removes the second set of cutlery, but I stick out like a sore thumb amid honeymoon couples and groups of friends. With no one to talk to, I rush through my meal, eager to escape for an evening stroll.

Using the torch on my mobile to light my way, I wander down to the beach. It's cooler now and the air filled with the smell of grilled fish and reggae music. The coarse sand is illuminated like a million tiny stars under my feet. A little way from the hotel, I stumble across a beach party – young people dancing salsa, while others laugh and chat, passing around a wine bottle. I feel old – old and vanilla.

Turning back, I head for the beach bar where the same guy is on duty. He's mixing drinks for a young couple. His display reminds me of a bird's mating dance as he throws cocktail mixers and bottles in the air before catching and pouring. He could be Tom Cruise.

When he's finished entertaining the punters, he moves towards me, raising a quizzical eyebrow.

'Diet Coke, please,' I say.

He shakes his head. 'You look as if you need something stronger.'

'No, I want to keep a clear head for my trip tomorrow.'

'Have a mocktail then.' He taps his nose. 'Let me surprise you.'

I laugh. 'Okay.'

He goes through as much of a rigmarole making my mocktail as he did for the genuine cocktails. When he's finished, he pours pink liquid into a glass, topping it off with an umbrella and setting it on a coaster. Si would love this!

I lean forward to take a sip. 'Mmm, that's delicious.'

'You booked an excursion then?'

'Yes.' I pull the flier from my handbag. 'Took your advice and went the bona fide route.'

He takes the leaflet and scans it. 'Good choice.'
'You've been to the Animal Rescue Centre?'
'Of course.'
'It's worth a visit?'
'Sure.'

I take another sip of mocktail, suddenly a little giddy. 'Are you sure there's no alcohol in this?'

'Definitely virgin.'

Virgin, vanilla… I sigh. 'What's your name anyway?'

'Mateo.'

'You know what, Mateo? I think I will have something stronger. I'll try a *Guaro Sour*.'

Mateo juggles three limes, before muddling slices with sugar syrup, adding Guaro, filling the glass with ice and topping with a sprig of mint.

'Gracias.' I taste it while he waits expectantly. 'It's nice. A bit like rum…'

Leisurely, I sip my drink as Mateo closes up for the night. As I slide from my stool, the sand shifts and I'm momentarily destabilised. I waggle a finger. 'You know, Mateo, if I'm not happy with this tour, you're going to owe me a drink.'

He leans closer, eyes twinkling. 'I guarantee, *senorita*, you'll be fully satisfied.'

CHAPTER FORTY-FOUR

The Uber driver sweeps under the archway. 'Animal Rescue Centre.'

'Thank you.' I hand him some notes. 'Can you come back and collect me?'

'What time, lady?'

'Three o'clock?'

'Sure.' He pulls away and a cloud of dust is thrown up from his tyres.

Brushing myself off, I walk towards the entrance. '*Hola*. Please can I buy a ticket?'

The woman takes my money before glancing at a clock on the wall of her kiosk. 'Next tour starts eleven-thirty.'

'Thanks.'

I move away to read the information board. Apparently, the rescue centre opened in 2006, and has been rescuing and reintroducing animals to their natural habitat ever since.

A young girl with orange braids appears at my side. 'Hi. You here for the tour?'

'Yes.'

'Great.' She beams. Her nose is covered in freckles, and she reminds me of *Pippi Longstocking*. 'I'm your guide. We'll give it another ten minutes and then we'll be off.'

'You're English? Whereabouts are you from?'

She giggles. 'Leamington Spa. I'm just here as a volunteer - a prerequisite of the uni degree I'm starting in September.'

'And do you like it?'

'I've only been here a week but I love spending time with the animals. Mind you,' – she leans forward to whisper – 'I do spend a lot of time slicing vegetables.'

An older couple pay at the kiosk and glance about nervously. Pippi bounces over to them. 'Welcome. We'll be off in just a few minutes. If you need the loo, it's in that building over there.'

The older lady shrugs off her rucksack and wanders across to use the conveniences. Meanwhile, a guy with a camera slung around his neck pays for a ticket and joins us.

Pippi checks her watch.

The lady returns and her husband helps her back on with her rucksack.

'Okay,' says Pippi. 'Welcome to the Animal Rescue Centre founded in 2006…' She proceeds to recite the wording on the notice board as she heads through a gate and into the compound.

'You'll find this tour unlike any animal experience you've had before. Here you'll be in close proximity with monkeys, wild cats, sloths and more. Guided by professionals' – her cheeks blush modestly – 'who have extensive training with our animals, you will see things you wouldn't even have known to look for and learn things you could never imagine.'

The rescue centre is impressive. I'd expected a zoo, but

this is more like a hospital. Pippi hands us over to a charismatic animal doctor called Alejo, who gives us a private tour of the medical centre. He's knowledgeable and very attentive.

Around the animal compounds there seem to be more volunteers than staff, but they're friendly, wisely deferring to more experienced staff members when our questions are beyond them. I'd never seen a sloth before, and they really are the cutest creatures imaginable.

Pippi encourages us to stroke a baby monkey rescued from a forest fire. 'Most of the other animals can't be petted as it might prevent re-entry into their natural habitat.'

The guy with the camera clicks away throughout.

'How long do the animals stay with you?' asks the older lady.

'It varies. We try to keep them for as short a time as possible, but some are badly injured and stay much longer. It's harder then to set them free.'

The tour lasts a couple of hours with stop-offs at various enclosures. When we've finished, Pippi walks us back to the entrance. 'There's a café if you'd like to buy refreshments, and a donation tin if you'd like to make a contribution to support our work.'

The small group burst into spontaneous applause and Pippi's cheeks glow with pleasure.

I wait until the others have gone before sidling up to her. 'Thank you. That was very educational.'

'You're welcome.'

I pull out my phone. 'I know you've only been here a few days, but I wonder if you could take a look at this photo.' I scroll through to find the picture of Angel and Si that Daniel gave me. 'This is a friend of mine. She may have visited. Do you remember seeing her?'

Pippi looks at the screen. 'She's very pretty. No, I don't know her, but I could ask Carlos. He's been a volunteer here, like, forever.'

'I'd be very grateful.'

She smiles and heads back into the enclosure. I follow as she leads the way to a tepee where several members of staff and volunteers are congregating for a late lunch. Pippi approaches a tanned guy sporting the rescue centre's logo on his T-shirt. I wait outside as she speaks with him. He follows her back out and I pass him my phone.

'Yeah.' He runs his fingers through his sun-bleached hair. 'That's Angie.'

My heart skips. 'You know her?'

'She works for us.'

'She works here?' My pulse quickens. 'Is she working today?'

'No, she's away this week, assessing the sea turtle beaches at Tortuguero. Nice girl is Angie. Want me to tell her you're looking for her?'

'No.'

My answer is abrupt, and Carlos shoots me a look.

'Sorry, but no. She's a good friend and I want to surprise her. Do you know when she'll be back?'

Carlos turns around and calls to his work colleagues. 'Hey, any of you lot know when the Tortuguero expedition returns?'

'Tomorrow, I think,' someone yells.

'Thanks, mate.' Carlos turns back to me. 'You got that?'

'Yes, thank you. Do you know if Angie's staying on site?'

'Nah. She's got a cabin on the beach at Playa Cocles. It's the surfing beach.' Carlos turns and wanders back to his colleagues.

Pippi walks me to the entrance.

'If you see Angie, don't say I've been asking,' I say, conspiratorially. 'It's a surprise.'

Pippi puts a finger to her lips. 'Mum's the word.'

My mind's in a whirl as I wait for the Uber. Angel's here, and tomorrow I'll see her.

CHAPTER FORTY-FIVE

I hire a bike from reception for the four-kilometre ride to Playa Cocles. As I near the resort, a red flag warns that the area is unsafe for swimming. I can immediately see why. Huge waves crash against the white beach, while daredevil surfers run into the water, flinging themselves headlong into breakers. Beautiful bodies are spread out on towels and suntanned girls wander between them selling jewellery. It's a young person's paradise.

Propping up my bike outside a beach bar, I head inside.

The bartender looks up. *'Buenas tardes.'*

'*Hola.*' I perch on a bar stool. 'Could I get a Diet Coke please?' I remove my sunhat as he pours my drink. '*Gracias.*' The glass is full of ice and the first sip tickles my nose.

I pull my mobile from my shoulder bag. 'I don't know if you can help me, but I'm looking for my friend.'

The bartender stops wiping the counter.

Opening the photos app. I scroll to the picture of Angel and Si.

He barely glances. *'No se.'*

'She lives in a cabin near the ocean. Do you know where that might be?'

He shrugs. 'Perhaps *cabanas de vacaciones?*'

'Where are they?'

He gestures along the beach. *'Un kilometro.'*

'Gracias.' I finish my drink and head back outside.

The sun is hot as I cycle along the road. Passing a wooden sign, I skid to a halt. *Vista al Oceano.* Underneath someone has scrawled the word – *cabanas.* This must be it. Dismounting, I wheel the bike across a sandy drive leading towards the beach.

The cabins are a little run down. I can't imagine any holiday maker being overjoyed to discover this is their accommodation, but perhaps the young surfers aren't bothered. Although identical, the wooden shacks have been personalised by the addition of brightly coloured curtains, rugs and plants and, judging from the assortment of swimming costumes and towels left out to dry, most are occupied.

Parking my bike against a wooden railing, I make my way along the row. The sand's ferociously hot, it's like traipsing across the Sahara and I'm grateful again that I'm wearing trainers. I scrutinise each terrace, but I've no idea which cabin is Angel's. A couple of lads head towards me with surfboards under their arms and I raise a hand in greeting. '*Hola.* Do you speak English?'

The shorter of the two nods.

'I'm looking for my friend.' I gesture to the huts. 'She lives in one of these cabins – *cabana* – but I don't know which is hers.'

Both lads look at the photo. The taller one says something in Spanish and the shorter nudges him and laughs before turning to me. '*No lo siento.* Can't help.'

I plod on, grains of sand flicking up to burn my ankles.

A woman steps out of a hut to bang a rug against the veranda railing.

'Excuse me…' I begin.

Ignoring me, she turns and hurries back inside.

Coming to a halt under a palm tree, I swig from my water bottle. The back of my neck prickles as I sense I'm being watched and spin around to see a boy sitting outside the hut the cleaning woman disappeared into.

'*Hola.*' I smile.

'Hello,' he replies.

'You speak English?'

'*Un poco.*'

I head towards him. 'Is that your mother?'

'*Si.* She not speak English good like me.' He pats his chest with pride.

I hold out my mobile. 'I'm looking for someone…'

The boy snatches it and for a moment I think he's going to steal it, but he simply taps the screen. '*Si.*'

'You know this lady?'

He jabs again. '*Si.*'

I gesture to the row of huts. 'Which cabin? *Que cabana?*'

He gives back my phone, takes my hand and drags me along the beach.

'Wait, slow down.'

Fifty metres along he stops, pointing at a cabin with two faded chairs on the decking.

'This one?'

'*Si, senora.*'

'*Gracias,*' I say.

He opens his palm.

'Oh, okay.' I fumble in my bag and retrieve a couple of coins. 'Thank you.'

The boy grabs the money and scampers back to his mother.

I step onto the veranda and try the door. It's locked. It looks as though, with a bit of a shove, I could force it, but I don't. Instead, I peer through faded yellow curtains. Inside is better than I expected. Quite cosy, in fact, with a small kitchen area, double bed, colourful throws and multi-coloured cushions. I sit outside on one of the old rattan chairs to wait.

An hour later, I've finished my water and wishing I'd bought something to eat. I could go back to the beach bar, but then I might miss her. A silk scarf is draped across the chair beside me. I lift it up, hold it to my nose and close my eyes. *Black Opium*. I'd know her perfume anywhere.

Another hour passes. As the heat drops, wind blows in from the ocean and I wrap myself in a blanket. This is stupid. She might not be home for hours and I don't fancy riding back in the dark.

I retrieve my bike and head back to my apartment.

Next morning, I'm up early to cycle back to Playa Cocles. My heart's racing as I tap on Angel's door, but there's no answer. I peer through the cloudy glass spotting a cup on the draining board that wasn't there yesterday. On the floor beside the bed is an overnight bag.

Damn it. Why didn't I wait longer last night? She could be anywhere now. I cycle along to the beach bar. As I pump the pedals with sea air in my face, my mood lightens. Perhaps she's gone for provisions? I'll treat myself to breakfast and try again.

As I cross the threshold of the beach bar, I stop dead. A

red-haired woman in a shady hat is seated at one of the small tables. I can't move.

The bartender sets a cup of coffee on her table.

'*Gracias,*' drawls Angel.

Turning away, he spots me. Recognising me from yesterday, he shoots a quick glance in Angel's direction before saying in a loud voice. 'You want breakfast?'

Angel looks around. Our eyes meet and I register her surprise. 'Sarah?'

My legs wobble as I approach her table.

She recovers before me. 'My friend will be joining me. *Mas café por favor.*'

I ease myself down on the chair opposite. 'Is it really you?'

Her eyes sparkle. Amusement? God, even in this heat she looks fabulous. I smooth down my own windswept hair.

The bartender returns with a jug of coffee and a second cup.

'*Gracias, Hugo*.' She pronounces it OO-goh. I watch as she pours coffee, a small smile playing on her lips. 'So, you found me.'

I nod, not sure I ever truly believed I'd see her again.

'You want breakfast?' She gestures to a plate of pancakes. 'Hugo's *chorreadas* are second to none.'

I shake my head. Reaching forward, I lift my cup. The coffee's stronger than I like and I grimace.

Angel studies me. 'I can't believe you came all this way.' Is that admiration in her eyes?

I set down my cup. 'I came to scatter Si's ashes on Arenal.'

'Arenal?' Her expression changes to bewilderment. 'But how did you…?'

'The picture on Si's wall, plus his blog. Arenal was a volcano he really wanted to visit.'

'How clever you are.' She cradles her cup like a bowl. 'It's great to see you, Sarah. How long are you here for?'

'Three more days.'

'Well, I'm delighted you looked me up. Perhaps we can grab a meal together before you go back?'

Her words are a stab in the heart. I've travelled halfway across the world and she might squeeze me in for a meal?

She glances at her watch. 'Actually Sarah, I'm sorry but I've got to go.'

She gestures for the bill, but Hugo waves his hand dismissively. '*Manana.*'

'Look, come and find me tomorrow. Hugo will explain where I live.' She leans across to air kiss me. 'I'll fix lunch and we can have a good old catch-up.'

I touch my finger to my cheek where her lips almost grazed my skin. She's gone.

CHAPTER FORTY-SIX

'*Gracias.*' I hand the Uber driver a note. 'No, keep it,' I say, as he rifles through a pouch in search of change. 'Can you pick me up around four?'

He mutters something under his breath.

'Sorry?'

'Four o'clock sharp. I have evening work. I can't wait.'

'Okay.' I clamber out of the car taking care not to drop the bottle of wine. My tummy's fluttering as I walk along to Angel's cabin. Stop it, I chide myself. This isn't a date.

Her door is propped open and I trot up the steps to the decking, calling a cheery *'Hola.'*

She rushes out to greet me, grasping my hands in hers. 'Sarah. I can't believe you're really here.'

I hold out the wine. 'Rioja. Hope it's okay.'

'I'm sure it will be. Sit down and relax.' She heads inside. 'Lunch is nearly ready.'

I get comfortable in one of the rattan chairs, now furnished with colourful fringed throws.

She returns with two glasses of wine. 'We'll eat out here. There's no room inside and anyway…' She waves expansively to where, not fifty metres from the deck, frothy waves lap against grainy sand.

'This view is fantastic.'

'I think I was in shock yesterday,' she calls, going inside again.

'Me too. I didn't really expect to find you.'

She returns with the food. 'So, you *were* looking for me?'

'Thanks.' I take a bowl. 'This smells amazing.'

'*Arroz con camarones.*' She winks. 'Shrimps and rice. A local classic.'

I taste a forkful. 'It's delicious.'

'Thanks.' She sits beside me and tries it herself. 'So, you were saying? You were looking for me?'

Of course I was looking for you, I want to scream. Instead, I play it cool. 'Valentina mentioned she'd had a postcard, so…'

'Oh fuck.' Angel laughs. 'I might have known she couldn't keep a secret.'

Her words sting. She didn't want me to know where she was. 'I had to come.' I set down my fork, reach for my shoulder bag and extract an envelope.

'What's that?'

'A cheque. The taxman sent Si a rebate. Twelve hundred pounds.'

She snorts with laughter. 'You've come all the way out here to give me that? Keep it. Consider it as costs towards scattering the ashes.'

Along the beach a fisherman drags his boat out of the water. My heart's racing. 'Why didn't you tell me you were leaving? We didn't even get to say goodbye.'

She shrugs. 'It all happened rather quickly. I'd written to the Rescue Centre and suddenly received a reply offering me an internship. I'm sorry, but it was a chance in a lifetime.'

'So, Costa Rica wasn't just Si's dream?'

'No.' She raises her glass. 'To friendship.'

I chink my glass against hers. 'Friendship,' I reply.

She nods at my bowl. 'Eat up. Plenty more in the pan.'

With bellies full, we linger, listening to waves lapping against the sand. 'I could stay here forever,' I murmur.

'More wine?' Angel tops up our glasses.

'Thanks.' The Rioja's not bad. 'So, tell me about your job at the Rescue Centre.'

'It's an internship, but if it goes well, they might keep me on.'

'A bit of a change from your previous career.'

She grins. 'You know my background. I always had an interest in protecting the environment, managing natural resources, conservation of wildlife…'

'So, you're their lawyer?'

'I'm offering legal advice, pro bono.'

'And no plans to return to the UK?'

'Not right now. *Carpe diem.* Grab life's chances when you can.'

'Perhaps that's what I should do?'

Her eyes widen. 'What?'

I sit forward, sincerity oozing from every pore. 'Seize the day. Things have changed since you left. Tom and I broke up.' My words come out in a rush. 'Suppose I stayed here? Could I find work?'

For a moment she doesn't respond. I try to read her face. She looks horrified. Then she's laughing, not *with* me but *at* me. 'You? In Costa Rica?' Chuckling, she picks up the dishes and steps inside the cabin. 'Honestly, Sarah,' she calls. 'You're a scream!'

My heart sinks like a stone. How could I have been so stupid? When I make my excuses and leave, she seems relieved.

Back at the hotel, I curl up on my bed, hugging myself. Angel doesn't care about me. Neither does Tom. I couldn't even find anyone to come to Costa Rica with me. What am I going to do with the rest of my life?

At eight p.m. I haul myself up. I suppose I should eat dinner. I have little appetite, but at least it's something to do. After freshening up, I head for the dining room, where I order a starter and proceed to drown my sorrows with a bottle of red.

The waiter looks on with concern. 'Nothing more to eat, *senora*?'

'*No gracias.*' Stumbling from the table, I go in search of more booze.

Mateo's manning the beach bar, sexy and charming as ever. '*Buenas tardes, senorita.*'

'*Buenas tardes, Mateo.*'

I climb onto a bar stool and watch as he mixes a cocktail, which he presents to me in a coconut. 'How was your day?'

'Unexpected.' I take a sip. Man, this guy can make a drink. 'I had lunch with a friend. We sat by the ocean.' I lean across the bar. 'Are you jealous?'

'Of course. *Perdoname.*' He moves away to attend to a couple who've come for a nightcap. As he shows off his cocktail-making skills, the girl giggles and I'm irritated. Perhaps I'm jealous.

After serving them, he moves back to me, remaining close as he polishes glasses.

'You like to impress, don't you?' I say.

'But of course.' Noticing I've finished my cocktail, he prepares another, this time presented in a pineapple.

I take a sip. 'Mmm.'

When the couple leave, I kick off my sandals. 'It's quiet tonight.'

Mateo checks his watch. 'I close in ten minutes.'

'That's early.'

He nods towards the hotel. 'The bar in the hotel stays open until midnight.'

'But you finish earlier?'

'Yes.'

I survey the optics behind him. 'I was thinking about a nightcap…'

He raises that sexy eyebrow. 'I can offer room service?'

Wow! 'You'd need my room number.'

'I have your number.'

'So you do.' Biting my lip, I slide off the bar stool. As I bend to pick up my sandals, I almost topple over.

'You okay, *senorita*?' asks Mateo.

'I'm fine,' I slur, pointing my body in the general direction of my room.

After letting myself in, I panic. What the fuck am I doing, acting like some sort of femme fatale? Mateo's gorgeous, but almost young enough to be my son.

Opening the minibar, I grab a tiny bottle of gin and neck it before heading for the bathroom to brush my teeth. Hurrying back into the bedroom, I rifle through the drawer for my black lace undies. Stripping off my clothes, I pull on the sexier underwear, topping them off with a silky beach kimono. Kicking my dirty clothes under the bed, I bundle all my clutter – make-up, jewellery, ticket stubs – into the top drawer and straighten the sheets.

Knock, knock.

'Oh shit, oh shit.' With a final despairing glance around the room, I open the door. 'Come in.'

Mateo enters, carrying a silver tray with an ice bucket and two glass flutes. 'Champagne?' He winks as he sets the tray on the chest of drawers. In moments, he's popped the cork.

I take the proffered drink. 'Cheers.' I clink my glass against his before taking a sip. Bubbles tickle my nose. 'So, what happens now?'

'Whatever you want.' He sips champagne before setting down his glass. 'This is room service, *senorita*. What would you like me to do?'

I giggle. It all seems so ridiculous, like a cheap porn movie. 'Perhaps,' – I sit down on the bed – 'take off your shirt?'

His eyes are fixed on mine as he tugs his shirt over his head.

I stare admiringly at his tanned torso and firm pecs. I don't know him. His body is a landscape yet to be travelled. My heart beats fast. I should be so lucky…

'What now?' he whispers.

I hesitate. Is this really happening? 'Everything else?'

His smile is slow and sexy as he kicks off his shoes, unfastens his belt and yanks it from his jeans like a whip. Leaning across, he relieves me of my glass. I feel the bed give as he kneels on it. I close my eyes as he kisses my lips, my neck… I run fingers through his jet-black curls and breathe him in. His smell is intoxicating – fresh spring water and sea air, coconut, watermelon, with a tinge of roasted coffee beans.

My kimono slips open, and his lips seek my breasts, my

stomach, my inner thighs. I groan with pleasure as he deftly removes my knickers.

'Close your eyes,' he says.

I close them, trying to block out memories of Daniel and that tacky hotel in Brighton.

Gently he lowers me down. I gasp at the sudden shock of cold and open my eyes. 'Ice?'

'I wouldn't be a very good bartender if I ran out of ice.' He slides the ice cube around my nipples and down my belly, teasing as he goes lower. I close my eyes again and hold onto the bed head. The ice is melting. Transferring it to his mouth, he holds it between his teeth and slides it sensually down and around my belly. Oh God, I'm so turned on.

When the ice reaches down there, it's replaced by hot, quick licks of Mateo's expert tongue. Oh fuck, that's good!

I thrust my hips upwards, panting. God, I'm climaxing already. How does this guy know how to do this stuff? Does he do it for all the single female travellers? Fuck it, who cares!

As I lay gasping, he removes his jeans and jockey shorts. I open my eyes to stare at his erection.

He smiles lazily. Reaching for his jeans he extracts a condom from the back pocket.

'Wait.' I've never particularly enjoyed oral sex but, right now, before he puts that on, I want to take this beautiful man in my mouth and taste him.

CHAPTER FORTY-SEVEN

When I wake, Mateo's gone. I blush at the thought of last night – flashbacks of tumbling between the sheets, thighs wrapped tightly around his torso… I lost count of orgasms.

Wow, just wow!

After using the bathroom and tugging on shorts and a T-shirt, I take the urn from my rucksack and check its contents. About a quarter left. I need to get this job finished and get out of here. I shove the urn back in, slip on flip-flops and step outside.

It's early but, not wanting to risk bumping into Mateo, I work my way around the side of the hotel where a noisy truck is making a morning delivery.

Hurrying along the road, I'm greeted by a woman setting up a fruit stall. '*Hola*,' she calls.

'*Buenas dias*,' I reply, cutting down the side of another hotel a few doors along.

On reaching the beach, I slip off my flip-flops to paddle in shallow waves. I pass a solitary jogger and a woman in downward dog practising yoga. To my left, birds sing a morning chorus from the trees. Further along, men prepare boats for a fishing trip.

I wait until I'm a couple of hundred metres past the fishing boats before slipping the rucksack from my shoulders and sinking down onto the sandy beach. Taking out the urn, I unscrew the lid and peer inside. 'This is it, Si. The last of your ashes. I'm sorry I didn't manage to scatter them all on Arenal, but perhaps it's better this way. Now you're all over Costa Rica. You've travelled to Arenal, to Cerro Chato, the rain forest and the beach. Quite a tour. I like to think I've trodden the path you'd have taken if you were here.'

Near the water's edge, I dig a shallow hole with my hands, before emptying the last of the ashes into the hole. 'As the waves lap, they take you with them. Who knows where you'll travel. Bon voyage, bro. I love you.' Closing my eyes, I listen as the waves take Si on his final adventure.

Standing up, I screw the lid back on the urn. My stomach rumbles and I have the beginnings of a headache. Time for breakfast, I think, as I trudge back towards the hotel.

'Hola.'

I spin around to see a little boy. Isn't he the one who told me where to find Angel? What's he doing so far from Playa Cocles? *'Hola,'* I smile.

He catches up and walks alongside me. 'You found your friend, lady?'

'Yes. Thank you.'

He nods. 'You know her boyfriend, too?'

'Boyfriend?'

He strokes his chin. 'Man with beard.'

'Man with beard?'

'Yes. He nice man. He give me five dollar.'

Harry? Is that why Angel was so cool with me? I grab the boy's hand. 'When did you see the man?'

The boy pulls away, eyes wide.

'Sorry.' I crouch down to his level. 'You saw this man recently?' I take two coins from my purse and hold them out.

'Yes, lady.'

One of the fishermen by the boats waves frantically. *'Eduardo, dense prisa.'*

The boy waves back. '*Si Papi.*' With a grin, he snatches the coins and scampers away.

Angel said she didn't know Harry. What are they doing here together? My pulse quickens. Have I got this all wrong? Did they have something to do with Si's death?

I check the time – ten past ten. On the way back to the hotel, I pass a rubbish bin and drop the urn into it, before fetching the bike and cycling to the Rescue Centre.

My stomach rumbles. I should have had breakfast before beginning a stake-out, but I daren't leave now in case I miss her. It's lunchtime before Angel cycles out. I consider tackling her but instead decide to follow.

She cycles south along the coast road for two kilometres. At a sign saying Playa Chiquita, she turns right, away from the ocean.

I keep my distance as we leave the tourist area to cycle along a dirt track through the trees. After passing old buildings and a few shacks, she comes to a stop beside a two-storey building. It's dated and run down, and a peeling sign reads Hostel Mango.

Leaving her bike propped against the fence, she runs up a flight of bright yellow wooden stairs and disappears inside the building.

I hide behind a bush to wait. I can see the building from

here. Is she meeting Harry? Has she come to tell him I'm in Costa Rica? Does she think I'm going to cause trouble?

Twenty minutes later she emerges, running lightly down the steps to collect her bike. As she mounts and pedals towards me, I step out from the bushes.

She skids to a halt to avoid hitting me. 'Sarah. What are you doing here?'

The laugh that emerges from my mouth is not pleasant. 'What are *you* doing here is more to the point?'

Her eyes flit side to side. I move forward barring her way. 'If you think you're doing a runner, think again.'

She looks down at the dusty road. 'Look, Sarah, I don't know what you…'

'It's not just your dream you're living, then?'

She shakes her head. 'We're not together.'

I gasp. I'd expected her to deny it. 'What did you and Harry do?'

Her eyes grow wide. 'Sarah, you've got this all wrong.'

'So, set me straight.'

She sighs. 'It's probably best I show you.' Turning, she wheels her bike back to the building. I park mine alongside hers.

Angel leads the way up the stairs. At the top I hesitate, staring at a rusty number seven on the door. What the hell am I doing? I can't trust them. Supposing they grab me?

But it's too late. She's already knocking.

Footsteps. The door swings open. A familiar voice. 'What did you forget?'

My legs crumple; the ground sways.

"Sarah?' says my brother.

CHAPTER FORTY-EIGHT

I'm in a tiny bedsit, seated on a tatty old wooden chair. Bob Marley's 'Jammin' is playing on a transistor radio and it's like I've slipped through a time warp.

Si places a glass in my hands. 'Here, drink this.'

The brandy burns my throat and I gag. 'I'm going to be sick.'

He pushes my head down between my knees. When the nausea passes, I look up.

He looks rough – tanned, but his beard, always so immaculate, has grown out, giving him a Tom Hanks in C*astaway* appearance. He's also put on weight.

'What the fuck are you doing here, Sarah?' he says.

'What the fuck am *I* doing here? What the fuck are *YOU* doing here? In fact, Simon, what the fuck are you doing alive?'

He wipes the back of his hand across his mouth.

I stare about the room, furnished with old pieces that would be junk back home. Washing up is piled in the sink, while empty beer bottles litter the floor and the unmade bed looks as if the sheets haven't been washed in an age.

Si shifts a pile of dirty clothes from the only other chair and sits down.

'Where's Angel?' I ask.

'Giving us some space.' He gazes around as if seeing the room through my eyes. 'It's a bit of a dump, isn't it? Why don't we go for a walk.' Picking up keys and a bundle of loose change, he opens the door.

We head back along the dirt track – him pushing my bike, me walking alongside. Si's alive. Am I dreaming? This can't be happening.

I break the silence. 'So, you're out here living the dream?'

'It's not what I expected. I got myself clean though' – he laughs – 'apart from beer and a few recreational drugs.'

'Are you working?'

'The owner of the hostel gives me a few shifts in exchange for my room. I've become a dab hand at breakfasts.'

A sweet fragrance tickles my nostrils. 'What's that smell, gingerbread?'

'Molasses. They spread it over the dirt track to keep down the dust. Dries like tarmac.'

This is surreal.

We're almost at the ocean when Si props up my bike and heads into a beach café. We sit down at a table and the waiter comes across with menus.

'Dos cafes por favor,' says Si. 'You want something to eat?'

I'm lightheaded. I should eat but I shake my head. 'Not right now.'

'Okay.'

The waiter goes to fetch our drinks.

'Sarah,' says Si, 'it's so bloody good to see you.'

'Is that all you've got to say?'

'No, of course not.'

Our coffees arrive and Si stirs two sachets of sugar into his. 'I guess I have some explaining to do.'

'Just a bit.' I can't believe I'm sitting opposite my brother. 'Why, Simon?'

'Hang on, I think I'm going to need something stronger.' He waves at the waiter. *'Dos tragos de tequila.'* When the shots arrive, Si knocks one straight back before turning to me. 'Things got messy. I feared for my life.'

'Why didn't you tell me?'

'I tried. I really did, but everything was such a mess, I didn't know how or where to start.'

'You know you could tell me anything.'

'I couldn't.' He puts his hands over his face. 'I couldn't tell you about my… needs.' He peeks through splayed fingers. 'I couldn't admit what a fool I'd been with the gambling.' He takes his hands away. 'I tried to get help, even attended Gamblers Anonymous. What they don't tell you is how to get the villains off your back. The ones you owe money to.'

'So, you planned this?'

'That's the strange thing. I didn't plan, it just happened.' He wipes his brow. 'Things had gotten really bad. I was on self-destruct. When Harry had a heart attack…'

'*Harry* had a heart attack?'

'Yes, and I didn't know what to do. I sent the girls away so I could think. That's when I came up with the idea to…'

'Wait. I cremated Harry?'

He shrugs. 'I guess so, yes.'

'And you think that was fair to Harry? To his family?'

'What family? Harry didn't have anyone. Only me.'

'How did you know the police wouldn't find out it wasn't your body?'

'I was sure they would. I had to leave the country right away. If the police got wind that it was Harry and not me who'd died, they'd have stopped me at the border.'

'That's why your passport was missing?'

'Uh huh.'

'I assumed the police took it to trace your next of kin. And because there were no suspicious causes, they had no reason to stop your passport?'

'Right.'

'So, you came here alone to start with?'

'I didn't come straight here. I went to Amsterdam first. Rented an old barge. That's when I contacted Angel.' He grins. 'It was touch and go when you wanted to view my body.'

I think back to when Angel and I were in the funeral home. Did she persuade me not to see Si? My cheeks flush with anger. 'How can you laugh about that?'

'I'm sorry, I'm not laughing. If there was any way I could have let you know, I would. But I had to keep quiet. I had to convince everyone that I was dead. It was the only way.'

'Does Daniel know?'

'Daniel? God no.' A shadow crosses his face. 'Daniel was a good mate, but it's safer he doesn't know. Only Angel. Anyway, tell me about you. How's Tom? And Jamie?'

'Jamie's fine. Tom left me.'

'Oh shit, Sarah. I'm sorry.'

'S'okay. Seems it's not just you who needs a new life. Oh God!' I reach out and grab Si's hand. 'You don't know about Dad.'

He squeezes my fingers. 'I do. Angel filled me in. Don't ask me to be sad about that, Sarah. It was his time.'

I shake my head. 'Si, you left me in such shit.'

He pales. 'Has Quinn been causing trouble? Did he hurt you?'

'No. I managed to convince him there was no money once Angel left.'

He exhales in relief. 'Good, that's good.'

'Do his powers reach as far as this?'

'No, he's not global. He'll drop it now.'

I hesitate, but I have to know. 'You and Angel are together?'

'Angel and I were never an item, not the way you're thinking, but she helped me, she really helped. You could say she saved my life.' He smiles. 'She told me you and she became close.'

I snigger. 'Right.'

'No, genuinely. She said you became friends. She felt bad leaving you behind.'

'Friends don't lie to each other. They don't just disappear.' I glare at him. 'And neither do brothers.'

He looks shamefaced. 'I'm sorry.'

'I can't believe I climbed a bloody volcano for you.' I thump his arm. 'I suppose you already visited Arenal yourself?'

'Course I did.' He grins. 'Almost as soon as I arrived.'

'So, what's going on with Angel now?'

He shrugs. 'She's moving on. Doing pretty well for herself. Got an internship at an animal rescue centre.'

'She's done well on the inheritance.'

'That's not fair. Anyway, she deserves it for all I put her through.'

'What about me, Si? What about all you put *me* through?'

'I know.' He reaches across and pats my arm. 'But we're okay, aren't we, sis?'

'I don't know. I need time to process all this.'

'You can't tell anyone, Sarah.' His eyes grow wide and I realise he's unsure. Grabbing the second shot, he throws it down his throat.

I sense the waiter watching. 'Come on.' I throw some notes down to cover the bill and we step out into the sunshine. Si takes my arm and we stroll along the beach. It's beautiful, like a tropical island.

'I wanted to get a bar on the beach. Like in that film *Cocktail*.'

I snort. 'That's not going to happen with you looking like that.'

'I know.' He sighs.

We find a shady spot and sit down. A sign beside us reads, '*Beware Falling Coconuts.*' I stare up into the trees. 'Is it safe to sit here?'

'Live dangerously,' says Si.

'I don't understand why you gave up on your life.'

'I didn't. That's the whole point. If I'd given up, I'd have checked out. For good.'

I wriggle my toes in the sand. 'I'm not sure I can keep quiet. I have to tell people there's been a mistake.'

Si's eyes survey me.

'I cremated someone who's not my brother. I need to tell the funeral directors and the coroner.' I press my hands to my cheeks. 'And the police. We have to tell the police.'

'No one knows it wasn't me.' Si's voice is calm and steady.

'But I can't just keep quiet.'

'Even if it means I'll be arrested?'

I stare at him. 'For what?'

'Don't you know it's a crime to fake your own death?'

'Tell me the truth. Did you plan all this?'

'No.'

'Then why? Why not go to the police when Quinn threatened you?'

'It wouldn't have done any good.'

'What did he have on you? I can't believe this was about a few grands' worth of debt.'

Si sighs.

'Tell me!'

'Harry's not the innocent you've built him up to be.'

'He was your friend.'

'We knocked about together, but he was never my friend.'

'But he was a real person with family and people who cared for him.'

'Not really.'

'Look Si, if you don't tell me the whole story right now, then I'm going to the police. We'll explain that you were being blackmailed. That you had no choice.'

'I'll still end up in prison.' He rubs his hands over his face. 'Harry was a drugs mule.'

'What?'

'He smuggled cocaine. From Columbia. Inside his stomach.'

'Oh my God.'

"When I got into debt, Harry set me up with some of his acquaintances. He told me one trip and I could clear my debts. Be free.'

'You actually considered it?'

'I didn't have a choice. If I didn't settle up with Quinn, his thugs would have beaten the crap out of me. Left me for dead.'

'You agreed to be a drugs mule?'

He has the decency to squirm. 'I guess.'

'So, what were you and Harry doing that night at your flat?'

'One final party. One last blow out before I made the trip. Harry convinced me it would be fine, but I was worried.'

'Did Angel know?'

'No. We'd had a falling out. I swear she knew nothing about the drugs.'

'Go on.'

'Harry and me were hitting it hard – ket and nitrous, you know. He had some sort of seizure. He suffered from high blood pressure. It's common for those of us carrying a few extra pounds.

'I tried mouth-to-mouth, but he was gone so I got the girls to leave. I intended calling an ambulance, but knew it was too late. I was clearing things up when it came to me. This might give me a way out. If Quinn thought I was dead, he'd leave me alone.'

'That's when you spoke to Angel?'

'Not then. I cleaned the flat, made sure there was nothing incriminating, grabbed my passport and left. After calling 999 of course.'

'And went to Amsterdam?'

'I caught the Eurostar. I was sure someone would be looking for me. I can't believe they were all so easily convinced that Harry was me.'

'So, when did you contact Angel?'

'A day or two later. I had to have someone on the ground. Someone to make sure everything was progressing as it should.'

'And she cooperated?'

'Why wouldn't she? I'd left her everything.'

'But she came out to Costa Rica a few weeks ago. Valentina got a postcard.'

'Yes, after the estate was settled, she insisted on coming to see me. She wanted to check I was okay. That I had enough to live on.'

'She's sharing the money with you?'

He shrugs. 'She's given me a bit to get by and promised me a little more to get my bar up and running, but I've got to clean up my act first.'

'She's still controlling your life.'

His smile is sheepish. 'I guess I like it.'

A thought occurs to me. 'Oh God! I should give you some money. You missed out on your share of Dad's inheritance.'

'No, Sarah. Money's not important to me anymore. And anyway…' He grins and, for a moment, he's the teasing Simon I know. 'It sounds like you're going to need it.'

'Hey…' A giggle escapes and just as quickly, disappears. 'Why Angel? Why didn't you call me?'

He raises his eyebrows. 'How could I involve you, sis?' He nudges me. 'Little Miss Goody-two-shoes. You'd never have gone along with it.'

'But Wendy and me… we thought you were dead.'

'Yes, and I am. As far as you and Wendy know, I'm dead and my ashes scattered.'

'Don't! Poor Harry…'

'You can't tell anyone, you know?'

'But Angel knows. You shared with her when you couldn't share with me. How do you know she'll keep quiet?'

'She will. But you, Sarah? What are you going to do?'

CHAPTER FORTY-NINE

I cycle back to Puerto Viejo. It's over six kilometres, but I barely notice. All the way the same words run through my head on auto play – Si's alive, Si's alive.

In my room, I replay the past couple of hours. How did I not know? Si and I are twins. I should have felt it. But then, did I ever feel he was dead? Hadn't I just got so caught up in the doing that I didn't really process his loss?

They'd never asked me to identify Si's body. The police had taken Michael's word that it was him. Si lived alone, who else would he have expected it to be?

I pick up the phone and put it back down. I want to speak to someone, but who? Wendy? Tom? No, they'll make me go to the police. Nicki? I shouldn't tell her, and certainly not over the phone. And, if I do, how do I know I won't be implicating her?

I rub my temples. My head's splitting. I shower before taking two paracetamol and climbing into bed. What am I going to do?

. . .

I dream I'm in the funeral home. I step into a dark room with sombre music playing and stare at a body in an open coffin, but it's not Simon.

I wake with a start. Why didn't I go and see my brother's body in the funeral parlour? If I had, I could have told everyone it wasn't him.

I sit up as black thoughts creep into my brain. How do I know Si's told me everything? Did he and Angel plan the whole thing? Perhaps they stumbled across Harry the Loner in a bar and noticed a resemblance. Did Si befriend him deliberately so that he could engineer his fake death? Did they groom him? Kill him?

I climb out of bed and use the loo, before downing a glass of water. No, it's too horrid. Si wouldn't do that. And anyway, Harry wasn't murdered. The post-mortem came back as natural causes. It must have been some weird coincidence. Perhaps they were drawn to one another due to similarities, got talking and realised they had even more in common. That night they were having the time of their lives until Harry clutched his chest. Si told the dommes to leave. Is that when he rang Angel? Did the two of them come up with the plan there and then?

I crawl back into bed. How much do I really know about my brother? I knew nothing about his secret life. I don't know what he's capable of. He staged his own death. That's fraud. But I did the executor thing. Have I committed a crime? Will the police think I'm involved?

Wearily I close my eyes. I dream of policemen knocking at my door. They lead me down the path in handcuffs. A policeman puts his hand on my head, so I don't bump it as they lower me into the police car. I look back to Tom and Jamie standing on the doorstep. 'I'm sorry,' I mouth.

The dawn chorus wakes me and I head for the beach. Ironically, I'm in time to bag a sun bed but of course I'm not in the mood.

The beach is tranquil, the sea softly dousing the sand, while my mind is in turmoil. I'm experiencing heart palpitations.

I know Si wants an answer, but I need to process everything first. What the fuck has he got me into? I should go to the police. Tell them the whole story. But I don't want Si to go to prison. No matter what he's done, he's my brother, my twin, yang to my yin…

Could I actually fly home and keep his secret? Pretend Si's dead? Close a door on the whole sordid chapter and go on as if nothing's changed? But how do I face Wendy, Jamie, Nicki? And how will I live with myself?

I feel so guilty. Why wasn't Si able to talk to me about what he was going through? I must be a crap sister. And I can't stop thinking about Harry and his family. Are they looking for him? Have they reported his disappearance to the police? Even if he wasn't the good friend to Si that I'd imagined him to be, I had him cremated. I scattered his ashes on a volcano. That's probably the last place on earth his family would want him laid to rest.

I wander along, turning everything over in my mind. I came out here to scatter Si's ashes and to search for Angel. Can I really keep Si's secret? If only I could talk to someone.

An hour later, I head back to my apartment and shower. On my way to breakfast, the guy on reception calls out. '*Senora* Edwards?'

'Yes?'

'You had a call yesterday, but we couldn't find you.'

'No, I was out, then went to bed early. Who was it?'

'Wait.' He rummages through paperwork. 'I wrote it down somewhere… ah.' He pulls out a scrap of paper. '*Senorita* Nicki. She said to please call her back as soon as possible.'

It's nine a.m. here, four p.m. in the UK. Checking my mobile, the signal's as bad as usual. 'Can I use your phone?'

He shows me into his office and places the call. The phone rings twice before she picks up. 'Hello?'

'Hello, Nicki.'

'Sarah. At last! How's it all going?'

'Okay'

'You scattered Si's ashes on Arenal?'

God, that seems a lifetime ago… 'Yes and no. It wasn't possible to get as close as I'd hoped.'

'Right.'

'So, I divided the ashes up and scattered the last of him on a beautiful beach.'

'You're doing an amazing thing. I'm very proud of you.'

I feel my cheeks colour. Proud of me? If she only knew…

'You're awfully quiet. When are you coming home?'

'I'm due to fly back tomorrow.'

'Right.' She hesitates a moment. 'But you *are* coming home?'

'Of course.' I hold onto the desk for support. 'Oh Nicki. I miss you.'

'I'm here.'

'I know.' I exhale. 'Look, I can't talk over the phone, but I'll see you in a couple of days, okay?'

'Now I'm really worried.'

'Don't be. I'm fine. I just wish you were here.'

CHAPTER FIFTY

'Hi.' Simon opens the door to his apartment.

I step inside to find Angel seated at the bistro table.

'Hi, Sarah,' she says.

I scowl. Despite what Si told me, I can't help thinking this is all her fault. 'What are you doing here?'

'I need to know your intentions. It affects me too.'

Of course it does. She's in this up to her neck.

'Coffee?' says Si.

'Sure.' I sit on the other chair. Si's had a tidy-up – the kitchen area's clean, the bed made and his clothes hidden away. He's trying to make a good impression.

'It's black, hope that's okay.' Si sets a mug down in front of me.

'Thanks.'

'You've not spoken to anyone?' asks Angel.

'Not yet.'

Angel exhales. 'Good. The fewer that know, the better.'

'I wish I could find out about Harry's family.'

'Didn't you try to do that before leaving the UK?'

'Yes. Everything came up a dead end.'

'Then you've done all you can.'

'Unless I inform the police.'

Her eyes widen. 'You wouldn't dob Simon in.'

'I don't know. He faked his own death. That's a crime.'

'But he hasn't defrauded anyone. It's not like he's made massive claims on life insurance policies or anything.'

'You got the pay out from his pension company.'

'Yes, but they'd always have had to pay that out at some point. If he'd stayed in the UK another thirty years, he'd have drawn it as an annuity.'

'But it means he can never go back.'

'I don't want to go back,' interjects Si. 'My life in the UK is over.'

'You say that now, but how do you know? You might feel completely differently in time.' I sigh. 'I don't want this hanging over my head. I don't want a knock on the door in ten years and to be charged with conspiracy to defraud.'

'That will never happen. There's no way you're implicated.'

'I cremated a stranger and scattered his ashes all over Costa Rica.' I put my head in my hands. 'His mother can never visit his grave.' Tears flow down my cheeks.

I feel Si's hand on my back, patting me as if I'm a Labrador.

'Don't touch me!' I shake him off. Can I really do this? Cut all ties with my twin brother?

I take a shuddering breath before raising my head and staring at each in turn. 'I came here this afternoon to tell you that I won't be reporting you.'

Angel and Si exchange a glance. It's congratulatory and almost makes me want to change my mind.

'Thanks, sis,' says Si. 'I promise to sort out my life. Perhaps one day we'll be able to…'

'No. I need to compartmentalise. Like you do, Si.' I continue. 'I can't live a double life. I can't lie to family and friends.' I stand up. 'We'll have no more contact. This is the last time I'll see you. Either of you.'

'*Pina Colada por favor.*'

Mateo smiles as he mixes my drink. 'So, your last night in Costa Rica?'

'How do you know?'

He taps his nose. 'Bartenders know everyone's secrets.'

Not mine, you don't, I think, sipping my drink as he serves the other customers. When he's finished, he places another cocktail in front of me. 'On the house.'

'*Gracias.*'

'So, you will tell all your girlfriends to come to Puerto Viejo?'

'I'm not sure… the bartenders here may be too much of a temptation.'

He grins as he takes a little bow. 'It has been a pleasure to serve you, *senorita*.'

CHAPTER FIFTY-ONE

As I ring the bell, Brodie launches himself at the door, barking excitedly.

When Nicki opens it, he leaps in the air, tail wagging nineteen to the dozen. 'Hello, boy.' I bend to stroke him, and he repays me with slobbery licks.

'Someone's pleased to see you.' Nicki hugs me. 'Come on in.'

I head out to her bijou patio while she opens a bottle of Sauvignon Blanc. 'So,' she says, following me out. 'Successful trip?'

'Yes, thanks.' Brodie, keen to ensure I don't disappear again, sprawls across my bare feet as I reach to take the proffered glass. 'But it's nice to be home. Only so much paradise a girl can take.'

She sits beside me on the wooden bench. 'It was beautiful, then?'

'The beaches were amazing. Like a tropical island. You'd have loved it.'

'Sorry I couldn't come.' She touches my hand. 'I feel like I let you down.'

'Don't be silly.' I sip my wine. 'To be honest, it was probably better I took the trip on my own.'

'One final sisterly act for Simon.'

'Hmm.' You have no idea, I think.

She eyes me suspiciously. 'What are you not telling me?'

I'll never tell Nicki. I can't risk incriminating her. 'Well…' I exhale slowly. 'I did do something silly.'

She leans forward, agog.

'I slept with a cocktail waiter.'

'You didn't!'

'I did. And young enough to be my son.'

'Fit then?'

'Very.'

We exchange a glance before dissolving into giggles.

'Well, good for you,' she says. 'I hope you enjoyed it.'

'I kind of did!'

She strokes her fingers across a potted shrub, releasing a heady fragrance of scented geraniums. 'So, what's next?'

'I don't know.' I set my glass down on the side table. 'Everything's changed.'

'Will you carry on teaching?'

'I don't think so. I'm a different person now. I feel like I need to try something new.'

'And Tom?'

'That's over. We've agreed to divorce. He'll probably marry Yvette. They might even start a family.' My voice breaks.

'I'm sorry.' She slides along to envelop me in a hug. Her skin is soft and warm from the sun, her hair scented with coconut shampoo. She smells like home.

When she pulls away, I shiver. Glancing up, I notice the sky clouding over.

'It's gone chilly, hasn't it?' She retrieves a blanket from the ottoman and tucks it around us.

'This is nice,' I murmur.

'Look, I hope I'm not overstepping,' she says, 'but will you be all right for money?'

'Yes.' I snuggle closer. 'Jamie's left home anyway, so Tom and I will sell the house and split the proceeds. With Dad's legacy, I might even have enough to invest in a little start up.'

Under the blanket, Nicki holds my hand. 'I had this idea. It's a bit mad, but…'

'Go on.'

'Well, you know I've inherited Mum's house in France. It's in a bit of a state, but I've decided not to sell. I'd like to turn it into a sort of retreat – walking breaks, perhaps even well-being classes…' She hesitates, giving me time to imagine. 'I wondered if you fancied coming into business with me?'

'Business partners?'

In the low evening light, her eyes are deepest violet. She reaches out, her fingers brushing a strand of hair from my face. 'I know. Told you it was bonkers…'

I smile. 'I'd love to.'

ACKNOWLEDGMENTS

With gratitude to my editor, Claire Chamberlain for developmental feedback and copy editing. Thank you to my beta readers - Fiona Campbell, Samantha Froud-Hill and Patricia M Osborne for feedback and advice.

I am grateful to Andy Keylock for the fantastic cover design. Special thanks to Samantha Rumens at Marketing Pace for marketing my books and providing ongoing advice for Broodleroo's social media platform.

Finally, thanks to my family and friends for their continued encouragement, support and love.

ABOUT THE AUTHOR

B.B. Lamett is a pseudonym of author, Suzi Bamblett.

Suzi lives in East Sussex and writes psychological thrillers, mystery and suspense. Her work has been published in literary magazines, anthologies and academic collections including Shooter Literary Magazine (2020) and the Performance and Communities collection - Storying the Self - (2022) and Performing Maternities (2024)

Other novels by Suzi Bamblett:
    The Travelling Philanthropist
    Three Faced Doll
    Prescient Spirit
    Pearl Seekers

For more information please visit Broodleroo.com where you can sign up to receive news.

Milton Keynes UK
Ingram Content Group UK Ltd.
UKHW031415231124
3022UKWH00006B/99

9 781838 255046